BLACK DIAMOND

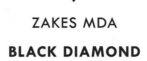

ZAKES MDA

BLACK DIAMOND

LONDON NEW YORK CALCUTTA

Sries Editor: Rosalind C. Morris

Seagull Books, 2014

© Zakes Mda, 2009

ISBN   978 0 85742 222 4

British Library Cataloguing-in-Publication Data
A catalogue record for this book is available from the British Library.

Typeset by Seagull Books, Calcutta, India

Printed and bound by Maple Press, York, Pennsylvania, USA

BLACK DIAMOND

1

FREE THE VISAGIE BROTHERS

No one will blame you if you think Kristin Uys is dressed for a funeral. Not the black folks' kind of funerals where women give the dead a glorious send-off in the same Versaces, Sun Goddesses and Givenchys that are a staple at such horse-racing events as the Durban July Handicap or the J&B Met. Not the joyful events where the living crack jokes about the dead and get sloshed and dance to loud music at those marathon parties known as 'after-tears'. But the sad and sombre affairs that pass for funerals in white communities. A calf-length black skirt, an off-white blouse with frills that have gone tired and a navy blue jacket that seems to be slightly oversized. The black gown, however, will soon disabuse you of any notions of bereavement and will place you squarely in a courtroom. She is the magistrate. The gown is almost threadbare, with bell-shaped sleeves and shoulder pieces of scarlet. Her blonde hair is tied in an old-fashioned schoolmarmish bun. But the austere look and the severe dress code fail to disguise her fine features.

She sits at the bench and looks sternly at the accused. One glares back at her unflinchingly. He is Stevo Visagie, the older of the two brothers in the dock. He is tiny and wiry. What he lacks in stature he makes up for in his menacing look. His sharp features, leathery skin and penetrating eyes tell us at once that he is tough. The other one hasn't got the guts to return the magistrate's gaze. He lowers his eyes. He is Shortie Visagie, a young man with the frame of a wrestler and a perpetually perplexed expression. Although he is obviously as strong as an elephant, he has an avuncular air about him. He may pretend to be tough but he is really a teddy bear.

The magistrate did not expect this kind of temerity from Stevo. She turns her gaze to the defence counsel. Mr Krish Naidoo stands up to address the court. Before he can utter a word, the magistrate says, 'You are not dressed, Mr Naidoo.'

'I beg your pardon, your worship?'

'Next time I will not allow you in my court in that suit, Mr Naidoo.'

He should have known better than to wear a light grey suit in Kristin Uys' court. Everyone is well aware that she is a stickler for courtroom decorum—a black suit, a white shirt, a bib and a black robe. But sometimes a lawyer forgets, especially because other magistrates are quite lax about such things.

'I expect such infringements from younger attorneys,' she adds.

The spectators in the gallery watch expectantly. Prominent among them are four women in the garish attire and exaggerated make-up of prostitutes. They are huddled together and are paying close attention to the proceedings.

Krish Naidoo suppresses his irritation and apologizes to the court. He then proceeds with his closing remarks.

His clients, the Visagie Brothers, are on trial for running a brothel.

'But the state has failed to make a case against them,' he says. 'Evidence given by their mother has shown that the girls found on the Visagie property were their cousins visiting from the *platteland*.'

The prostitutes in the gallery seem to enjoy this characterization of their peers. They give the court what they think are coquettish smiles. The magistrate has nothing but disgust for them. All they need to do is give her the slightest excuse and she will have them thrown out of the courtroom. Just as she did this morning when she asked Ma Visagie, the boys' mother, to leave after she uttered an exclamation of disagreement at something the prosecutor said. It was after she had given her evidence for the defence, had been cross-examined by the state and had taken a seat in the gallery.

Ma Visagie joined the demonstration in the parking lot in front of the courthouse and took over from Aunt Magda—who is really not anyone's aunt—to lead the protesters. The scrawny but feisty matriarch sings with gusto. The small group—consisting of five hookers, three drag queens and about ten women in black who call themselves the Society of Widows—is waving crude placards with bold letters: *Free the Visagie Brothers*! and *Release Shortie and Stevo*!

The demonstration is Aunt Magda's brainchild—she of the missing front teeth, like a lot of Cape Town people of her generation. She came all the way from the Mother City as soon as she got the message that her boys were in jail. Although she retired two years ago from her long service as the Visagie maid, she is still very attached to the boys. After all, she brought them up from the time they were babies and looked after them until they were grown men. Stevo lost his virginity to her in his early teens one drunken night. She even had a tryst with old Meneer Visagie himself before cancer stole him away. She returned to her beloved Athlone after her knees gave up on her because of arthritis, although one can't see any evidence of that today judging from the *toyi-toyi* she is performing outside the courthouse—a dance that has mystified her fellow protesters, most of whom have only seen it on television when workers' unions are on strike and are overturning dustbins.

Most of the women in the group of protesters are community members who are beholden to the Visagie family.

In the same way that mass action brought the apartheid government to its knees, it was bound to bring the post-apartheid justice system to its senses. Aunt Magda assured her supporters that she had studied the methods used by the Release Mandela Committee of old and would apply them to force the magistrate to free her innocent boys. If mass action worked for Mandela, it would surely work for the Visagies. The group has even appropriated 'Free Nelson Mandela', the song by the ska band Special AKA, as its anthem. Of course, they have changed the words 'Nelson Mandela' to 'Visagie Brothers'.

Ma Visagie does not understand anything about demonstrations, mass actions and organizing committees. Her community was never part of that culture. But she is willing to try anything to get her sons freed. If Aunt Magda says people were released from jail through such actions, then there is no reason why they will not be effective now that those who were once prisoners are the rulers of this country.

The Society of Widows is the culmination of Aunt Magda's organizing prowess. Some of its members are indeed widows whose husbands or boyfriends may have died in some car hijacking misadventure or armoured-vehicle cash heist. Others are not necessarily widows in the literal sense. They may be single mothers who have benefited from the generosity of the Visagies or wives whose husbands are useless layabouts. In the tradition of South African criminals who have become folk heroes in their communities, the Visagies often operate on a semblance of the Robin Hood principle. When South African criminals have been gunned down by the police in car chases, or by fellow gangsters in turf wars, you often hear in funeral speeches how generous they were, and how many young people in the community have achieved their dreams of studying at universities, becoming lawyers and doctors as a result of funding from the man now lying in the coffin.

It is the same with Ma Visagie's boys. That is why Aunt Magda tells a newspaper reporter, 'The government has failed the widows of this country. The Visagie Brothers have made big donations to our society. They always help those in need. They even pay school fees for kids from poor families.'

Ma Visagie, however, will not let Aunt Magda hog all the limelight. She sings the loudest in her shaky voice. After all, she is the mother of the heroes in question and Aunt Magda was only their nanny.

But the demonstrators' protest songs cannot penetrate the thick walls of the Roodepoort magistrate's court, and Kristin Uys presides over the case unperturbed.

In his summing-up Krish Naidoo dismisses the evidence of the policeman who arrested his clients. The policeman, he says, entrapped the girls after one of them turned down his proposal. The Visagies are respectable businessmen who own a scrapyard selling used car parts.

'They are well known in the community for their good deeds and charitable work,' he adds.

'You are wasting this court's time with irrelevancies, Mr Naidoo,' says the magistrate. 'The accused may be the reincarnation of Mother Teresa herself but that has nothing to do with this case.'

The attorney is deflated. The court is adjourned to the next day.

Outside the courthouse Ma Visagie is telling another reporter, 'My boys are innocent. They have been framed by the police. They're the most angelic children any mother could wish to have.'

But at that time, the Visagie Brothers don't look angelic at all as they are led in handcuffs and leg irons from the courtroom to the holding cells by two burly policemen. One may think they are the deadliest criminals that the police have ever laid their hands on.

As the magistrate walks out of the building the demonstrators sing even louder. They stop short of jeering at her though. She pays no attention to them and walks to the parking lot.

Kristin Uys arrives home in her battered Fiat Uno. She gets out of the car as the electronic gates close automatically behind her. Hers is an average suburban house that once knew glorious days but now looks neglected. Not dirty, just the worse for wear. Those who have lived here for decades would say that the suburb itself—known as Weltevreden Park, which means 'well satisfied'—has known glorious days as well. It used to be a paradise for the Afrikaner white-collar workers. Those were the good old days of apartheid, before the place was invaded by the black professional classes, middle-management apparatchiks of big corporations and chief executives of smaller corporations—chief executives and executive chairpersons of the big multinationals are in Sandton and Constantia Kloof. Now the suburb is completely non-racial, though a passer-by wouldn't notice since the residents hide themselves behind high security walls. The only vestiges of the pure Afrikaner past are the streets that still bear the names of apartheid's dead presidents and prime ministers, such as Jim Fouché, John Vorster and J. G. Strijdom.

A nondescript but well-fed cat purrs its welcome at the door.

The furniture in the house is old and the walls are bare of any pictures. There are papers, files and other items strewn on the sofas, the floor and the coffee table. Kristin Uys plays Antonio Vivaldi's 'Four Seasons' on an old-fashioned hi-fi. She draws a cork and pours herself a drink from a wine bottle on a sideboard. She likes her wine at room temperature. She sits on the sofa and the cat jumps on her lap. She shuts her eyes while caressing the cat and taking an occasional sip from the glass. The cat purrs with contentment.

She continues to drink into the evening. Even as she takes a bubble bath, she has a glass of wine. She looks at herself in a hand-held mirror and kisses her image. She is embarrassed by what she has just done and places the mirror on the floor. She takes another sip of wine, then places the glass on the floor next to the mirror. She examines herself. She is self-conscious about her tiny breasts, she is almost flat-chested. In this private world she seems unsure and uneasy, quite a contrast from the brash and confident magistrate of the courtroom.

The cat is playing with a bottle of bath oil near the tub. As it leaps at the bottle, it knocks the glass over and the wine spills on the floor. She gets out of the bath, wraps herself in a towel and wipes the wine from the floor while the cat plays around with the cloth she is using, frustrating her efforts. She laughs as she pushes the playful cat away. So she *can* laugh, after all!

After nibbling at a ham sandwich she goes to bed.

The bedroom is a far cry from the living room. It is decorated in garish pink and black. White lace predominates—it is on the curtains, on the lampshade and on the cloth on the dressing table.

She is in bed in a delicate, frilly nightie that belies the tough exterior we saw in court. She is reading a book—Xaviera Hollander's *The Happy Hooker*.

The cat is cuddled up on the comforter between her legs.

Don Mateza can hear Aunt Magda's song seeping in through the window: 'Free . . . free . . . Visagie Brothers!' Although she sounds drunk the voice has the breathiness of the jazz singers he likes. From his office across Dieperink Street he can see a small group of demonstrators at the parking lot in front of the magistrate's court.

He chuckles at the antics of one of the widows who breaks into a silly jig, then turns his attention to his client, an elderly white woman. He is demonstrating surveillance equipment and enthusiastically assures her that the camera is state-of-the-art and the price includes installation. It will be mounted on the wall under the eaves.

'Oh, *ja*?' says the customer. 'Like the one the robbers blasted with their guns before they broke into my house?'

'That one, ma'am, was not installed by VIP Protection Services. We disguise it, ma'am, so no one will know it's there. This is a weatherproof dome surveillance camera . . . vandal proof! Once it's up it stays up. And it's high resolution too.'

The customer is impressed. Don explains how the equipment can detect the slightest movement and switches on the recording machine, and how it automatically zooms to the intruder.

He is interrupted by the phone. It's his boss.

'Are you busy, Don?'

'I'm with a client, Jim. Did you want something?'

'Dr Mbungane is entertaining a few cabinet ministers and visiting businessmen from the Congo. He needs a number of bodyguards at his Sandhurst mansion.'

VIP Protection Services is short-staffed at the moment, what with the increase in highway robberies and the need for extra armed guards to accompany the armoured vehicles transporting cash. But Molotov Mbungane (the doctorates are honorary after a number of South African universities fell over themselves dishing out degrees to him when he became an overnight dollar billionaire) is a very special client who must have what he wants when he wants it. Don Mateza will therefore withdraw three guards from protecting other facilities and will post them and himself at Comrade Capitalist's house—which is what Dr Molotov Mbungane's comrades, with whom he fought in the guerrilla forces during the liberation struggle, call him behind his back.

There was a time when Don resented such assignments. You see, he used to be Molotov's commander back in the bush, until Molotov bungled a mission to bomb a power station in Pretoria and was arrested and sent to

Robben Island. There, of course, he met and befriended the leaders of the struggle and got some university education, while Don continued living in guerrilla camps in Angola and Mozambique and leading expeditions of sabotage inside South Africa. Now Molotov is the richest black man in South Africa and Don is middle management at a security company—often becoming a foot soldier when there are not enough bodyguards to go around.

Don returns to his client and shows her where to sign on the contract forms.

'Thanks for your business, ma'am. We'll install the equipment first thing tomorrow morning.'

When the happy customer departs, he dials Tumi at her TM Modelling Agency. 'Ah, Tumi, darling! How's my Tumza?'

'Don't you Tumza me, Don. You should have been here by now. You know I don't like to be late for gym.'

He has forgotten that Tumi's Jaguar X-Type was in for service today and that he had promised to take her to the gym at Melrose Arch after work.

'I'm sorry, Tumi, I have to do overtime.'

He does not tell her that the overtime involves standing guard at Comrade Capitalist's private party. Whereas Don has long accepted his menial status, Tumi has never forgiven any of his former comrades for being successful beneficiaries of the government's Black Economic Empowerment policy, or BEE as it is fashionably called, while her fiancé has to work for a security company. It is a sore point with her that Don's comrades forgot about him when they reached Paradise, after he sacrificed so much in exile fighting for the overthrow of the apartheid state. He, a child of a single mother, sacrificed even his mother who was tortured to death by the Boers in a vain attempt to get at her son. His name lives on only in songs that the youth sing at parades on such national holidays as Freedom Day, Human Rights Day and Youth Day about AK Bazooka and his battlefield exploits against the enemy. None of the youth knows that AK Bazooka was in fact Don Mateza's *nom de guerre*, he who is today a security guard at *VIP Protection Services: Your Preferred Company for Personal, Facility and Events Protection*.

'I'll call Nomsa to give you a ride.'

'I can call her myself,' she says abruptly and hangs up.

She is angry but she can't have it both ways, Don concludes. She is the one who is always pushing him to work harder and prove himself worthy of promotion. Jim Baxter, who founded the company after he was honourably discharged from the South African Defence Force of the old South Africa, will be retiring soon and the board of directors is on the lookout for a new chief executive. Tumi believes that if Don plays his cards well, he can take over—not only as the man at the helm but as a majority shareholder—and finally be on his way to becoming a Black Diamond—as the fat-cat BEE beneficiaries are called. For Tumi, 'playing the cards well' means networking with the BEE dealmakers and using his leverage as an ex-guerrilla to outmanoeuvre any competition for the position. But the only way of 'playing the cards well' that Don knows is working hard, even to the extent of personally taking on tasks that Tumi deems demeaning, instead of assigning them to underlings.

She believes there is nothing more degrading than having Don act as Comrade Capitalist's bodyguard. She became even more convinced of this last year when the billionaire wanted to spend Christmas at his vineyard in the Western Cape. He ordered a group of bodyguards from VIP Protection Services and Jim Baxter could trust no one but Don to lead the squad. This spoilt the couple's plan to spend Christmas in Soweto with Tumi's parents.

'Why *you* all the time?' she had asked. 'Surely a man like Molotov has his own personal bodyguards who are permanent staffers.'

'He usually supplements his permanent bodyguards with our men when he has more guests at his events.'

Tumi smarted for a while but ended up offering to go to the Western Cape and booking in at a hotel so that she could spend as much time as possible with Don whenever he was free.

Molotov organized a Christmas party for his staff and Don went with Tumi. She found it ridiculous that both Molotov and his white wife Cathy addressed the bodyguards as 'comrade' as if they were all equal, whereas the bodyguards called him 'chief'. Previously she had only seen him on television or read about him in the newspapers and was struck by how he was such a jovial man who mixed freely with everyone, without the slightest air of superiority or arrogance. She admired the way the man carried himself. Until he hit on her, right there in the reception hall while his wife was chatting away with the other guests and Don was giving instructions on the walkie-talkie to guards who were patrolling the sprawling grounds with dogs. When Tumi expressed her shock, Molotov said, 'You were one of the top models in South Africa and now you own a successful model agency. What are you doing with a *mantshingilane* like Don?'

'In other words, according to you, I have no taste in men. How would that change if I went out with you?'

Tumi walked away without waiting for an answer.

What offended her most was his use of the demeaning word for a security guard, often used to insult country-bumpkin nightwatchmen. She vowed to herself that one day Don would show everyone what he was really made of—he was going to be a Black Diamond in his own right.

The next day she told Don she was flying back to Johannesburg, without giving him any reasons. He put it down to Tumi's ever-changing moods. It is 2 a.m. The security guard must be sleeping on the job. Don hoots, but no one comes to open the gate. He can see through the window of the gatehouse that there is no one there. If the nightwatchman worked for VIP Protection Services, he would long have been fired. Each resident of the Three Oaks townhouse complex in North Riding is given a code for opening the gate in the absence of the security guards. But Don always forgets it because he rarely needs it. He will just have to call Tumi on his cellphone.

'Sorry to wake you up. What's the damn code?'

'I was not asleep. I was waiting for you, Don.'

She gives him the code. He punches it and the gate opens. He parks his Saab convertible at its assigned parking spot under the canopy next to Tumi's spot. Her Jaguar is still at the garage. He walks to Number 42.

The living room is expensively furnished, boasting the extravagant trappings of new money. The walls display a sgraffito by an accomplished artist and charcoals and acrylics of township art. An exhausted Don throws himself on the genuine black leather sofa, kicks his shoes off and begins to relax. A big fluffy snow-white Hima-layan cat leaps on to his lap and purrs happily. He closes his eyes and begins to doze off as he strokes it.

Tumi walks out of the bedroom. She is alluring in a skimpy nightie—her tall shapely figure and her catwalk gait attest to the fact that she was indeed once a top model. She perches herself on the arm of the couch.

'So what was the overtime all about?'

'Oh, just an assignment . . . you know . . . the usual stuff.'

'Ah, when you say that I know exactly what. Comrade Capitalist!'

'I cannot pick and choose the jobs I do, Tumi. Anyway, what do you have against Molotov?'

'You wouldn't want to know.'

'I know . . . I know . . . I've heard it many times . . .'

She grabs him by the scruff of the neck and silences him with a kiss. Then, like a magician who has just performed a trick, she says with a flourish, 'Ta . . . dah . . .!'

But Don does not see the magic trick.

'Don't be blind, Don. Look round you.'

For the first time Don notices a new chaise longue.

'Hey, what did you do with my old chair?'

'Like you say, it was old . . . too out of sync with my lounge suite.'

He is not happy about this. That was his very special La-Z-Boy recliner that he enjoyed particularly when he was watching television. By way of furniture it was his only contribution in the house.

'You don't like it?'

'It's nice, Tumi, but . . .'

'Nice? Only nice? It's from Bakos Brothers, Don. From Bakos Brothers! And all you can say is nice?'

'You know I don't like it when you spend all this money on me, Tumi. Unlike you, I worry about money.'

Once more she shuts him up with a kiss.

'You gonna get that promotion, baby. You gonna be the chief executive of VIP Protection Services. You're a Black Diamond, Don. You should learn to live like one.'

Don chuckles at this and says, 'An aspiring one, Tumi. An aspiring Black Diamond.'

After all, real Black Diamonds are not behind with instalments on a sports car they can't afford. The car was Tumi's choice and she paid the deposit for it, and promised she would help whenever Don had problems with the monthly payments. He didn't tell her that he was having difficulties and now gets threatening letters from the finance company, which he hides from her. Black Diamonds don't live in their girlfriends' one-bedroom flats either!

'With an attitude like that, you won't get anywhere, Don. Positive thinking! That's what you need. I wouldn't be where I am now if it was not for positive thinking. That's one thing that people like Molotov Mbungane have that you lack—positive thinking!'

Dr Mbungane's name always comes up whenever Tumi is giving Don what she believes is a pep talk. It used to hurt Don but he has since learnt to accept it. He no longer even bothers to argue with Tumi about Comrade Molotov's advantage over him because she always dismisses that as an excuse for Don's failures.

Comrade Molotov does indeed have what Don lacks—political capital. He was able to morph from a poor kid growing up in the village of Engcobo in the Eastern Cape to a Marxist guerrilla to a political prisoner to a member of parliament and cabinet minister in the first Mandela government. In the last stages of that process he accumulated the political capital that he was able to convert into financial capital and equity in some of the biggest corporations in the land as soon as he left government service. It is the political capital that made him palatable to white business. Banks plied him with cash, until he became known as Comrade Deal-a-Minute because he put together consortia that acquired huge stakes in the mining industry. In less than five years, he was the owner of some of the most lucrative diamond, gold and platinum mines, and had interests in the banking, health care, wine and engineering industries. When his former comrades gossip about him in the township taverns, they say it didn't hurt his palatability at all that he was married to an Afrikaner woman. During their days in political power the Afrikaners knew how to create affirmative action for themselves. Now they are teaching the art of accumulation to their son-in-law, Dr Molotov Mbungane.

How can Don compete with that? His only training is that of a guerrilla fighter and when he came back there was no place for him in the government. He never got to rub shoulders with the cream of the leadership of the country. He therefore never acquired any political capital.

Tumi has no sympathy with this line of thinking. Molotov played his cards well. Why couldn't Don? After all, Molotov had been his subordinate out there in the bush. Don was the one who strategized, the one who decided where and how the likes of Molotov would next attack. He was the hero who acquitted himself well when he was only in his mid-teens fighting alongside Zipra forces against the Rhodesian Ian Smith. He is the one young people sing about even today. He is Comrade AK Bazooka in person! Surely that should be political capital enough? Surely if he went out there, put together a BEE consortium, the white corporate world would recognize his worth, and would give him a slice of the cake.

But Don realizes that he would be bringing nothing to the corporate table since he has no political clout that can be converted into capital. He returned from exile and became one of the ex-combatants who spent their days *blomming*—hanging out, that is—in the taverns of Soweto. When he received his compensation from the government he spent it on lawyers, fighting to get his mother's four-roomed house back from the family that acquired it after she was killed. He lost the case, took to drink, and was broke. He continued to *blom* at taverns with his best friends and ex-combatants, Fontyo and Bova. But thanks to the fact that he and his childhood sweetheart Tumi rediscovered each other, he pulled himself together, got a job as a security guard and worked his way up. Even then Tumi had high hopes and big plans for him, and was determined to groom him, not only into the clean, fresh and urbane man he is today but into a Black Diamond. It is a determination that was reinforced by such insults as we have heard at Comrade Molotov's Christmas party.

'Ja, positive thinking! That's the only way out, Don,' she says once more, her eyes daring him to argue with that.

The cat is rubbing against her legs. She screeches and pushes it away with her foot. Don is horrified. He reaches for the cat and caresses it.

'You don't need the damn cat, Don. We don't have mice in this townhouse.'

'It's not for catching mice, Tumi. Snowy is my very special pet.'

'You no longer need *Snowy*. You have me.'

Don does not respond. Instead he takes his cat and walks to the bedroom, holding it like a baby.

3

AN INJURY TO ONE IS AN INJURY TO ALL

Stevo and Shortie are back in the dock. Our prostitutes are in the gallery as before. Kristin Uys is on the bench and Krish Naidoo is seated at the table for the defence. This time, he is properly attired in a dark suit and robe. The magistrate takes a long disapproving look at the prosecutor before asking him if he would like to rebut Mr Naidoo's closing remarks. He has no rebuttal.

'Why am I not surprised?' asks the magistrate, giving him a smile that is both sarcastic and condescending. The prosecutor fidgets uneasily.

The magistrate thinks that the state has presented a very shoddy case, and she says so. The state has failed to prove its case against the Visagie Brothers and she has no choice but to find them not guilty.

The prostitutes in the gallery applaud raucously.

'This is a court of law, not a shebeen,' says the magistrate. 'I will cite you all for contempt.'

'Bullshit,' says Stevo, almost under his breath. But not softly enough. The gallery laughs. The magistrate's dignity is injured but she tries to look unruffled.

'What did you say?' she asks.

'Nothing,' he says.

'The Visagie Brothers . . . especially you, Stevo Visagie . . . you are the scum of the earth. I'm going to nail you one day.'

The attorney objects. It is not proper for the magistrate to threaten his clients when she herself has just found them not guilty. But Stevo doesn't make things any better for himself when he bursts out, 'I'm sure you'll enjoy it, lady . . . nailing me. Every lady who has nailed me has enjoyed it.' He accompanies this with a rude sexual gesture.

Once more the gallery laughs.

Kristin Uys has never experienced such impudence in her court. She is beside herself with anger, and this time she cannot hide it.

'I'm citing you for contempt, Stevo Visagie. I am sentencing you to six months without the option of a fine for contempt *ex facie curiae*.'

Latin used to be the staple of South Africa's Roman-Dutch law system and the particular phrase refers to a common law remedy when the court is being insulted to its face. Unlike most legal practitioners who have allowed the dead language to fall into disuse in the courtrooms of South Africa, Kristin Uys is a stickler for tradition and has been known to utter lengthy quotations in Latin, if only to bamboozle young attorneys.

Despite Krish Naidoo's protestations Stevo is dragged away by two policemen, and is taken back to the holding cells, where he will await transportation to Sun City, as Diepkloof Prison is derisively known.

'You can't do that,' yells Krish Naidoo.

'I can,' says Kristin Uys smiling at him patronizingly. 'I am the magistrate.'

Outside the courthouse, the demonstrating crowd is smaller than yesterday's. People have been protesting for three days now and some of them are beginning to lose interest. But the members of the Society of Widows are still there in full force. Ma Visagie and Aunt Magda are competing as to whose privilege it should be to lead the songs. Some think Aunt Magda is best because her voice was made for singing. She has the poise of a jazz singer on a professional stage. Others favour Ma Visagie because even though her voice is rough and out of tune, it is so loud that the powers that be cannot ignore it. That's what protest is all about anyway—to be heard.

Aunt Magda wants to assert her rights as the organizer of the mass action; Ma Visagie thinks she has natural rights as the mother of these celebrities. The protesters suggest a compromise—Ma Visagie should lead when the song is a church hymn, since she once belonged to the women's union of the NG Kerk, and Aunt Magda should lead in the singing of protest songs, an area in which she professes expertise as an alleged veteran of anti-apartheid marches.

Ma Visagie is singing at the top of her voice when Shortie appears at the entrance to the courthouse surrounded by the prostitutes. The song suddenly stops and the demonstrators surge forward to hear what news he brings. It can only be good news for the man has been in jail awaiting trial for three months, and here he is now walking free with his guard of honour.

'Where's Stevo?' asks Ma Visagie.

'Stevo and me . . . we were both found innocent.'

The crowd cheers. Aunt Magda yells, 'I told you so! I told you mass action works!' She begins a new song but stops when Shortie raises his hand to indicate that he is not done recounting Stevo's fate.

'But guess what?' Shortie says. 'They still took Stevo to jail.'

Is this what the new South Africa has come to? People mutter things to this effect. A hothead widow hurls an empty Coke can at a nearby parked car. Other protesters try to follow suit, but the parking lot is clean and there are not enough missiles to throw around. Aunt Magda tries to stop the riot.

'Discipline, comrades,' she shouts. 'That's the only way we'll gain victory.'

But the freedom fighters are too angry to listen to her. In no time, a small contingent of policemen is on the scene spraying tear gas. It is not difficult to contain the small crowd and an officer warns them that next time they create a riot outside the courthouse they will find themselves in jail.

The demonstrators' morale is broken but they are determined to have the last word on the matter. Like the wounded soldiers they are, they walk away chanting, 'An injury to one is an injury to all; an injustice to one is an injustice to all!'

Krish Naidoo wants to consult with Shortie and his mother on the next course of action, but they are already marching down Dieperink Street surrounded by the protesters. He watches from the entrance to the courthouse as they try to lift Shortie on their shoulders. But he is too heavy—they stagger, almost falling with their load.

Kristin Uys is in her chambers. She is busy on some paperwork when Krish Naidoo barges in. She raises her eyes briefly to look at him, then returns to scribbling something in a notebook.

'You have caused quite a riot outside,' he says lightly.

'I don't pander to mobs, Krish. You should know that.'

'Come on, Kristin, it's a joke.'

'What do you want, Krish?'

Krish Naidoo confronts her about Stevo Visagie. The sentence was unfair, he says. The maximum sentence a magistrate can give for contempt is three months. That is the law.

'The Visagie boy insulted me twice,' explains Kristin. 'First he said "bullshit", then he made that dirty sexual innuendo. Two three-month sentences that will run consecutively.'

Krish tells her that he is going to appeal the sentences. He thinks he has very strong grounds because the magistrate provoked contempt by calling the Visagie Brothers the scum of the earth, even though she had no case against them.

'There is no need for you to appeal,' she says.

All summary judgements have to be reviewed by the high court automatically. She is obliged by law to send Stevo Visagie's case to the judges and she is confident that they will agree with her.

'You're on a crusade, Kristin,' says Krish. 'It's not in the interests of justice for a magistrate to be on a crusade.'

'I don't care if you call it a crusade, Krish. I'm going to throw the book at pimps and their whores. I'm going to clean this town of brothels.'

She believes she is racing against time. The new government of the post-apartheid South Africa has already shown tendencies of being too liberal on issues of morality. The government has legalized homosexuality; sexual orientation is in the constitution. Gay people can marry. Now there is talk of legalizing prostitution, and having designated red-light districts in the city. Even if she cannot stop that tide by herself, she is determined to make life hell for prostitutes and their pimps before the new age of utter degradation is visited upon the upright citizens of the land. 'You're using the bench to fight your personal wars. And you know exactly what I mean, Kristin,' says Krish.

Kristin ignores him and continues with her work. He stands there for a while, not knowing what to do next. Then he bursts out in frustration: 'What happened to the law-school Kristin, the compassionate Kristin, the Kristin who was going to temper justice with mercy?'

He is disgusted and leaves in a huff as the nonchalant Kristin pages through some files and drafts a letter. But he changes his mind and returns.

'Can you join us for dinner on Friday, Kristin? My wife will be happy to cook you *mattar paneer*. I remember how much you used to like it.'

Kristin smiles and says, 'So now you want to bribe me with food?'

'It will be like old times.'

'You know it can't be like old times, Krish.'

'Damn it, Kristin! For how long are you going to mope? Yours was not the first marriage in the world to end in divorce.'

She stands up and glares at him as if she will pounce on him and strangle him with her bare hands. He knows that now he must leave.

4

ACCUMULATION CANNOT BE DEMOCRATIZED, COMRADES

When Tumi and Don talk of home they mean the Southern Western Townships—better known as Soweto. That's where they were born and raised. Like most Sowetans who have since moved to the formerly all-white suburbs of Johannesburg, they continue to have a deep attachment to the sprawling townships to which black people were confined during apartheid. True Sowetans, even BEE Fat Cats and sundry Black Diamonds, make regular visits back home just for the smells, the tastes and the noises—for the Sunday lunch of *chakalaka*, curried chicken, *dombolo* steamed bread soaked in tomato and onion gravy, fried cabbage, mashed pumpkin, green beans cooked with potatoes and grated carrots, beetroot salad, custard and jelly; and to be fussed over by aunts and uncles and neighbours; and to talk football with people who really know something about the 'beautiful game'; and to enjoy the latest gossip in the taverns; and to have their gaudy Hummers and Lamborghinis admired by urchins playing football on dirt streets with tennis balls.

Gone are the days when it used to be BMWs and Mercedes Benzes! Now these German sedans are as common as dirt and can be seen parked in township yards.

More than anything else, former Sowetans return to Soweto for the homeliness as well as the nostalgia—being in Soweto is like being enveloped in the ample bosom of a much-loved matriarch.

This Sunday morning Tumi and Don are driving home in Tumi's Jaguar. Actually she is the one who is driving. He sits next to her reading *City Press*. But it is a bumpy drive, which makes for uncomfortable reading. When Tumi is in Soweto she drives like Sowetans—speeding on the streets without any respect for lanes, when they happen to be there, and disobeying traffic lights on the township highways. Sometimes she swerves to avoid cars parked in the middle of the street while their owners are shooting the breeze over cans of beer.

The couple's township in Soweto is Orlando West, and kids wave at Tumi as she drives on Mooki Street to her home. Older ones may remember seeing her picture in *Drum*, *Bona* and other magazines or on billboards when she was still a *modlara*, as they call models in Soweto. Even today she occasionally features in the newspapers and on television as one of the rising stars in business—the owner of a prestigious model agency with a whole new breed of models, even white ones, in her stable. Seeing her in the flesh sends the kids into a frenzy of excitement. 'Hey, that's Sis' Tumi! There's Sis' Tumi!' they screech, jumping up and down. One boasts, 'Yes, and she lives in my street.' Others look at her incredulously and laugh mockingly—a celebrity like Sis' Tumi cannot live in anyone's street.

Some of the kids are in school uniform even though it is Sunday. There must be an event, perhaps a concert, at one of the schools. From the maroon and black uniforms, Tumi can tell that they are from her alma mater, Belle Primary, of which she is not proud at all. It was reputed to be the worst school in the area where students failed in great numbers. Tumi suffered the fate of all the kids from that school who never got any respect. She was the laughing stock of those who went to better schools, and everyone expected that she would amount to nothing. No one imagined that one day she would be a top model because those days she was a tall, gangly tomboy with a silly giggle. Even her parents thought she needed more feeding so that she would fill up a bit. They would never have sent her to Belle Primary School in the first place but for the fact that they were too late to enrol her at better schools.

Don, on the other hand, went to Tloreng Primary—just across the street from Belle—and wore the black and gold uniform with pride because the school had a good reputation. Tumi chuckles to herself as she remembers how spoilt Don used to be—a real mama's boy. His mother was a staff nurse at Baragwanath Hospital, and as an only child, he was one of the few boys whose pants were not patched and who wore shoes all the time, not just on Sundays.

Tumi's thoughts are interrupted by the sight of an old friend crossing the street from the Hector Peterson Memorial Museum.

'Hey, there's Oupa,' she says and stops the car.

Don looks up from the newspaper and says, 'That old man can't be Oupa.'

They argue about it. The Oupa that Don remembers was a handsome toughie who used to be very popular with girls. The likes of Don both looked up to him and envied him. He used to walk the streets with an arrogant swagger, a far cry from the skeletal man in greasy tattered overalls, with a rough, peeling face that has been devoured by alcohol, who is now staggering among the young men and women selling arts and crafts on the pavement.

It is Oupa all right. Don laughs.

'Don't laugh,' says Tumi. 'Maybe you would have been like that too if you had stayed.'

'I'm not laughing at the guy's misfortune,' says Don. 'I just remember that he was once your boyfriend.'

Tumi giggles and says, 'I just remember that he beat the hell out of you once.'

Tumi had 'crowned' Oupa, which meant that she accepted his love proposal, after he had pestered her for a long time and even twisted her arm, literally, when he waylaid her after school. And then she met Don while they were both waiting in a long queue to buy *vetkoek* and *snoek* at the Makgetha Supermarket, which was not really a supermarket but a tiny store whose claim to fame was the *vetkoek* that were popular with school kids who would fight over them during break. She knew him as the dandy son of Staff Nurse Mateza who was never allowed to play beyond Lembede Street where he lived. He knew her as the awkward girl from Mooki Street who was all over the place and was known for being forward. At first he didn't think much of her because she went to Belle Primary and was one of Oupa's girlfriends—Oupa had a girlfriend in every street in Orlando West. He even encroached on some pastures in Orlando East and Diepkloof.

But despite their reservations about each other, a friendship developed in that long *vetkoek* queue. Almost every day they met during break since their schools had their recess at the same time. He always had lunch money and would buy her the *amagwinya vetkoek* with mango *atchaar*. She taught him how to eat fresh white bread with fish crumbs or with battered fishbone. When he had stolen more money from his mother's purse, he bought her French polony, Russian sausages and chips, which was quite a treat because no primary school kid could afford that kind of fare.

Oupa got wind of what he interpreted as a relationship between Don and one of his girlfriends. He confronted Don about it and did not believe him when he tried to assure him that his friendship with Tumi was confined to sharing *spykos*, as that kind of food was known. Instead, he gave Don a black eye and forced him to give him all the money he had in his pockets.

'Only Bra Oupa will buy his cherries *spykos*,' Oupa said. 'And from now on you'll have to pay tax every day so that I can continue to buy Tumi the treats you have made her accustomed to.'

For months after that, Don took a different route whenever he saw Oupa approaching. His friendship with Tumi came to an end. He did not want to have anything to do with her even after he heard that the 'silver cup was broken' between Oupa and Tumi.

A few years later Don and Tumi met as students at Matsike Secondary School. They renewed their friendship and became lovers. They both remember that period as the best time of their lives, despite the political upheavals that were sweeping Soweto and the rest of South Africa. But the affair was not to last. Don was taken up by the struggle even before he could matriculate and was active in street committees and protest marches. One day he disappeared. He and two of his close friends, Fontyo and Bova. Not even his mother knew where he had gone. Later Tumi learnt that the three had 'skipped the country' and had joined the freedom fighters in exile. Her hurt turned into pride. She boasted to other girls that her boyfriend was a guerrilla fighter, which was misinterpreted by the gossiping old ladies at prayer meetings who wondered what there was to be proud of in a man who fought against gorillas in the forest.

Oupa staggers to the Jaguar and begs for a few coins. He is too drunk to recognize Tumi and Don. To him, they may just be some of the tourists who flock to the Hector Peterson Museum. They give him a ten-rand note and he staggers away singing their praises, promising them that the good *amadlozi*—the ancestors—will bless them with more Jaguars than they already have.

Tumi pulls out and negotiates her way among the tour buses, cars and minibuses that have brought tourists to the memorial site. She has to drive only a few blocks before she parks the car outside her parents' yard. Except for a blue awning over the stoep and the fence of concrete slabs known as 'stop-nonsense', the red-brick four-roomed house has not changed from the time Tumi was a little girl. Most of the other houses in the neighbourhood look different because the owners have extended them from the uniform matchbox design of the past, to different shapes and sizes, some of which would not be out of place in the suburbs. Only the small yards stop further extension. The houses are now roofed with red, black or green tiles instead of corrugated iron sheets. Some of them are surrounded by high brick walls, just like in the suburbs, whereas when Tumi and Don were kids all the houses had waist-high broad-meshed fences over which young men running away from the police could jump with ease.

Tumi's father, Rre Molefhe, is sitting on a rocking chair on the red stoep smoking a pipe. He is wearing his sixties' eight-piece Ayres cap and is tapping his sixties'

Florsheim shoe to Miles Davis' trumpet wailing from the speaker near the door.

Don observes with satisfaction that the jazz generation has not yet died out in Soweto. He remembers when he was growing up that on Sundays jazz blared from most homes. His mother, however, had no time for that kind of meaningless music; she listened to the Dark City Sisters' harmonies and Spokes Mashiyane's pennywhistle instead. But everywhere else people sat on the black, red or green stoeps listening to John Coltrane, Charlie Parker, Sonny Stitt, Milt Jackson, Duke Ellington, Count Basie, Sonny Rollins and Dizzy Gillespie. These were the big names that every jazz collection in the township would have. There were others who were more obscure and would only be known by aficionados of the first order. The more obscure the jazzman, the more respect the collector gained. Tumi's father, for instance, discovered Eric Dolphy when no one else in the township knew about him. He had visited a nephew in Lady Selbourne, Pretoria, which was the jazz capital of South Africa those days, and learnt of this new guy. He came back to Soweto with his LP and boasted to everyone about Eric Dolphy. Soon Eric Dolphy had joined the staples in Soweto. That was why when Sowetans wanted to learn more about jazz they secretly went to Pretoria but would never openly admit that the black townships of that city were more advanced in the fine art of jazz appreciation than Soweto.

Rre Molefhe had stacks and stacks of LPs and would sit with friends over bottles of beer arguing about the sidemen. They had only to listen to a few bars of a song they had never heard before and knew at once who was playing the bass or the drums or the guitar. They could identify Barney Kessel's guitar or Max Roach's drums in the midst of complicated instrumentation by many musicians. They shared their disgust when Joe Zawinul messed up with the great idiom by introducing electrification in Miles Davis' music, beginning with *In a Silent Way*. When the bluesman Champion Jack Dupree sang of how his mother-in-law was the ugliest woman anyone had ever seen, and that she was so skinny she could hide behind the broom, they laughed heartily and ribbed each other about their mothers-in-law. Even though they had heard those lyrics over and over again and knew them by heart, they still found them hilarious.

Sometimes the ribbing turned nasty, like when Rre Molefhe had a fist fight with a neighbour who has since joined that great jam session in the sky. Those days Rre Molefhe was a snob who despised the home-grown jazz giants. The neighbour was sold on saxophonists Eric Nomvete and Kippie Moeketsi and would play his new stereo at full blast, drowning Rre Molefhe's *Canadian Suite* by Oscar Peterson. Rre Molefhe made snide remarks to his drinking buddies about his neighbour's lack of taste, which reached the man's ears and he came storming to Rre Molefhe's house to demand an apology. But Rre Molefhe stood his ground and continued to say disparaging things both about the man's music collection and the man's ethnicity.

'It is because you are a Venda, that's why you don't know good music,' he said.

This was too much for the neighbour. He floored Rre Molefhe with a right jab on the stomach and a left hook on the jaw. But Rre Molefhe quickly jumped to his feet and paid the man back in kind. They exchanged blows on Rre Molefhe's front lawn and in the ensuing fight some of Ma Molefhe's zinnias were destroyed. The children of the neighbourhood came to watch and to egg on the side they favoured. No one tried to stop the fight until Ma Molefhe was woken from her nap by the commotion outside. She came running and got in between the men. She reprimanded both of them for acting like children.

'The Boers are killing our children in the streets and you are killing each other over jazz?' she asked.

The neighbour went back to his house to nurse his bruises and Rre Molefhe went to wash the blood from his nose under the backyard tap.

There was a chill between the men for many months. And then one day Rre Molefhe heard the sound of a flute coming from the neighbour's house. At first he thought it was Roland Kirk but, no, it was not. He listened intently again because the volume was quite low and thought it was Herbie Mann. But the sound was different. So were the drums and the guitar. The guitar accompanied the flute in a unison that knelled like the music of the spirits and the drums had the full-bodied boom that could only be produced by a combination of cowhide drums and a demented drummer. Rre Molefhe stood outside for a while and listened. The neighbour came out of the house and approached him suspiciously.

'Are you missing something, Molefhe?' he asked.

'Who is playing there?' asked Rre Molefhe.

'It's Malombo Jazzmen. Don't tell me you haven't heard of Malombo Jazzmen. That song is called *Foolish Fly*.'

Then he told him about the line-up—Abe Cindi on the flute, Julian Bahula on the Bapedi drums and Philip Tabane on the guitar. From that day not only did Rre Molefhe become friends with his neighbour again but he gained new respect for local jazz. He began a relentless collection of LPs by Morolong, Victor Ndlazilwana and the Jazz Ministers, the Jazz Epistles, Hugh Masekela, Chris McGregor and the Blue Notes, Dollar Brand and many others. It was as though he was making up for lost time. On pay day, which was every Friday, he stole away from the Bramley ball-bearings factory where he worked to Kohinoor Stores in the city to spend most of his money on LPs. When wives were complaining that there was no food in the house because their husbands had gambled or drank the money as soon as they got the pay packets, Ma Molefhe was complaining that Tumi was going to school without eating a proper breakfast and did not have the required school uniform because Rre Molefhe wasted the money on LPs.

When some members of Malombo Jazzmen broke away to form the ill-fated Malombo Jazzmakers, he took the matter so personally that there was no peace in the home for months. It was a schism that was as earth shattering in his life as the one that happened later when some renegades broke away from Orlando Pirates to form Kaizer Chiefs in January 1970.

No wonder! After being harassed by the police and by the white bosses and even by the nondescript white nonentities in the streets of Johannesburg, or after spending the night in jail for not carrying their reference books with them, men came home to be soothed by jazz.

Don remembers some of these events with fondness and finds it amazing that the culture of the period endures in the hearts of people like Rre Molefhe, who have refused to change with the times both in their taste in music and in their fashion statements. They have even refused to embrace the new jazz generation such as Terence Blanchard and Wynton Marsalis. Though Rre Molefhe's generation grudgingly admits that these youngsters are geniuses, it nevertheless does not see any contradiction in regarding them as upstarts. For Rre Molefhe and his mates only things that were produced in the fifties and the sixties or, if they want to be magnanimous, the early seventies, are of any value. That is why the eight-piece Ayres and bebop are his trademarks even in his dotage.

Ma Molefhe has been expecting the children, as she calls them, since morning. Why did they come so late? She didn't even go to church because she was waiting for them. Then she fusses over her daughter. She looks thin and is not eating enough. 'I know, I know, you *modlara* people have to starve yourselves,' she adds. 'It is a strange profession that requires people to be as thin as ghosts.'

At least for today her daughter will be well fed. She has cooked her favourite Setswana dish—tripe that has been cut into tiny bits with a pair of scissors and is served with *ting*, a fermented sorghum hard porridge. Don loves *ting* too, and has often begged Tumi to teach him how to cook it. Even though his mother taught him how to cook from an early age, in the same way that she taught him how to scrub and polish the linoleum floor with Cobra and the red stoep with Sunbeam until they shone like a mirror, she never taught him anything about *ting* since it was not part of the isiXhosa culture to which she belonged. But Tumi pretends that she never learnt any cooking skills from her mother. It is because she hates it when Don cooks—it is not in keeping with the status of a Black Diamond.

Rre Molefhe is in good spirits as usual and during the meal regales everyone with funny stories of how he used to escape the police when he worked at a factory in Bramley during the days of apartheid when there was a curfew for black people in the city. He is obviously very proud of his daughter's achievements and even prouder of Don, who used to be a freedom fighter and is now a BEE Fat Cat.

This last one, of course, embarrasses Don and he knows that Rre Molefhe got it from Tumi. He dare not tell him that he is not a Fat Cat, at least not yet, but is a security guard. It is a good thing that Tumi is not privy to his thoughts at this moment, otherwise she would have yelled some sense into them: 'You are not a security guard, Don. You are a manager and soon will be the chief executive. And then you'll own that security company, and many other companies. Positive thinking, Don. Positive thinking.'

Ma Molefhe shares her husband's sentiments. She embarrasses Tumi when she praises her right there in Don's presence for at last settling down with a real hard-working man instead of the layabouts she used to date. It is a *bonsella* that she is not bringing a stranger into the Molefhe home, but a son of Orlando West who has done well in life and whose mother was the township's beloved staff nurse. She was a hero in her own right because she died at the hands of the Boer torturers.

'Oh, yes,' says Rre Molefhe. 'It is clear to me that one day, Don will be like Comrade Molotov Mbungane. I have just read in the *Sowetan* that he has now acquired new mines in the Congo.'

Don has heard about the Congolese gold and diamond mines. He also heard that these were acquired in partnership with former Mobutu Sese Seko cabinet ministers. Don finds this odious and wonders what happened to the moral high ground on which the leaders of the liberation movement used to stand. He finds it even more tragic that many members of the Zairean elite who looted the coffers of their country during Mobutu's dictatorship have bought mansions in the suburbs of South Africa and have gone into business with the likes of Molotov Mbungane—injecting money stolen from other African countries into the South African economy. But he does not voice these thoughts to the enthusiastic Rre Molefhe.

'Ja,' says Rre Molefhe, 'that Comrade Molotov is a good man who loves his people. Do you know that now he is spending five million rand to sponsor the soccer league?'

Then father and daughter argue about which team will win the league. Tumi is an ardent soccer fan and supports Orlando Pirates—'Once a Pirate, always a Pirate'. Before she got to be so busy at her TM Modelling Agency, she used to attend all their matches in full gear of black and white and skull and crossbones. Even today, occasionally, she and her friends fly to such countries as Mauritius when the national team Bafana Bafana is playing there. The father, on the other hand, changed from Orlando Pirates years back and is now an unshakeable supporter of Kaizer Chiefs—which disproves the once-a-Pirate-always-a-Pirate theory. Don is always left out of any argument about soccer because he does not bother to follow the politics of the game. He does, however, enjoy the matches he occasionally attends with Tumi and, like Rre Molefhe, he supports Kaizer Chiefs.

After lunch, while Tumi helps her mother with the dishes, Don borrows the Jaguar and goes to see his pals, Fontyo and Bova. Although Tumi does not approve of them, this is one relationship she has to stomach because she understands the bond they share as childhood friends who, during the freedom struggle, endured the kind of hardships she can never even imagine. Of course, she hopes gradually to wean Don from unproductive friendships based only on sentimentality. Don needs to take up golf and associate with fellow Black Diamonds who will throw lucrative deals his way.

Don knows exactly where he will find his friends—at Wezile's Restaurant, which is more of a tavern really, on Vilakazi Street, famous as the only street in the world that has produced two Nobel Prize winners: Nelson Mandela and Desmond Tutu. In fact, the restaurant is next to Tutu's house, and the owner has been hauled to court once for making too much noise for the Tutu family.

Don finds his two friends hanging out with a group of European tourists. This is what they do all day long, ever since their demobilization compensation ran out. They sit here all day long moaning about how Black Economic Empowerment has failed them and waiting for a friendly patron, most likely a tourist, to buy them beer. Bova remains an ardent Marxist and blames all his problems on capitalism. He never stops telling everyone how the liberation movement sold out the struggle by taking a Thatcherite route.

The comrades are happy to see Don because they know that more beer will flow.

'So, how's our *mantshingilane* doing these days?' asks Fontyo.

They tease him about his good fortune to have a girl like Tumi who waited for him during all his years of exile.

Don knows that Tumi was not really waiting for him. In fact she has confessed that in the long run she forgot about him completely and had other relationships. Don was just fortunate that when he returned she was not in any serious relationship and they were able to rekindle their love again, which then became even more intense. But Don does not correct his friends. Instead, he tries to encourage them to follow his lead and look for any job they can find instead of complaining in the taverns. But they are so disillusioned with life, with what they call crony capitalism in South Africa, and with the betrayal by such comrades as Molotov whose mantra is that 'accumulation cannot be democratized, comrades', that they have given up even trying.

'The fruits of liberation are not for the foot soldier, Comrade AK,' says Bova, placing a sarcastic emphasis on Don's *nom de guerre*. This is news to Don because cadres never saw one another as foot soldiers or anything like that. They were all comrades.

Bova takes out a newspaper cutting from his pocket, unfolds it and says, 'Now I want you to tell me, Don, who says these words.' Then he reads: *The true fact of life is that you'll not succeed equally the same. There are people sometimes I know and I believe that they would like to hold successes against those of us who succeed.* Then he stops and looks at Don expectantly. 'Don't tell him, Fontyo. I want him to guess who is saying these words. These words were spoken by this man on an American television programme called *60 Minutes*. He never thought they would reach our ears. Who is speaking here, Don?'

Don has no idea.

Bova continues to read: *And remember, we carry those political prisoners and former exiles by putting them as shareholders in our businesses. By the way, we don't have to. It's our pure philanthropy of thinking about those you were with in prison. There's no law, no rule to help anyone.*

'Are these words truly from a comrade?' asks Don.

'Who else but Comrade Dr Molotov Mbungane!' announces Bova.

'They called him Comrade Capitalist in that programme,' adds Fontyo.

'We are the object of his philanthropy,' says Bova with a pained look. 'We who made it possible for him to be where he is today. He's now a philanthropist. He's now Bill Gates.'

'The motherfucker steps on our heads to be where he is,' says Fontyo, trying very hard to copy Bova's pained look. 'Now he talks of us in terms of philanthropy. Whose bloody philanthropy made him a billionaire?'

Don takes all their bitching with good humour and buys them more beer. He is not so worked up about Comrade Molotov's utterances because from what he has come to know of the man he cannot put anything past him. Before he drives back to Tumi, he gives his comrades some money, pleading with them not to spend it on beer but on paraffin, cooking oil, maize meal and salt.

Back at Three Oaks, in the quiet suburb of North Riding, Soweto is ringing in Tumi's and Don's heads. And when Soweto is ringing in your head you make love. No, you fuck. That's what you call it because making love sounds too clinical. Too neat and clean and proper. You wear your Rough Rider ultra-ribbed, lubricated latex and fuck like you are back at Matseke Secondary School. Of course, during those carefree days it was always flesh-on-flesh. You fuck like Tumi has sneaked into your bedroom for illicit sex when your mother is doing night duty at Baragwanath. Like you must ravage each other very quickly, which becomes even more breathtaking, because Tumi has to rush home before Rre Molefhe discovers that the person sleeping in her bed is a rolled up blanket and beats her black and blue with his belt until her buttocks are sore to borrow an expression from Ma Molefhe who could only threaten whenever Tumi was becoming a problem child: 'When your father comes back from work, he will give you a thorough hiding until your buttocks are sore.' Yes, you fuck like you have just discovered Tiger Balm and Pau Yuen Tong from the gossip of fellow smokers behind the school toilets, and have applied it to your penis to enhance both your pleasure. Only now the enhancement is a natural one. It is not a result of experimentation with dodgy Chinese ointments, but of the juices that flow with abandon between your bodies, culminating in explosions that raise the roof. And the neighbours.

5

SOMEHOW THE BITCH MUST PAY

Kristin Uys cooks out of habit. After a long day at the Roodepoort magistrate's court she usually only has time for a sandwich for dinner. But on some days cases are shorter than originally envisaged, especially because she knows how to make attorneys and prosecutors get to the point without wasting time on arguments that are too clever by half, and then she gets home before three in the afternoon. It is on such days that she cooks an elaborate meal and sits down to a candlelight dinner all by herself. She always cooks more than she needs, and by the end of the week she is confronted by many Tupperware containers in the fridge filled with yellow rice, mixed vegetables and meats of different kinds—on occasion even *bobotie*, a spiced mincemeat pie baked with an egg-based topping.

On Saturdays, she takes a walk to the park two blocks from her Sonneblom Avenue house. Her cat is at her heels. She is laden with the Tupperware which she carries in paper bags. She also has serviettes, plates, knives and forks in the paper bags, all from her best china and silver collection that was used only on special occasions during the glorious days that have since receded into distant and murky memory.

The denizens of the park are waiting with drooling anticipation. They are the types who would never have been tolerated here in the past, when flowers bloomed and white children's laughter filled the air. The only black faces that could venture into these hallowed grounds were municipality workers in brown overalls who tended the flowers, and the nannies in pink or yellow dresses and white *doeks* who sat on the grass—not on benches, for those were for whites only—and gossiped about their madams while the little ones played on merry-go-rounds. Or who pushed the swings whenever the tykes demanded it.

Kristin Uys was one of those kids once. Forty years ago, this was her park too. Every Saturday afternoon, her nanny brought her here while her mother hosted a bridge party at her home which was then on Jim Fouché Road and her father, a *dominee* of the Dutch Reformed Church, ministered at weddings and funerals. This was decades before the government did away with the Group Areas Act—the law that confined each racial group to its own residential and business area—and black hoboes began to invade sacred spaces at the same time as democracy was invading the rest of the land.

She took the changes in her stride. She did not mope about the hoboes. She accepted them as one may accept a benign tumour on a part of the body that can easily be covered by clothing. They were fine as long as they stayed in the park. As long as they didn't make themselves a nuisance in the well-kept suburban streets and didn't buzz at neighbourhood gates for alms. She didn't need the park anyway; they were welcome to it.

She forgot about the hoboes until the habit of cooking made her remember them. Now she has grown to love them. They serve a useful purpose—they eat her food.

They see her even before she enters the gate and greet her with grins, wishing her a long healthy life resplendent with blessings and happiness. She does smile back but never returns their good wishes. Without a word she lays a tablecloth on the grass among the broken swings and jungle gyms. She dishes the food out on to the plates and sets out the knives and forks. The hoboes attack the food without ceremony.

She has her own plate and sits on a bench with her cat and eats quietly. The hoboes, on the other hand, chew loudly and vigorously while arguing about things she cares nothing about. Even in destitution the habit of segregation cannot be broken. The white hoboes huddle together in a broken-spirited and timid manner while the blacks sprawl confidently at the opposite end of the tablecloth as if they own the place. When Kristin began bringing food to the park three years ago, only black hoboes could be seen. Now there is an increasing number of whites, and they come with a political axe to grind. They blame the black hoboes for their dire situation.

'It is your Mandela who created all this mess,' one says, emitting fumes of methylated spirits. 'I lost my job because of affirmative action.'

A black hobo laughs and says, 'Every one of you white guys blame affirmative action, even those who never had an honest job in their lives in the first place . . . those who had been cushioned by the welfare state that the Afrikaner had created for himself. Where is this affirmative action that none of us here can see?'

This is the black hobo that everyone hates—both black and white. He is the hobo who is always reading newspapers instead of just sleeping under them. The white hoboes think he is uppity while the black ones wonder what he is doing among them when it is so obvious that he is a learned man who should be working in an office somewhere. They resent him for being too smart for everyone's good. The black hoboes call him Professor —which may or may not be derisive—while the white hoboes don't call him anything at all. When he makes a stupid statement like the one about the Afrikaner welfare state, they do not respond to him directly but mumble among themselves that in the new South Africa blacks can talk shit with impunity.

After the meal Kristin Uys clears the china, silver and Tupperware and places them in the paper bags. The hoboes thank her profusely and shower her with more blessings. With her cat in tow she walks back to Sonneblom Avenue.

A service truck is parked near her gate. In the cab Shortie Visagie is watching the house with binoculars, which really shouldn't be necessary since he is not so far from the house as not to be able to see over the wall with the naked eye. Kristin Uys does not pay any attention to the truck as she walks past it through the gate which she has opened with her remote key. Shortie's binoculars follow her until she and the cat enter the house. He quickly scribbles something in a notebook and then drives away.

Shortie's mission was a simple one. Find out what the magistrate's 'weakness' is and report back to Stevo at Medium B Section, Diepkloof Prison. These were the instructions he received when he visited his brother yesterday.

One thing that impressed Shortie was that Stevo still had a lot of power even at Sun City. For instance, the prison warders stood a distance away, overtly giving them some privacy. He was also encouraged by Stevo's optimism, unlike an earlier visit when he seemed to be down-spirited. He believed that he was going to be free soon.

'And I tell you, china, I'm going to make life hell for that magistrate.'

This last bit made Shortie nervous.

'That's dangerous talk, Stevo. Let's forget about the magistrate and focus on getting you out of here. Krish Naidoo is working hard to get you out of here.'

But Stevo is stubborn. When he has made up his mind about something, it stays made up.

'I'm going to make that bitch pay, Shortie,' he insisted, 'and you're going to help me do it.'

'Don't make things worse, Stevo,' Shortie pleaded. 'It doesn't pay nothing to revenge against a magistrate.'

'We are the Visagies, man,' said Stevo. 'We're not afraid of nothing. I want you to go out there and find her weakness. I'm gonna use it to destroy the bitch piece by piece once and for all.'

When Shortie was about to leave, his brother instructed him to give some money to the warder. Stevo could see that Shortie was not pleased at the prospect of parting with cash. He warned him, 'And be generous, Shortie. These are the guys who make my life comfortable here.'

And indeed one can buy comfort at Sun City. Stevo has a cell to himself, despite the much publicized overcrowding in the prison system. The reason given to senior management for this special treatment is that it is for his safety because some gangsters are plotting his death—a threat concocted by warders on his payroll. In his cell, he has a portable television and a microwave oven. This is not because he is a hot-shot gangster. Anyone can have such comforts for a high rental fee paid to corrupt prison guards. This, of course, means that Shortie must bring more money, even though he has been complaining both to his brother and his mother that their coffers will soon run dry because there has been very little income since their arrest.

When Shortie got home, he shared Stevo's intentions of vengeance with Aunt Magda, who was still pissed off that the magistrate exposed her to ridicule when she sent Stevo to jail, despite the mass action she had guaranteed to her followers would succeed.

'Do as Stevo says,' said Aunt Magda. 'Stevo knows best. But don't tell Ma Visagie about it. We don't know what her reaction will be.'

That is why we see Shortie at Weltevreden Park spying on the magistrate.

He continues the stake-out for some days, noting down the time the magistrate leaves for work in the morning and returns in the afternoon, never to leave the house again until the next day. Her only companion is a cat. She receives no visitors, nor does she visit anyone. The cat has a lot of freedom to roam about but is always waiting for her at the door when she arrives. Her face lights up and she plays with it a bit even before she unlocks the door and the folding security barrier.

She must live a very lonely and sad life, Shortie concludes.

Before the week is out, he returns to Sun City to report to Stevo. There are many other people visiting prisoners—mostly women talking to their menfolk in their orange prison jumpsuits. Shortie is already waiting when Stevo is brought in. His orange prison uniform is oversized and Shortie cannot help laughing.

'I don't see nothing funny, china,' says Stevo, looking at his brother suspiciously. 'I hope you got something to tell me instead of sitting there giggling like a schoolgirl.'

But he has nothing to tell him. The magistrate lives alone. Just she and her cat. There is nothing that he saw as a weakness that could be exploited to make her suffer.

'You didn't do the job right, Shortie,' says Stevo. 'There must be something we can use. You didn't watch that house right, china. You didn't follow her right.'

'Sure, I did, Stevo, starting on Saturday. She came back from somewhere with paper bags and stuff. After that she didn't leave the house. Sunday she drove to the Dutch Reformed Church in Roodekrans. She came back and stayed in the house. Monday she went to work . . .'

'She came back and stayed in the house,' Stevo completes the sentence for him.

'I can't spend all the time watching that house, Stevo,' says Shortie. 'I gotta work, Stevo. Nobody's doing the work at the scrapyard if I spend all my life waiting in Weltevreden Park. Ma is beginning to ask questions because there's no money coming in.'

Stevo is disgusted. If Shortie is not of much help then he'll have to think of something else. Somehow the bitch must pay.

Kristin Uys has not been an attorney for more than a decade—since she left the Transvaal side-bar to become a prosecutor and then a magistrate. Though she did practise as a conveyancer, even then she hated that aspect of the law. It is the same today. She finds it tedious when she has to settle a case that involves disputes over transfers of immovable property. Today's case was particularly irksome and it dragged on for the whole day. She is looking forward to a bubble bath and a glass of warm wine.

She is about to walk out of her office when the phone rings.

'You bitch!' says a strange muffled voice. 'You whore! We gonna get you. We gonna fuck the shit out of you and then kill you.'

'Who's this?'

Whoever it is has hung up. The magistrate is shaken. She stands there for a while as if she does not know what to do next. Then she decides to dismiss the telephone call with the contempt it deserves.

She gets into her Fiat Uno and drives home.

It is almost eight-thirty in the morning but she is still in bed. Her cat cuddles up beside her. She oversleeps sometimes, especially when she has had a lot of wine the previous night. She will make it to the courtroom by ten. One of the joys of being a magistrate is that the cases cannot begin without her.

Both she and the cat are rudely awakened by the phone. She reaches for it.

'Bitch!' the voice screeches into her ear. It may or may not be the same voice as yesterday's. It is muffled, so she can't tell. 'I am going to mess your face up so you'll never want to show it anywhere again.'

'Who gave you my private number?' she asks.

The caller is no longer there.

Her number is not listed. What if the caller is already in the house? For a moment she panics, but soon gets in control of herself. She is a bit groggy as she climbs out of bed. The room is in a mess. A skimpy skirt, fishnet stockings, stilettos and various items of frilly underwear are strewn all over the floor. There are three empty bottles of wine and a wine glass on the floor. It looks like there was a hell of a party here.

She trips on a feather boa as she stumbles to the bathroom for a shower.

As soon as Kristin Uys gets to the Roodepoort magistrate's court, she asks the security office to trace the two threatening calls, and in no time she gets the report that both calls came from Diepkloof Prison. She is relieved because now she thinks she knows who is behind the threats—Stevo Visagie. She can handle the petty gangster and will not make him feel important by reporting the matter to the police. Instead, she will go to the prison to face him and to show him that she cannot be frightened by the likes of him, and that she will continue to do her work, which to her is more of a calling, without fear or favour.

She examines the roll—there is no matter that is so urgent that it cannot be postponed. She calls the prosecutor.

'We'll start a bit late today,' she says. 'I have an emergency to attend to. Inform the attorneys of the accused.'

She gets into her Fiat Uno and is about to drive away when her cellphone rings. After rummaging through the stuff in her handbag, she retrieves the phone.

'Hello, sweetheart.'

It is the impudent voice again.

'My cellphone number too?'

'This is only the beginning. We are going to get you, and your family, and your cat,' says the voice with muffled glee. 'I bet you're shitting in your pants by now.'

The magistrate laughs mockingly.

'You and who, you coward? You can't face me, can you? You have to make anonymous calls?'

She is the one who hangs up this time. She is determined more than ever to have a showdown with Stevo Visagie, once and for all.

At Medium B, a warder ushers the magistrate into the room that is used by lawyers to consult with their inmate clients. She takes a seat facing the door. A few minutes later Stevo is led into the room in shackles and handcuffs. As soon as he sees the magistrate he displays a defiant smirk.

He turns to the warder and winks.

'A date with the magistrate!' he says. 'You guys really do spoil me.'

The magistrate indicates to the warder to leave. He shoves Stevo on to a seat across the desk and goes to stand guard outside the door.

'I have come to warn you, Stevo,' says the magistrate calmly. 'Stop the stupid calls.'

'You sent me to jail for nothing, lady. Now you come to threaten me?'

'You stop threatening me, Stevo. I know you are behind the phone calls.'

Stevo almost spits out the words: 'I am in prison, lady. How the fuck do I threaten you?'

'I've been receiving some dirty telephone calls . . .'

'Oooohhhhhh!' swoons Stevo lasciviously. 'Dirty phone calls, hey!'

'And they have been traced to Diepkloof Prison.'

'How do you know I made the calls? Obviously you are the most popular girl among the boys at Sun City.'

'I am just warning you, Stevo, that's all.'

Stevo explodes like a volcano, yelling at the top of his voice that the magistrate will first have to prove that he has something to do with the calls. This brings the warder rushing in. He does not leave even after the magistrate assures him that she can handle the situation. He stands to attention next to Stevo.

'Instead of harassing me, lady,' says Stevo, 'I think you better focus on looking after yourself, in case someone decides to do something bigger than the phone calls.'

The magistrate stands up and hovers over Stevo Visagie. The warder is really worried now.

'If you think I'm a frightened little girl, you've got another think coming, Stevo,' she says. 'You're not man enough to carry out your silly little threats. That's why you're a pimp . . . playing with little girls . . . when bigger and better criminals carry out cash heists and run big syndicates.'

Stevo is livid, the more so because he is powerless in his shackles. The best he can do is hyperventilate.

'You're nothing but a scared little boy, Stevo. A scared little boy. A worm, Stevo. A wiggly little worm.'

At this she wiggles her index finger like a worm in front of his eyes. Tears stream down Stevo's cheeks. She glares at him with satisfaction.

He says feebly, 'You'll regret you ever said this to me.'

'Do I look like someone who ever regrets anything? And by the way, Meneer Visagie, who is going to make me regret? A crybaby like you? Get real, *boytjie*! You call yourself a gangster—you're just a tickey-line gangster.'

Now he weeps uncontrollably.

The magistrate sings as in a lullaby, 'Cry, baby, cry!'

She has put him in his place. She is convinced that she will never hear from Stevo Visagie again.

Her gait is light and cheerful as she walks back to her car.

6

THE CAT THAT CAUSED ALL THE TROUBLE

Don Mateza cooks for the love of it. He likes to experiment, fusing dishes from various cultures to create something unique. It is a gift he inherited from his mother. Like most boys growing up in Soweto those days, he learnt that there was no work for boys or for girls. There was just work. Boys in Soweto were taught by their mothers and big sisters how to cook, wash dishes and polish the floors. The problems only came later in life, when boys reached their late teens and thought they had outgrown what they suddenly recognized as women's work and, like their fathers before them, felt the need to assert their manhood after the emasculation they suffered at the workplace and everywhere else they confronted the white world. Staff Nurse Mateza made sure that Don did not outgrow housework. She needn't have worried. Don had no intention of outgrowing at least one aspect of domesticity—cooking.

Unfortunately, he does not get to practise his culinary skills that much, living in the fast-paced middle-class world of Johannesburg where men and women are busy chasing the almighty rand and cooking is left to the maids. Tumi hasn't got a live-in maid though; only a part-time woman who comes twice a week to do the washing and clean the house. But her pots rarely need cleaning because only once in a while does anyone cook in them. The couple lead such hectic lives that usually the only meal they get to eat at home is a bowl of cereal in the morning. Lunch finds them both at work. For Don it is normally a *boerewors* roll from the Greek corner cafe and for Tumi it may be a chicken salad at some restaurant in Sandton where she may be treating a client or a favoured model to a light meal. Most evenings Tumi is not home because of a fashion show or a meeting or a photo shoot or a cocktail party; Don, if not working overtime, orders a pizza for delivery or buys takeaways.

Sometimes he comes home early enough to cook a meal. Like tonight. Tumi phoned to say she didn't have an engagement and would be coming home earlier than usual. For dinner he is going to surprise her with *ting*, the favourite Setswana dish for which she goes especially to her mother's place in Soweto when she has the time to spare. Tonight she is going to have it right here in her apartment in suburbia. And she is going to have it with *tshotlo*, the pulled beef briskets that are overcooked and then pestled until they look like little strings in a brown paste. He has cooked it with scallions and seasoned it with salt, mixed masala and cayenne pepper. That's all it needs.

It took him a lot of planning to come up with this meal. He has always wanted to surprise Tumi with *ting* but didn't have any idea how to cook it—until he learnt that one of the office cleaners at VIP Protection Services was from Botswana. He took notes as she explained how to mix sorghum meal with a fermentation agent, also made of sorghum meal, and how to cook the mixture as one would cook porridge. She told him that the best meat to accompany *ting* was *tshotlo* rather than tripe. This morning, she brought him the fermentation agent in a small jar that women use to preserve fruit.

The meal is almost ready when Tumi arrives. Don is still in his apron doing the finishing touches in the kitchenette. In the dining area, the table is extravagantly laid with shimmering silver and expensive china and two unlit candles. Tumi is in her business executive-type trouser suit and is carrying a load of files and catalogues. She starts sniffing and frowning as soon as she enters.

'What's up, Don?' she asks.

'I thought I should surprise you with a wholesome meal of *ting* the way your mama cooks in the township. And guess what? I have cooked *tshotlo* too. Do you know *tshotlo*? The Basotho call it *lekgotlwane*.'

When Tumi is enthusiastic about something she shows it. Now she just stands there looking dumbfounded. Maybe she had a difficult day. She overworks and often comes home almost half dead. Don thinks he will give her time to sit down and relax a bit. The cat is comfortably curled on the sofa. He picks it up and holds it in his arms.

'Let's rather get Chinese takeaways,' says Tumi, putting the files on the coffee table and spreading herself on the sofa.

'Hey, I went to all this trouble, Tumi.'

'Give it to the cat. Let's get Chinese.'

Don knows that Tumi has her 'moods', as he calls them, but he cannot quite believe this.

'You like *ting*, Tumi. We go to Soweto especially for *ting*.'

'It has its place, Don. Back there in the township. What if my friends come and find this foul smell? They'll think that's what I eat.'

'But that's what you do eat. That's what we eat.'

'They don't know that. That's why we eat this kind of stuff in Soweto and not in North Riding. Here, as far as everyone knows, we eat sushi and the like. Plus, you know, Don, I don't like my man to stand in an apron in the kitchen cooking.'

'You know I love cooking, Tumi. It's my thing, man.'

'I guess it was OK when you were in the township. But you're going to be a Black Diamond now, Don. You must learn to behave like one. Cultivate more class. If you like home-cooked meals that much, then I can employ a full-time helper for you.'

When affluent blacks talk of a helper, they mean a maid. It is one of those euphemisms that are meant to assuage the guilt of having your own kind as a servant.

When things get tense between him and Tumi, Don always takes refuge in his cat. He is stroking its fluffy fur with one hand while holding it to his bosom with the other. This infuriates Tumi no end.

'You're not listening, Don,' she yells. 'That cat has mesmerized you.'

'Of course I am not listening,' Don yells back. 'What is there to listen to?'

'It's either me or the cat, Don.'

Don does not respond.

'Get rid of it, Don,' Tumi says firmly.

'It's a pedigreed Himalayan cat, Tumi. How do I get rid of it just like that?'

'I don't know,' says Tumi dismissively. 'Take it to an animal shelter or something.'

Even at this time of the night, the tranquillity of the suburb is marred by illegal immigrants waiting on the side of the road, hoping to be picked up for work. They must have been waiting for the whole day. Some were indeed picked up, did odd jobs such as gardening or loading and unloading goods and then returned to the spot to be picked up again by other employers. These remaining ones will wait here until the morning so that they are the first to be picked up when new employers come to look for the cheap labour they can hire far below the minimum wage stipulated by law.

Tumi and Don are on Beyers Naudé Drive in her Jaguar. She knows just the right place to get them

Szechuan tea-smoked duck at a Chinese kiosk at a mall in Blackheath. He is still sore about the *ting* but has decided he'll take it to the office and share it with his black colleagues. He doubts if the white ones would want to venture into strange African dishes.

At the traffic lights two blind young women come to the window to beg for money. They come from a Zimbabwe that has been devastated by Robert Mugabe's mismanagement, corruption and savage violence against his own people. Blind people in South Africa receive monthly grants from the government and the younger ones are in educational institutions that cater for the handicapped. Rarely does one see them begging in the streets. Except for buskers with their guitars and sighted assistants. And scammers of different kinds. The blind beggars at traffic lights are a new phenomenon. It is as though one morning, Johannesburgers woke up and intersections were populated by blind Zimbabwean women, in addition to the regular vendors of coat hangers, flowers and bootlegged CDs and DVDs.

Tumi rummages in her handbag for some coins.

'Don't give them money,' says Don, grabbing Tumi's hand. 'You are perpetuating the problem.'

Tumi gives him a disapproving look. The traffic lights turn green and she drives off without giving the beggars any money.

'It's like Zimbabwe has dumped all its blind beggars in South Africa,' he says.

Tumi, like other black South Africans who consider themselves progressive, cringes at the xenophobia that infects some of her compatriots and hates it when her own Don seems to suffer from the same malady. It must be the influence of the people he associates with at work. Security guards and nightwatchmen, like most unskilled and semi-skilled South Africans, always complain that foreigners are stealing their jobs. And their women.

'They welcomed you with open arms when you were refugees in their countries,' she says.

Don is resentful that she, who never experienced exile, should be so presumptuous as to teach him his responsibility to the Africa that gave him succour during the bad days of apartheid.

'Only when we had documents,' says Don. 'We had to be legal in their countries. It was not the free-for-all that everyone wants you to believe it was.'

He emphasizes that South Africans did not flock into other African countries in their thousands and live any-where they wished. They had to be registered as political refugees, were closely monitored and were kept in refugee camps. Only those with the skills the host coun-tries needed were integrated into the community—the teachers, the lawyers, the nurses and so on. It was only in very few countries, like Lesotho and Swaziland, where South Africans were not kept in refugee camps.

'Even in Botswana I lived at Dukwe Refugee Camp, and when I left the camp for Gaborone to socialize with fellow South Africans who were working there, I was arrested and later sent back to the camp,' he says.

Tumi drives quietly for a while. Then she decides that if she can't win the argument over the illegal African immigrants, she will surely win it over the cat.

'You know, Don,' she says, 'I am serious about that cat.'

Don is amazed that she should, out of the blue, bring back the subject of the cat.

'That is my cat, Tumi,' he says. 'It is not going anywhere. You are not going to discard Snowy like you discarded my chair.'

'Don't tell me you're still sulking about that old La-Z-Boy.'

'I don't sulk—I'm not a child.'

At this he sulks. They drive quietly for some time.

After a while Tumi bursts out, 'You're an ex-combatant, Don. A hardened guerrilla fighter in the liberation struggle. What are you doing with a cat?'

7

STEVO HAS A DREAM

Carcasses of cars of all makes and models cover about an acre at the Visagie scrapyard in Strijdom Park. Shortie is sitting on the bonnet of a wrecked late-model BMW, the golden hair on his head and arms bristling in the sun. He is annoyed at the three men who are not doing a proper job stripping a Volkswagen Beetle. He barks his instructions, liberally mixing them with expletives about the workers' miserable origins.

That's what you get when you employ casual labour on the cheap, he blames himself. What choice does he have but to pick up illegals at the roadside? With Stevo's continued incarceration things have been tight. What makes things worse is that Stevo demands too much of his time for his mission for vengeance, and when he is gone from the scrapyard the workers rob him blind by selling car parts and pocketing the money.

A car honks at the gate and the workers give a collective sigh of relief as Shortie goes to open it. It is Ma Visagie in her Volkswagen kombi—a rickety sixties' model painted with flowers and peace signs all over its body. It is older than the boys and is her own special pride that she used to drive to music festivals as far afield as Durban and Port Elizabeth during those heady days of free love and psychedelia. Inside it is still plastered with fading memorabilia of the bands of the time—Dickie Loader and the Blue Jeans, the Four Jacks and a Jill and the Freedom Children. The roof is wall-to-wall with their tattered posters. These days the kombi stays parked and covered with a tarpaulin most of the time, and Shortie knows that when his mother is driving it she means business.

He notices that there are four or five young women in the kombi as well as Aunt Magda. He knows immediately what his mother has come to complain about.

Ma Visagie gets out of the kombi and Shortie follows her into the office, which is a shipping container near the gate.

'What gives, Ma?' he asks.

'You gotta do something, Shortie. The girls have got to start working again.'

'But, Ma, that's Stevo's side of things. My side is the scrapyard.'

'Stevo's rotting in jail right now, boy. Things can't stand still till he comes back.'

Shortie tries to assure his mother that Stevo will be back soon because Krish Naidoo is working hard to get him out. He is appealing to the high court to overturn the unjust sentence. The high court judges must be taking their time because they are giving serious consideration to the matter, as Krish Naidoo has assured them. All they need at this trying time is patience because Krish Naidoo knows what he is doing. He is a good lawyer like all Indians are. Just like the Jews.

'Well, maybe we should have gone to a Jew 'cause Stevo is still in jail,' moans Ma Visagie.

'For now we gotta cool it a bit, Ma,' Shortie says. 'Till Stevo tells us what to do. Plus the law will still be sniffing around.'

'We are the Visagies, boy,' says Ma Visagie. 'We're not afraid of nothing.'

She orders Shortie to get into the minibus because they are going to Diepkloof Prison.

'All of us?' asks Shortie. 'They won't let us see Stevo with all this gang.'

Only Shortie and his mother will see Stevo, explains Ma Visagie. The rest are going to 'case the joint' because Aunt Magda has come up with a new plan of taking mass action right to the gates of hell, otherwise known as Diepkloof Prison or Sun City.

Shortie barks orders at the workers to continue working without messing things up and without stealing any of his parts because he will know if they have and will chase them out of South Africa after giving them a thorough beating that they will remember for the rest of their lives.

Ma Visagie nurses her kombi as it coughs along the N1 Highway amid zooming traffic. Shortie reassures her once again that Krish Naidoo will get Stevo free.

'How do you know this Naidoo has not been bought by the magistrate?' asks Aunt Magda. 'Lawyers can easily be bought, you know. My uncle was a lawyer, so I know all their tricks.'

'Just like you know about mass action,' says Shortie and the girls giggle.

'It's nothing to joke about,' Aunt Magda says firmly. 'Lawyers go to the highest bidder.'

They shouldn't have worried about Krish Naidoo going to the highest bidder. At that very moment, he is running after the magistrate as she walks out of the building and down the steps. She has her black briefcase and her gown over her shoulder, and is going home for the day. Krish Naidoo calls after her but she does not stop.

'I don't have time, Krish,' she says as she hurries on.

Krish Naidoo catches up with her.

'It's wrong, Kristin,' he says, almost out of breath, 'seeing my client behind my back. It's improper. It's not procedural.'

The magistrate keeps on walking and the lawyer walks alongside.

'Your client is harassing me, Krish. I just wanted to warn him to stop.'

'How do you know it's him? He denies he has anything to do with those calls. He heard of them for the first time from you.'

She stops in her tracks when Krish Naidoo tells her that if she does not cease and desist from harassing his client he will lay an official complaint with the Department of Justice.

'You wouldn't dare.'

'Try me,' he says and walks away.

She calls after him, 'You don't walk away when I'm talking to you.'

He doesn't stop but walks on to his car parked in front of the building. She rushes after him and grabs his arm just before he opens the door.

'We don't have to fight about this, Krish,' she says, pleadingly now.

'I have to look after the interests of my client, Kristin,' he says. 'That's what attorneys do. Have you even sent the matter to the high court for review?'

The magistrate does not answer. It becomes obvious to the attorney that she has not sent the matter for review. He loses all patience with her. She was obliged to send the case to the high court within three days of the summary judgement. That is the requirement of the law with all summary judgements. He threatens to appeal to the high court on behalf of Stevo Visagie. He will put it to the judges that his client had no intention of insulting the court but merely responded to the provocation and uncalled for remarks by the magistrate. The law expressly states that there must be an intention on the part of the accused to insult the court.

'I hope you have a good night, Krish Naidoo,' she says as she leaves in a huff.

Krish Naidoo gets into his car but before he drives off he calls after her, 'Next time you receive threats on the phone you call the police, Kristin Uys. You don't go around harassing innocent people.'

At the Medium B Section, Diepkloof Prison, the warder says he will allow Stevo only one visitor for the day, unless the visitors can buy him a cold drink so that while he is drinking it he can turn a blind eye to the extra visitor. Both mother and son know that a 'cold drink' means not just the actual price of a can of Coke but a number of hard-earned bank notes. Ma Visagie is not in any mood to enrich prison warders and orders Shortie to go see his brother so that he may brief him on what has been happening to the business and why the girls can't lie low for ever but need to start working. She herself will wait in the kombi with the rest of the gang that is 'casing the joint'.

Stevo is in high spirits, which makes Shortie nervous because it is not normal for Stevo to be in high spirits even when he is not in jail.

'I have a dream, Shortie,' he tells his brother as soon as he takes a seat. 'I have a dream.'

'*Ja*? So what did you dream about, *my broer*?'

Shortie can be so *dof* sometimes, which irritates Stevo no end.

'I didn't dream about nothing, you fool.'

'Don't play games with me, Stevo. You said you dreamt.'

'I said, I have a dream,' says Stevo, his eyes looking up at the ceiling and his open hands raised in a prophetic fashion. 'I have a dream that when I get out of here, we gonna be big, Shortie. Real big, my china. Nobody's gonna call us small-time hoodlums no more. Nobody's gonna call us tickey-line gangsters.'

'We're not tickey-line gangsters *mos*, Stevo,' says a perplexed Shortie.

'And nobody's gonna call us that no more, my china,' says Stevo. 'And you know why?'

'I don't know why, Stevo. I don't even know what you're talking about.'

'Because we gonna be big, my china. We gonna run big-time syndicates. We gonna go international, Shortie, and nobody's gonna stop us. We gonna be kings of the world.'

But Shortie has more urgent things to worry about.

'What about the girls, Stevo,' he asks. 'They are getting restless. And Ma is getting restless too.'

'Ma's always restless,' says Stevo dismissively.

'*Ja*, but now she's more restless because I can't run the girls and the scrapyard at the same time.'

Stevo bursts out laughing.

'That's our Shortie. Can't chew Chappies and walk at the same time.'

'I don't wanna chew Chappies, Stevo,' says Shortie desperately. 'I just wanna know what about the girls?'

Stevo loses all patience with him.

'To hell with the girls,' he says through clenched teeth. 'The more urgent thing is the damn magistrate. We need something drastic, china. Something she will not forget in a short while.'

On the way to their home in Strubensvallei, Aunt Magda teaches the passengers in the kombi a song that will come in handy when a new wave of mass action takes place outside the prison gates. It is one of those Zulu protest songs about shooting a number of named Afrikaner leaders with a *mbayi-mbayi*, supposedly a machine gun. The irony of the song is lost on mother and son whose leaders these used to be because the song is in a language they don't understand. They cannot even identify the names of the leaders in question—some of whom are long dead anyway, such as the bad Doctors Verwoerd and Malan—because their names have been Zulufied. Verwoerd, for instance, is Velevutha, which means 'he who appears engulfed in flames'. But then even an expert in the Zulu language would not have followed what the song is about because Aunt Magda herself is a stranger to the language and mangles the words of the song and invents her own whenever she gets stuck.

Mother and son have to shout above the cacophony at the back of the kombi to hear each other. He tells her that he is worried about Stevo—he seems to be losing his grip in prison. He did not address the question of the girls at all but kept on repeating something about the strange dreams that are haunting him.

Two evenings later, the magistrate arrives home from work and is greeted by smoke that fills the whole house. There is a stench that is so strong that even the cat cannot stand it. It caterwauls and scratches the carpet. She dumps her briefcase and files on the floor and runs to the kitchen. There is a boiling pot on the stove. A thick slimy liquid is seeping through the lid on to the red hot plate, causing the smoke. She lifts the lid and a wave of steam and stench assails her. The slime bubbles over, creating even more smoke.

It is rotten tripe.

Pinned on a cupboard above the stove is a note written in letters cut from a newspaper and pasted on a page from an exercise book in kindergarten manner: *Next time it will be your cat!*

She switches off the stove and opens all the windows. She has a good mind to take the whole pot to Diepkloof Prison and dump its rotten contents on Stevo Visagie's head. But common sense prevails; she would not like to see herself in the dock for assault. Instead she goes to her bedroom, sits on the bed and dials Krish Naidoo.

The attorney is still adamant that his client is not capable of such skulduggery. He is, after all, still in jail, as the magistrate well knows. She must look elsewhere for the culprit. Perhaps someone who has just been released from serving time to which she had sentenced him. The police are sure to find whoever is responsible and she will be disappointed when she discovers that the Visagies have nothing to do with it.

'What pisses me off even more is that they used one of my best waterless pots,' says the magistrate. 'You're not supposed to use water in these pots.'

'Never mind the pots, Kristin. Call the cops now.'

But Kristin Uys is defiant and stubborn. She is determined not to be intimidated by small-time thugs, as she calls them.

'They are amateurs,' she says. 'They think they can scare me.'

It is just bravado. She is scared. For instance, when the cat leaps up from behind the bed, she is startled and almost jumps out of her skin. Then she becomes embarrassed that she has displayed this outward sign of fear, even though there was no one to witness it. She needs to steel herself for the war of nerves that lies ahead and must never show weakness, not even to herself.

'They gained entrance to your house in your absence, Kristin,' says Krish Naidoo who sounds genuinely worried about her. 'Clearly, you're not safe. If you don't call the cops, I will.'

But the magistrate thinks that would be playing into the criminals' hands. She wants to show them that she is not a little girl who can be terrorized by bullies.

'At least report this to the chief magistrate,' pleads the attorney.

The magistrate is adamant that she will do nothing of the sort. The only thing she will do is to change the locks.

She consults the Yellow Pages for a locksmith who works all hours.

In no time all her doors have different sets of locks and chains and the folding security barrier is reinforced with iron bars so that it cannot fold open again.

The next day Shortie visits his brother to brief him on his first real success. He is surprised to find that Stevo already knows about it. So as to leave Shortie mystified, Stevo does not tell him that he had an earlier visit from Krish Naidoo who wanted reassurance from his client that he had nothing to do with breaking into the magistrate's house and cooking rotten tripe in her pot. Of course, Stevo denied all knowledge of it. He was convincing, the more so because he really knew nothing about it, although he suspected that his brother had finally had the gumption to do something about the damn magistrate.

'I swear I had nothing to do with it, my china,' he told his lawyer. 'I am as innocent as a newborn baby.'

At this he assumed a look that he hoped passed for the angelic face of a newborn baby.

'If I ever discover that it is your work, Stevo, you'll have to get yourself another lawyer,' said Krish Naidoo.

Stevo Visagie scowled and said, 'You law people stick together like a bunch of thieves.'

Then he broke into uncontrollable laughter at his own joke.

His good spirits continue as Shortie fills him in on the details. It was not easy breaking into the house. Shortie had to get help from Fingers Matatu, a well-known cat burglar who is long retired from the trade because of old age but still rents out his services to whoever wants locks picked. It is said that a lock has not yet been invented that Fingers Matatu cannot pick.

'It was a good one, Shortie. A very good one, my china,' Stevo enthuses. 'Rotten tripe! You can be a genius sometimes.'

Shortie has the broadest of grins because he has never been called a genius by anyone before, let alone by his brother.

'Now for the big one, Shortie,' Stevo announces like an impresario on stage, or perhaps like a circus ringmaster. 'Next time the bitch comes home, she must find her cat cooking in that pot.'

This horrifies Shortie.

'I can't kill a cat, Stevo,' he pleads. 'It's one thing to buy tripe from the street vendors, keep it for a while until it stinks . . . but to kill a cat, Stevo!'

'We are the Visagies, man. We're not scared of nothing. You'll kill that cat and cook it.'

'Come on, Stevo, what do you hope to gain from all this?'

He wants to run the magistrate out of town before she gets the opportunity to carry out her threat to close down their operations once and for all and send the whole Visagie clan to prison.

'Don't make the mistake of thinking that the bitch is only after nailing my ass,' says Stevo. 'She's after your ass too, and after Ma's ass, and after the ass of all the Visagies dead or alive.'

She will stop at nothing, unless she is run out of town.

'Think of Ma, Shortie,' says Stevo. 'Think of all the work she put into establishing the business from the time we were teensy little babies. What will Ma say, Shortie? What will Ma say? You've always been a coward, Shortie. But think of Ma.'

At that moment the magistrate is drawing her own battle plans. She has a map of Roodepoort and environs in front of her and is highlighting all the spots she suspects are red-light districts. The decaying city centre especially has buildings that have been taken over by pimps and madams and by run-down hotels where johns and their low-class street walkers can rent rooms for 'day rest'. Despite the complaints of attorneys that she has been authorizing police invasions of suspected brothels without probable cause, or reasonable suspicion that a crime was being committed there, she will continue to sign search warrants indiscriminately. It is part of her crusade against the moral decay that has overwhelmed the city. She hates the whores for the power they can unleash in their bodies to render men so insane that they part with fortunes, and with their wives and families.

The phone rings. The chief magistrate for the Roodepoort district, Mr Bangani Mbona, is summoning her to his office. She suspects it must be about a search warrant that she signed without so-called reasonable suspicion. Some attorney must have complained.

Mr Mbona is sitting behind his desk as Kristin Uys enters. He is one of the youthful sharp legal minds that are taking over the South African legal system and who insist on misguidedly sticking to the letter of the law even when it defeats justice and criminals go scot-free. Yes, Kristin herself is a stickler for tradition. But she considers herself smart enough to know when the law is becoming an ass and can carefully bend it in order to see to it that the guilty are punished. Especially if they are pimps and prostitutes.

Even before she takes a seat, he addresses her.

'Why did I have to hear of this from Mr Naidoo?' he asks.

So, it is not about a search warrant; Krish Naidoo has ratted on her.

'Because he does not mind his business,' she says.

'You cannot afford to be flippant about this, Ms Uys. I'm going to ask the Police Commissioner to post police guards at your house.'

This is the last thing Kristin Uys wants. She will not have her house crawling with police. That would be sending the wrong message to the petty gangsters who are trying to intimidate her. This is between Stevo Visagie and her, and she intends to win it on her own terms.

'Police don't crawl, Ms Uys,' says Mr Mbona. 'And in my experience, petty gangsters are the most dangerous. They don't think twice. They don't reason. They don't consider the consequences. They just act.'

'What I meant to say, sir, is that the police are short-staffed as it is. What with all the crime in the city.'

'OK, we'll hire a private security firm. I know just the right one. It's across the street on Dieperink. VIP Protection Services. They'll assign a bodyguard who will be with you 24/7.'

Kristin Uys's protests are in vain. She will have a bodyguard and that is final.

8

CADRES IN THE TRENCHES

These are hectic times for Tumi Molefhe, what with her TM Modelling Agency gaining more international recognition and her involvement in a consortium that is bidding for a free-to-air television station. But despite all this she will not miss going to the gym. She must stay in shape and must look as good as any of the younger models in her stable. She leads by example. That is why we find her at the Virgin Active Classic Club in Melrose Arch this afternoon sweating it out in a virtual-reality enhanced spinning class. She comes here at least four times a week.

Her two best friends are with her—Nomsa, a dentist, and Maki, who is serving articles with a leading firm of attorneys. Even though the three women come from different worlds they have been very close since they met at a book club a few years back. One thing they have in common is the ambition to hit it really big in some BEE deal one day. Hence they are all part of the consortium that is bidding for the television station. They are always on the lookout for investment opportunities and for white corporations that are searching for BEE partners. For instance, Nomsa dabbles in construction and last year hit the jackpot with a low-income housing contract.

The pace is very fast and the women look good in their spinning shorts and Pedal Power jerseys that cling to their bodies. Although Tumi's friends are not built like models, they are both beautiful and well groomed. Both are younger than Tumi, perhaps in their late twenties. Maki is petite with gleaming Jabu Stone dreadlocks while Nomsa is buxom and, like Tumi, sports cornrows today.

The three cannot but ogle the guy in front who is wearing padded leggings that highlight all his endowments and a tight tee that displays his pecs to full advantage. They covertly make naughty gestures and giggle.

After the class the women meet at Kauai Health Food and Juice for long fruit cocktails. They are still in their spinning gear and are full of good cheer and laughter.

'*Sies*, Maki,' says Tumi. 'You were practically drooling at him.'

Maki laughs and declares that the man is not her type; the person who was actually drooling was Tumi herself.

'Not your type?' asks Nomsa. 'You know who that guy is? One of the BEE Fat Cats. He's worth millions.'

'Who cares,' Maki finally admits. 'With a body like that, he can be worth zero and I'd still go for him.'

'Good for you, Maki,' says Tumi. 'This is the new South Africa. The sisters are doing it for themselves, as they say. You don't need a guy with big bucks—you make your own.'

'And create your own man too,' says Nomsa. 'Like you're doing with Don.'

'What do you mean?' asks Tumi. The laughter has vanished from her face. Nomsa realizes that her friend is offended by her remark and tries to hide her embarrassment with giggles.

'You guys wouldn't understand,' says Tumi quite seriously. 'Me and Don, we come from far. Don has got connections. He was a freedom fighter. He's going to be a Black Diamond too one of these days.'

Of course Don is a great guy, the women agree. You don't find guys like Don in Johannesburg any more. There is a drought of men in the city, not because the species is extinct but because it is intimidated by successful women. Yes, the typical Jozi sophisticate would like to take a woman like Tumi or Nomsa or Maki to bed and boast about it to his buddies at the country club the next day, but he certainly would not like to take her to the altar. Women like these are far too independent-minded for the altar. For a wife these men prefer a beautiful young thing with not too many brains. Someone they can display at cocktail parties where, pray to God, she must not open her mouth lest she says something stupid or, worse still, something that will betray her common origins and her lack of education and finesse. Someone who will get all her fulfilment from shopping and whose greatest achievement in life will be featuring in the society pages for nothing more than wearing particular French and Italian labels with poise. Someone who will be at his beck and call at all hours of the day and night and who will wait patiently and uncomplainingly while he spends the night pub-crawling or bonking schoolgirls in the apartments he is renting for them. Someone who will be completely dependent on him and will be dead scared of being sent back to the poverty of Soweto or of some village in KwaZulu-Natal if ever she showed the slightest sign of rebellion. Someone whose main task in life is to stand next to him and smile. Until she is replaced by a younger version when the skin begins to sag a little.

After a boisterous group shower reminiscent of carefree schoolgirl days, the women go for a massage. Then they cruise down Corlett Drive and Oxford Road to the consortium meeting at Sandton Square in a showy convoy of Tumi's Jag, Nomsa's Mercedes Benz SLK and Maki's BMW 3-series—she already has plans to upgrade it to a 5-series as soon as she completes her articles of clerkship.

The meeting is intense as usual. It has been going on every evening for the past two weeks. The bid for the television licence is spearheaded by the Mabanjwa Trust, a group made up mostly of former political prisoners on Robben Island, but also from various inland prisons. Tumi is amazed how they have evolved into savvy businessmen who speak the jargon both of the television industry and the corporate world, albeit occasionally mixing it with military terms since they continue to see themselves as cadres of the liberation struggle. They already own radio stations and newspapers in some of the important markets in the country, and now have this great opportunity of owning a television station that will broadcast nationally and will focus on entertainment with two thirty-minute news slots per day.

The meetings are long not because there is any waste of time on cheap talk and petty digressions, but because each section of the proposal is examined and debated thoroughly and strategies are mapped out in fine detail. Nothing is left to chance. At first Tumi was out of her depth in this company, but she was not ashamed to ask questions and read up on the technical aspects of the free-to-air television industry. She also went to the library at Wits University and read extensively on the subject. Now she can hold her own in the debates and is the one who explains concepts to Nomsa and Maki who are still out of their depth. They marvel at her brilliance, especially because she doesn't even have a junior degree. They find it hard to believe that they are taking lessons from a woman who was discovered as a model before she matriculated at high school and who then never had the incentive to complete her studies after she established herself as South Africa's top black model of the time.

In addition to the members of the Mabanjwa Trust who are the principal shareholders, the consortium is composed of a Malaysian broadcasting company who are providers of expertise and of some of the capital, the women's group led by Tumi and her two friends, an orphanage and a church youth group that runs a shelter for homeless people and street children. These three groups have a very small equity of about 3.3 per cent each, and serve the important function of proving to the Independent Broadcasting Authority that the television station will benefit the most disadvantaged members of society. The tiny equity does not bother Tumi. All she wants is to have her foot in the door—she and her group are already devising strategies of acquiring more shares should the bid succeed.

The proposal has to be presented to the IBA at noon tomorrow and Tumi is one of the three who have been selected by the consortium to defend it at a hearing where all the proposals of other bidders will be competing. She will be with the chairman of Mabanjwa Trust, Kenny Meno, and the old lady who runs the orphanage. The two women will be a clear demonstration to the committee of the IBA that is assessing the proposals that this bid truly is representative of the disadvantaged in society and, more importantly, of women.

Kenny Meno invites Tumi for a late dinner at the Country Club after the meeting so that they may thrash out a few points about their presentation tomorrow. Tumi can see through him—he has more on his mind than just discussing business.

'Sure, let's do dinner,' she says. 'I'll call my boyfriend to join us, if you don't mind.'

'We'll be talking shop, Tumi,' he says. 'I don't think third parties should hear our strategies.'

'He'll sit at the bar when we talk shop. You'll be glad to meet him.'

That is the whole point. Whereas Kenny hopes to have his way with her, she hopes to introduce him to Don. She is always going out of her way to introduce Don to Black Diamonds so that he may network his way to BEE deals. She does not wait for any further debate on the matter but whips out her cellphone and calls Don.

Don is in his silk pyjamas watching television in the bedroom. That's another one of Tumi's innovations—silk pyjamas. He has always enjoyed sleeping in the nude but Tumi weaned him from that—Black Diamonds don't sleep naked. When the phone rings he first lowers the volume on the television with a remote and then reaches for it on the nightstand.

'Tumza, what's up? I've news for you. When are you coming home?'

'I'm working late, Ma-Don-za.'

When she calls him Ma-Don-za, his Matseke Secondary School nickname, he knows immediately that she is going to ask him to do something he hates doing. And true enough she says, 'Please meet me at the Country Club as soon as you can get there.'

'Country Club? The Roodepoort Country Club?'

'The Johannesburg Country Club in Auckland Park.'

'I didn't know you're a member of the Johannesburg Country Club.'

'I am not. At the door tell them you're Kenny Meno's guest.'

Don knows that name. The man is always in the news as one of Comrade Molotov Mbungane's protégés. He is reputed to have mastered the art of accumulation by using the Mabanjwa Trust—Comrade Molotov is also a member—to acquire equity in a number of companies. Don knows why Tumi wants him there. He has resigned himself to participating in this networking game, though he was reluctant at first. Who knows? Something may come of it and then he will feel worthy of Tumi at last. He dresses quickly in a lemon Versace suit that Tumi bought him on a trip to New York. He knows the dress code at the country club is 'smart casual' when it is not a formal occasion; he has been there a few times before, but only as a bodyguard to some politician or visiting mogul.

In one of the restaurants of the ranch-style clubhouse, Tumi and Kenny are sitting by a window which reflects their uneasy images. If it were daytime they would be admiring the sprawling gardens with manicured lawns, gigantic oaks and indigenous shrubs and bushes with flowers of many different colours. Birdsong would be filling the air and those club members who are birdwatchers would be creeping about with their binoculars and cameras, and squash players would be quenching their thirst on the terrace.

A waiter comes for their orders. Both opt for chicken salad, and Kenny orders a bottle of Moët et Chandon Champagne.

'Wow! What are we celebrating?'

'Ourselves,' says Kenny. 'Our presentation tomorrow that will go excellently thanks to the formidable team of Tumi Molefhe and Kenny Meno and the orphanage woman whose name I forget. And what else are we celebrating? Oh, yeah, the fact that my divorce will be through soon!'

'I didn't know you were divorcing.'

'Now you know,' says Kenny winking. 'And you also know that there is room in my heart for a beautiful woman like you.'

Tumi bursts out laughing.

'That's the dumbest line I've ever heard,' she says.

'Are things serious then between you and the guy who'll be joining us?'

'Do you think if things were not serious between Don and me, I would not think your line is dumb?' she asks jokingly, although it is obvious from Kenny's face that he does get the message. But he gathers his dignity soon enough and smiles amiably.

Their orders arrive and they eat quietly for a while. Occasionally, young black men in business suits—sometimes with their ladies in ball gowns, or in the company of white-haired or balding white gentlemen also in business suits—stop to exchange pleasantries with Kenny.

These are the new Black Diamonds or Fat Cats, depending on who you are talking to, who revel in their membership of a club that was out of bounds for them only a few years ago. Although it opened its doors in 1906, four years after Cecil John Rhodes' death, those who knew him well and worked with him walked through these halls and dined in these very restaurants. The Black Diamonds see themselves as the new Randlords. Like the original Randlords, our Black Diamonds come from humble backgrounds and suffer the same prejudices that were piled on their predecessors by the snooty English establishment which accused them of being the nouveau riche with garish tastes. Now the critics who pile these insults on the new guys are the heirs of the original Randlords, who have long settled comfortably into old money with its supposed lack of pretension and ostentation.

When Don joins the party, he says he'll only share their drinks since he has already had dinner. At first, both men are resentful of being brought together in this way, but Tumi is determined to make this meeting work.

'I am surprised you guys haven't met before,' she says. 'After all, you were both in the struggle.'

'Every black person, just by virtue of being black, was in the struggle, Tumi,' says Kenny.

Don begs to differ. What about those blacks who supported the system—the Bantustan leaders who benefited from the grand apartheid design, the black policemen who were even more enthusiastic about enforcing apartheid laws than their white counterparts, the black bureaucrats and junior clerks eager to please white bosses?

'We work with them now because of Mandela's reconciliation policy,' adds Don, 'but we cannot claim that they were in the struggle too. Reconciliation must not make us rewrite history.'

'Reconciliation is between blacks and whites,' says Kenny. 'I don't know of any reconciliation programme between those blacks who supported the system and those who were fighting against it. What I meant is that all of them were struggling for something. All of them were victims of apartheid.'

'We are not going to argue about this now, guys,' says Tumi. 'What I was saying is that Don was a guerrilla fighter and you were on Robben Island. You have a lot to talk about.'

Kenny Meno begins to look at Don Mateza with new respect. He never fought any war. He served five years on Robben Island for throwing stones at white policemen who were patrolling his township with armoured vehicles. In prison he met some hardened fighters who had lived in refugee camps and had trained as freedom fighters in such places as the Soviet Union, East Germany, Libya, Cuba, Tanzania, Mozambique and Angola. He was in awe of them, and suspected that behind his back they despised him because he had never really seen action but was in jail for some petty rioting in the streets. That was where he met men like Comrade Molotov Mbungane, who took him under his tutelage. He looked after the needs of the older comrade in prison; now he was reaping the rewards.

'This man, Kenny,' says Tumi, 'is Comrade AK Bazooka himself.'

Don cringes at this and gives Tumi a disapproving look.

'Come on, guys, that's a song we used to sing in prison.'

'It was about him, Kenny. You were singing about this man.'

Don can't take it any more. He yells, 'Please stop it now. All this is unnecessary. Why should anyone care who the fuck I was in some past life?'

'I care,' says Kenny, standing up and shaking Don's hand vigorously as if meeting him for the first time. Tumi smiles; her job here is done. The man is in absolute awe of Don. The next step is to get him to invite Don for a round of golf.

As the night progresses, more bottles of Moët et Chandon are demolished and Kenny is telling them how he got to where he is today. With Comrade Molotov becoming a cabinet minister after liberation, he was deployed into government service as a director general in his department. When Comrade Molotov was deployed into business Kenny remained in government for a while. Two years later, he was deployed to establish the

Mabanjwa Trust so as to gain equity in some of the important corporations in the country for the benefit of those who suffered in apartheid's prisons in the cause of freedom. Comrade Molotov was highly instrumental in the establishment of the Trust.

With all this talk of deployment, Don cannot help wondering how the government became so enamoured of military vocabulary. In this brave new world, accumulation of personal wealth is dressed up in militarism, as if capitalism is the continuation of the guerrilla warfare that was fought during apartheid. It is as if they are compensating for the fact that most of those who are enjoying the fruits of deployment are not the freedom fighters—the foot soldiers—who bore the brunt of the war. It is mostly the leaders whose fight against apartheid was in the capitals of the world and the trade-union bosses who crossed to the other side to be at one in body and spirit with corporate bosses. Or perhaps it is compensation for the fact that the actual war itself was a very limited one and the liberation movement was denied the glory of an outright military victory when liberation was won mostly through the ordinary black civilians who made the country ungovernable, and the workers who brought the economy to its knees, and of course the Western community which pressured an erstwhile ally to negotiate with the blacks now that the fear of the Soviet Union was a thing of the past. More than anything else, the so-called mass action brought the government to a standstill; we did not see platoons of cadres in a triumphant march into Pretoria after felling Boer forces.

But today we see platoons of cadres fighting a new war of accumulation and the trenches are the boardrooms of South Africa. When a party loyalist with no experience in health matters is made a director general in the Department of Health, the ruling party calls that deployment. When that party loyalist, as it happened with Kenny Meno, resigns from government service in order to take up directorships in the corporate world, the ruling party announces that Comrade So-and-So has been deployed in the trenches of business.

Tumi wonders aloud how her Don was left out of all this deployment.

'I don't know,' says Kenny. 'After all, he is a hero of the freedom struggle.'

'Perhaps I missed some seminars on how to convert my political capital into capital capital, as my friend Bova would say,' says Don sarcastically.

'You don't need a seminar on how to convert political capital into equity in the biggest conglomerates in South Africa,' says Kenny earnestly. 'White capital has a way of finding you. When you have political clout, white capital comes knocking at your door to drag you screaming into its boardrooms. That is why I am not in government service today. They badgered me until I gave in. Even those of us who may resist at first, professing some misguided conscience, we always end up with a broad self-satisfied grin and the dazed eyes of a cat that has eaten too much cream. What I am saying, Comrade AK, is that if they haven't yet come knocking at your door, you're not worth anything to them.'

This is old news to Don. The only freshness here is that Comrade Kenny, assisted by Moët et Chandon, is putting things quite bluntly. Even small white businesses need black partners in order to be awarded tenders. But they are careful to have the right kind of black—either a pliable figurehead or one who has strong political connections that can be used to access bigger government contracts, such as the mammoth arms-procurement deal that made quite a few people overnight millionaires.

Don has mapped out his own path despite Tumi's reservations. He will do whatever it takes to prove himself to the board of directors of VIP Protection Services; they will have no choice but to appoint him chief executive. That is the only thing he can do because, as Bova and Fontyo have observed before, he has no political clout that would make him attractive to those who have shares to dish out. This particular meeting with Kenny Meno has finally convinced him that all this 'networking' that Tumi is always organizing for him is futile. Nothing will ever come of it except his humiliation.

The party continues until closing time, after which Tumi and Don drive home in their separate cars. Tumi is not the least surprised that throughout the dinner and the drinking afterwards Kenny did not bring up the subject of the television presentation, which was what the appointment was purported to be about. It is exactly as she suspected—it was a ruse. *Ja*, she says to herself as she drives along Beyers Naudé Drive towards her North Riding townhouse, that's Jozi men for you.

'Every time there is a serious discussion, you bring up your useless friends,' says Tumi as soon as they enter the apartment. 'It was silly to quote the "wise sayings" of Comrade Bova about seminars to convert political capital at our meeting with Kenny Meno.'

'To you, Fontyo and Bova are an embarrassment, Tumi. To me, they are the real heroes of the struggle.'

'Heroes? What heroes? Fontyo and Bova have not come to terms with the success of their own struggle.'

'Don't you start on that again. Those men went through hell and when they come home, what do they find?'

'We are enjoying the fruits of the struggle, Don. It is their problem if they want to sit on the sidelines.'

'That's very insensitive.'

'Your friends, Don, are sitting in the taverns afraid to go out there and compete with mainstream society. Instead, they are blaming those who are not afraid to face challenges. You'd be like that too if I had not taken you out of Wezile's. You would be guzzling beer all day long, blaming your misfortunes on discrimination.'

'You don't see the discrimination? It's no different from the days of apartheid. Only now it's black discriminating against black.'

'And what stops them from being on the right side of discrimination? Positive thinking, Don—that's all they need.'

Don won't argue against 'positive thinking'. Instead, he walks to the bedroom and finds his cat sleeping on a mat on the floor next to his side of the bed. He reaches for it and cuddles it. Meanwhile Tumi takes out her laptop from its bag and prepares to do some work while curled on the living-room sofa.

'You must call Kenny and arrange for a round of golf,' says Tumi, as she goes through tomorrow's PowerPoint presentation on the screen.

'He said he will call,' says Don.

'Why would he call? He does not need anything from you. You must take the initiative and call him.'

'And invite him to his own country club for golf?'

'Don't be silly, Don. Make him invite you to his country club for golf.'

'You know I hate golf.'

'You think those fools you see trudging the fairways swinging golf clubs and being followed by caddies carrying heavy golf bags love golf? They don't. They're there because that's where deals are made.'

'Are you not coming to bed? It's almost midnight.'

'Later, Don. I have a presentation tomorrow. Kenny Meno expects me to be ready for any questions those IBA guys will ask.'

'To hell with Kenny Meno. He cannot have you even during my time. This is my time, Tumi, not Kenny Meno's.'

Don walks back to the living room, still holding his cat to his bosom. Tumi is busy punching the laptop which is uncomfortably perched on the armrest. She stops work and gives Don a long surprised look. Then she bursts out laughing.

'What exactly are you saying, Don? Are you jealous or something? Do you think there is something between Meno and me?'

'You don't think I saw the way he was looking at you?'

'He's got to look at me that way, Don. He's a man. You know how silly men are, baby.'

Then she laughs again. But Don does not see anything funny in all this. He just stands there fuming and looking a bit foolish. Tumi, still with an amused look on her face, pulls him down to her and gives him a peck.

'I just want to make sure I don't let my team down, Don. I've got to rehearse this presentation. So please, go to bed, baby. I'll catch you later.'

She returns to her computer. He makes to leave but turns back.

'When you called I told you I had news. Don't you want to know what it is?'

Tumi looks up and excitement slowly creeps to her eyes. Don just stands there and says nothing.

'Don't toy with me, Don. Did you get the promotion?'

No. It is not about the promotion. Jim Baxter called him to his office this morning and asked if he would be willing to act as a bodyguard to a magistrate who is being threatened by gangsters. Because the bodyguard has to live at the magistrate's house and accompany the magistrate everywhere she goes, Baxter thought Don would be the right man for the job. Unlike other guards at VIP who are less polished in their manners, Don will be able to communicate with the magistrate and will not feel out of place in a magistrate's house. He was about to say no, thanks, when Baxter mentioned that in fact this would count in his favour and would show the board of directors that he was fit to take over as the chief executive when Baxter retired. Don knew that the competition for the position was stiff, even from highly experienced applicants from outside the firm, and saw this as his chance to prove himself not only to the board of VIP Protection Services but also to Tumi. So, he accepted. He has to begin this new assignment tomorrow—at the very time Tumi will be making her presentation.

For a while, Tumi does not know what to say. She just stares at him with a dumbfounded expression.

'I don't understand why they should choose you for this menial job,' she finally says. 'It's a demotion.'

'It's a test, Tumi,' says Don. 'I suspect the board wants to see how willing I am to sacrifice for the company before they give me the big position.'

Tumi cannot hide her frustration with this man—he just doesn't get it.

'You're a Black Diamond, Don. Don't allow them to treat you like a minion.'

'I hate it when you call me a Black Diamond,' says Don.

'That kind of attitude won't take you anywhere. Positive thinking, Don. Positive thinking.'

At this, she taps her forehead repeatedly with her forefinger.

'Jim Baxter thinks I am the best man for the job.'

'He's trying to humiliate you—that's what he's trying to do. He knows that, come what may, you're going to take his job when he retires next month. But before that, he wants to give you the final humiliation. And you're allowing him to.'

'Tumi, you are too distraught. Let's go to bed.'

'And you look too stupid with that cat. I'm surprised it's still here.'

He leaves for the bedroom. But Tumi does not move from the sofa. Instead, she hammers on the computer with a vengeance. He places the cat on its mat and it immediately curls itself up to sleep. He changes into his silk pyjamas and sits on the bed waiting for a while. He reaches for the remote and turns the television on. But he switches it off again and walks back to the living room. Without a word he reaches for her and gives her a long passionate kiss. She submits for a while, then pushes him away gently and returns to her computer. He is wounded. He walks back to the bedroom and promptly falls asleep.

When he opens his eyes in the morning Tumi is applying lotion to her tall, slender body after taking a shower. He does not know when she finally came to bed, if she did at all. She notices that he is awake, sits on the bed and caresses his head.

'I am sorry about last night, baby,' she says. 'It's just that this TV presentation is very important. I'm doing it for us, baby. We don't want to live in a townhouse for ever, do we?'

9

AN INTRUDER IN THE HOUSE

Kristin Uys is sitting on a sofa in the living room. She is not doing anything at all, not even reading the papers on top of a file on the coffee table in front of her. Instead, she is fidgeting anxiously, even nervously. She looks at her wristwatch constantly as if she is expecting someone who is late. She stands up and walks to the sideboard. She pours herself a brandy and swallows it in one swift swig. She is about to pour another one when the buzzer sounds. She presses the remote at the door to open the gate. Then she realizes that she has done something stupid. She should have established the identity of the person at the gate first. But it is too late now—the car is already driving into the yard. She pours herself the drink and takes another swig.

The doorbell rings. She tiptoes to the door and looks through the spyhole. She is filled with dread. She unlocks one of the three bolts on the door and then stops before unlocking the second one. Instead, she sits on the sofa and sighs deeply. After a few beats, the doorbell rings again. She stands up and with trepidation unlocks all the bolts. She opens the door and there is Don Mateza standing between her and the iron security grille. He is well dressed in a dark grey suit and a matching silk necktie. Even to her untrained eye in the world of fashion, his whole attire looks very expensive. He has a suitcase and two smaller bags, all made of black soft leather.

'I am here to protect you,' says Don.

She looks him over. Consternation registers on her face. She unlocks the grille which now opens like a gate and he enters. While she is locking the grille and bolting the door he looks the living room over. It is very untidy as usual. Consternation registers on his face.

'It was very careless of you,' says Don.

Kristin stops and looks at him curiously.

'To open without knowing who was at the gate,' Don adds.

She is offended by his temerity and lets her face show it.

'Let me show you to your room,' she says abruptly. 'Follow me.'

Don stretches out his hand and says, 'Let me introduce myself. I'm Don Mateza. VIP Protection Services.'

But she ignores his hand and walks on to the guest room. Don follows with his bags. She just opens the door and leaves him to his own devices.

There is a double bed and a sofa in the room. He opens the built-in wardrobe hoping to find some bed linen but there is nothing. He unpacks his suits and hangs them in the wardrobe. Then he goes back to the living room and finds her about to pour herself another drink. She stares at him like a rabbit caught in headlights.

'Nobody told me I was supposed to bring my own sheets and blankets.'

She walks away without pouring herself the drink. Don just stands there not knowing what to do next. He is saved by the arrival of a nondescript cat that squeezes itself into the living room through a cat flap in the door. A cat flap is a great idea, he thinks. It would give Snowy, his Himalayan pure breed, freedom to come and go as she pleases. But of course, Tumi would never entertain the idea of having a kitty door on her front door. Not when a day doesn't pass without her demanding that the cat must go.

Don bends down to caress its back as it curls up at his feet and purrs. This must be the cat that, according to his brief, is the target of assassins. Jim Baxter had shown him the next-time-it-will-be-your-cat message.

She returns with blankets and sheets, puts them on one of the chairs without a word and goes back to finishing the task of pouring herself a drink. He looks at her and smiles but she remains stony faced. He shakes his head and takes the bedding to his bedroom.

After a while he returns and asks, 'May I take a seat?'

'Please yourself.'

He sits opposite her. The coffee table, laden with papers and files, forms a buffer between them.

'I'm not your enemy, you know? I'm here to protect you.'

'I didn't question that,' says Kristin.

'Who are these guys who want to harm you anyway?'

'Just some petty gangsters I sentenced to prison. I can handle them. I don't need anyone's protection.'

'The chief magistrate doesn't think so. That's why he engaged our services.'

She stands up and says it's been a long day and she wants to have an early night.

'Nobody told me I should bring my own dinner,' says Don as she makes to leave.

'I'm not going to be making *you* dinner,' says Kristin. 'There is the kitchen. See what you can make for yourself.'

She leaves for her bedroom.

'You don't need to worry about that,' says Don. 'I'm quite handy in there.'

The kitchen is quite a mess. The sink is full of dirty dishes. The magistrate uses plates and pots and piles them up in the sink and they stay there until Monday when the maid, who works one day a week, comes to clean the house and do the washing. He will only have a peanut butter sandwich for now. Tomorrow he must buy the sort of food he likes and charge it to VIP Protection Services.

He has been ready since six-thirty because he does not know what time the magistrate leaves for work and she is not cooperative about anything. So, he waits in the living room studying the walls that are bare of pictures and are crying out for a new coat of paint. In his dark suit, white shirt and olive silk necktie, he looks more like a business executive than a bodyguard. Except for the bulge of a Walther PPK/S semi-automatic pistol in a holster concealed under his jacket. As a back-up he carries the more compact S&W .38 Titanium revolver in his pocket, whose bulge rather spoils his well-defined and neat outline.

It is only at about nine that the magistrate appears from her bedroom, ready to leave for work. Don wonders if she ever eats at all. She didn't seem to have any dinner last night, and now no breakfast. Perhaps, like him, she plans to have something at the Greek cafe on Dieperink Street. Or she will have something delivered to her office.

'We can use my car,' says Don.

The magistrate looks at him enquiringly.

'To take you to work,' he adds.

'Oh, no, you're not coming with me to court.'

'I've got to protect you, ma'am,' Don insists.

'You stay here and look after the house,' she says.

'I'm a bodyguard, not a house guard.'

'Nothing has harmed my body so far—it does not need a guard. My house does—the scum broke into it and cooked rotten tripe in my kitchen. I'm afraid you'll just have to be a house guard.'

As she opens the heavy-duty bolts, he wonders whether he should follow her willy-nilly but decides against it. He walks with her to her old Fiat Uno, which is parked next to his gleaming Saab convertible in front of the house. She never bothers to park her car in the double garage. She cannot imagine any self-respecting thief scaling the walls and breaking the gate to steal a battered Fiat Uno.

For a moment she is stunned. She looks at the Saab, and then looks at him. He responds with a smug smile.

'I hope you don't plan to follow me,' she says.

'No. I'll stay here until I get further instructions from my boss. I'll see what he and the chief magistrate have to say about guarding your house and not you.'

'Make sure all the doors are locked at all times.'

'Of course. But I need to have my own set of keys. I also need a remote for the gate.'

'We'll talk about that when I come back,' she says as she gets into her car.

'In the meantime how do I get in and out of here? Or do you expect me to be a prisoner in your house until you return?'

'OK, here are the damn keys,' she says, throwing them at him. 'There's a remote for the gate there as well.'

Don watches her drive away and the gate closes after her. Then he decides to take a walk in the garden. One can see that it used to be expertly landscaped, but now the rockeries are overgrown with weeds and flowers that have got out of control. But in its own way, it remains beautiful in its wildness. The jacaranda tree on the front lawn is imposing and the lawn has obviously been mowed not too long ago. Don wonders why whoever mowed the lawn didn't also weed out the rockeries.

In the back garden there are three gigantic jacaranda trees, a number of bushes, a jungle gym that is falling apart and a fenced-in swimming pool. The lawn here has been mowed recently as well but the swimming pool is dirty with slimy algae floating on the green water. The smell from the pool is foul, and as Don walks away, he is amused by the Parktown prawns—the fat light brown king crickets with black stripes and long whip-like antennae—that feed on snails and slugs, and the large dark grey short-legged hadeda ibises that feed on the Parktown prawns. Nature has a weird sense of humour. The hadeda ibis laugh their raucous laughter *ha-ha-hadeda* and fly away.

He walks into an enclosure with an outdoor clothes line. There is a small building attached to the double-door garage—the two-roomed servants' quarters, now disused since no servant has lived here for years. The water in the toilet is brown and the chain from a flush tank that is so high it almost touches the ceiling is broken. It reminds Don of the outdoor toilets that one finds in the poorer areas of Soweto. Give the servants the lifestyles to which they are accustomed.

He goes into the house and changes into more casual jeans, a loose shirt and sneakers. He relaxes on the sofa and watches television. He has carelessly left his hand-guns on one of the easy chairs. He watches his favourite soap opera, *Isidingo*, for a while but it is a repeat of an episode he has already seen. He surfs the channels but the magistrate doesn't have the DStv satellite television. Her viewing is therefore limited to the three public broad-casting channels that are free-to-air. When Tumi's group gets the licence, he thinks to himself, at least there will be the fourth channel that will be independent and will be watched by people who can't afford to subscribe to satellite television with its exorbitant monthly rates. Although he can't really say Kristin Uys lacks the luxury of the eighty-plus channels of DStv because she can't afford them. She is the magistrate, after all. Well, she's a strange one, isn't she?

Daytime television is boring and the mess in the room seems to suffocate him. He decides to do a little bit of vacuum cleaning both in the living room and in his room, and dusts the furniture. Because the living room is in such a mess, his cleaning really makes no difference. He gives up in exasperation and looks for something else to do. He examines the books on the shelves—mostly law books and some airport fiction. And a number of *Rebus* law journals and *South African Law Reports*.

He is paging through a dusty clothing catalogue of the eighties when his cellphone rings. It is Tumi. She is anxious to know how her Ma-Don-za is doing. Did he sleep well? She herself didn't sleep a wink thinking of him. Did he think of her too? Did he miss her?

'I miss you, Don,' she adds.

'I miss you too, Tumza,' he says. 'Did you remember to feed Snowy?'

'Guess what I'm wearing.'

'You forgot to feed the cat again!'

This reminds him that there is also a cat in this house that may need some attention. Although he received no instructions about feeding it he goes to the kitchen and searches the cupboards for cat food as he speaks to Tumi.

'Is that all you can think about, Don?'

She is clearly irritated. Then she demands firmly, 'Guess what I am bloody wearing!'

He has found a can and an opener. He feeds the cat, and then walks back to the living room, a process that makes it impossible for him to respond immediately.

'Don, are you listening?'

'Are you in bed?' he asks.

'Of course I'm in bed. Why would I make you guess what I'm wearing if I'm not in bed?'

'Are you not going to work today?'

She is getting even more annoyed.

'I had a late night preparing for the Johannesburg Fashion Week. I'll go to the office at noon. Two of my models have a photo shoot in the afternoon. Are you going to guess what I'm wearing or not?'

He sits down on the sofa and the magistrate's cat jumps on his lap. He pets it.

'Is it one of your La Perla numbers?'

'Don't cheat, Don. You know it's either my birthday suit or La Perla. Which one?'

He is now getting into the spirit of the game.

'The red bra and thongs . . . no, wait . . . the black slinky one.'

Tumi giggles naughtily and says, 'Right the first time. The La Perla Black Label. And where are my hands? What am I doing with them?'

'Are they where I think they are? Are they doing what mine should be doing to you?'

'Oh, I miss you, Don! It's like you've been gone for ever.'

Now he is really aroused. He gently puts the magistrate's cat down and mimes holding Tumi close to himself.

'You know what I'm going to do to you when I get back?' he asks, almost out of breath. 'You know what I'm going to do, Tumi baby?'

She is just as breathless.

'What are you going to do, Don?' she says. 'Tell me every little detail . . . step by step. Start from the time you peel off my La Perla Black Label.'

But his detailed description of how his hands will traverse the contours of her slinky body, a movement he replicates on his own body, is stopped short by Tumi's searing scream: 'What the shit!'

'Tumi? Tumi?' shouts Don.

'It attacked me, Don. Your damn cat attacked me!'

Not really. What actually happened was that the cat gently leapt on the bed and purred while it rubbed its head on her hand. It took her by surprise and she was startled.

'I think it's just hungry, Tumi,' says Don. 'Snowy would never attack anybody.'

'You always take the cat's side against me,' moans Tumi.

'Please, Tumi, try to be reasonable just this once.'

'You promised, Don. You promised to get rid of it.'

'I didn't make any such promise, Tumi.'

'You promised. You promised.'

Then she hangs up. He tries to phone her back, but it takes him straight to her voicemail. So much for phone sex.

He finishes up the feather dusting, makes himself a mug of coffee and relaxes in the easy chair. His attention is drawn to a stack of old magazines and folders on the floor near a bookcase. At first he wonders why the magistrate would be keeping all these old copies of *Fair Lady*, *Sarie*, *Rooi Rose*, *Huisgenoot*, *Femina* and even *Scope* with its 'blonde bombshell' covers and centre spreads. All these date between fifteen and twenty years back. When he pages through them, he realizes that they all feature Kristin Uys on their glossy society pages. Not the dowdy magistrate we have come to know, but a young, beautiful blonde fashion plate. There are pictures of Kristin Uys in a fashionable hat at the horse races; that year she won the fashion stakes. And then there is Kristin Uys with her husband, Barend Uys, at some charity event at the Roodepoort Country Club. According to the caption Mr Uys was a city councillor and a leading light in the ruling National Party circles. He practised as an attorney in the same firm as his wife. In another magazine, there are Barend and Kristin in a group photograph of the Weltevreden Park Bowling Team. Everyone is in crisp white.

In all the magazines, Kristin Uys, sometimes with her husband, at other times with ladies in big hats, is featured at social events, fund-raisers, cocktail parties and church conferences. In a *Scope* issue that dates much earlier there is Kristin in a skimpy bikini, her arms covering her breasts which are much smaller than those of the usual *Scope* centrefold whose claim to fame lay solely in the oversized bosoms, hence the 'bombshell' title. Kristin's own claim to fame was that she was that year's Tukkies Rag Queen—she was a law student at the University of Pretoria. Unlike the regular voluptuous *Scope* girls, she was more of a Twiggy-type, with a beautiful oval face and big come-hither eyes.

The folders contain press cuttings from *Beeld*, *Die Burger* and the *Sunday Times*. All the articles are about the Uyses' acrimonious divorce. There are no details about the cause of the divorce; only the lament that the couple were the pillars of the Roodepoort community and were active in charity work, especially in Weltevreden Park where they lived. In another article there is a picture of the dogs and a cat which were at the centre of a custody battle since the Uyses did not have children to fight over.

Don can hear the gate opening, the car doors closing and the security grille being unlocked. He is too engrossed in the articles to pay much attention, although at the back of his mind, he is aware that it must be the magistrate returning.

'I didn't know you came home for lunch . . . all the way from Roodepoort,' says Don as soon as she enters.

'I come home any time I want to. It's my house.'

'Well, the house is still here . . . still standing,' says Don, and goes back to paging through the folder. The magistrate will not respond to any of his impertinence and is about to walk to the kitchen when she notices the guns on the sofa.

'I don't want guns in my house,' she snaps.

'You don't want guns?' asks Don with a smirk on his face. 'What kind of an Afrikaner are you?'

'I don't want you and your impudence in my house either.'

'I'm a bodyguard, lady. Bodyguards carry guns. As for not wanting me in your house, do you think I want to be here?'

She leaves for the kitchen in a huff but returns immediately to make sure she saw what she thinks she saw. Indeed, the impudent man is reading her papers.

'Who gave you permission to touch my personal stuff?' she asks. She is quite livid.

'Nobody,' says Don, continuing to page through the folder. 'The magazines were just sitting there so I read them.'

'You have no right to touch my things.'

'They're just magazines and newspapers, for crying out loud. It's not like you're hiding secrets. They are in the public domain.'

She snatches the folder from his hands.

'Give me back my stuff,' she screeches and grabs some of the magazines from the coffee table.

'You are very beautiful in those pictures,' he says, as he takes the magazines back to their place on the floor near the bookcase.

'What happened to your husband . . . to your ex-husband, I mean?'

'It's none of your business.'

'If I'd known you were coming home for lunch I would have cooked something for you,' says Don, hoping to relieve the tension between them. But she does not respond. She takes her handbag and leaves the house. Don decides to follow her. He will not let her bully him into staying in the house this time. He will follow her and protect her whether she likes it or not. He has no time to change into his suit, but wears his holster under his shirt and leaves the smaller revolver in his suitcase.

Don quickly locks the door and the security grille. He jumps into his Saab just before the Fiat Uno drives out of the gate. She turns left into J. G. Strijdom Road and then right into Jim Fouché. She then turns right into Beyers Naudé Drive and drives towards Cresta Shopping Centre. This is not the road to the Roodepoort magistrate's court. It is not the road to Roodepoort at all but to the city of Johannesburg. The traffic is always heavy on Beyers Naudé and she tries to weave her way into different lanes. Don chuckles to himself because he can see that she is trying to lose him.

When she gets to Melville, she drives into the narrow streets, away from Main Road, and meanders into alleys and then back to Main Road. He stays close to her. She tries a new tactic, that of driving way above the speed limit, but he is relentless. They play this cat-and-mouse game until they get to the city of Johannesburg where she zooms through Smit Street, beating traffic lights. He does likewise. Fortunately they are not stopped by traffic police.

After more than an hour she stops at Bruma Lake. He parks his car three cars from hers. He follows her through the gate of the mammoth Bruma Lake Flea Market.

'The flea market!' says Don. 'Don't tell me you put me through all this trouble for a flea market. I thought you were meeting a secret lover.'

She ignores him and walks through the stalls of various goods until she gets to those that sell women's apparel. She buys a blue dress with yellow flowers and a black skirt, similar to the kind she wears in court. Don is impressed that she knows exactly what she wants without bothering with the labels. All she cares about is the price. He marvels at how a magistrate can live such a no-name life. He has lived in a society of walking labels all his life. Even in the heydays of apartheid, young men like him had to boast of Bang Bang jeans, or at least Levis. They had to wear Crocket and Jones shoes, Bostonians and Ballys. They had to seek refuge in *jewish*—as sartorial elegance was known—because they had no other way of expressing themselves. Now, in the post-apartheid era, what is their excuse? Well, this is the great epoch of freedom. And freedom comes with conspicuous consumption and instant gratification—people of his class don't only wear brands but see themselves as brands. They package and market themselves as such. And here is a magistrate, with all her power and money, living an unbranded life. He feels sorry for her.

He offers to carry her shopping bags but she will not let him touch her stuff.

The drive home is much shorter because she does not try her circuitous tricks.

10

SHE NEEDS SOME LOVING

An all-white congregation is singing an Afrikaans hymn. This is an NG Kerk service in Roodekrans. An old balding *dominee* is in the pulpit. In the pews, Kristin Uys is singing from a hymnal while she keeps throwing nervous glances at Don Mateza who is standing next to her wearing a self-satisfied smirk. He is obviously enjoying her discomfiture. He is in his bright and hip casual attire and is out of place in this conservative-looking, dark-suited congregation. There is general awkwardness because no one seems to know what to make of the stranger. At first there were whispers that were passed from elder to elder until they reached Kristin's ears. She had no choice but to whisper back that the man was her bodyguard, and the elders passed that message on to the pastor. Only then did he seem to relax a bit and to preach the gospel as if the stranger was no longer among them.

Today's sermon is on charity and brotherly love. You are your brother's keeper, the *dominee* says. Don finds it interesting that the gender-sensitive vocabulary of the new non-racist and non-sexist South Africa has not yet permeated the ranks of the NG Kerk. Each one of us is our brother's keeper. Why, then, should we look away in embarrassment when an Afrikaner woman is standing at the traffic lights with a begging bowl and a board that speaks of the pain of hungry children and betrayed dreams? How have the *volk* come to this, they who were chosen by God to lead the dark tribes into His light? Jesus said the poor will always be with us, and we have always looked after our own. But these are trying times for the Afrikaner, even for those liberal ones among us who accepted the changes with grace and who indeed voted for the changes when F. W. de Klerk put the matter to a referendum. Never before have we seen so many poor whites begging in the streets of Johannesburg among young black male vendors. Why do we look the other way? Is it enough to feel their shame without extending a helping hand? Shouldn't we say that it is our duty as Christians to ensure that there is no Afrikaner begging in the street? Are we still our brother's keeper, as the Bible commands, or are we only concerned with our own individual selves?

The congregation responds to these questions with another hymn. Although Don is not familiar with the words, it is a well-known Protestant tune and he hums along. He signals to Kristin to share her hymnal with him but she ignores him. He takes her hand, the one that's holding the hymnal, and brings it closer so that he is able to read. Then he sings like an opera basso, which attracts the attention of all those round them. She remains frozen in place until the end of the hymn.

At the end of the service, the congregation trickles out of the church. Kristin hurries out as if something is chasing her and does not even stop to shake the extended hand of the pastor who is at the door greeting people as they leave. She almost runs down the steps. Don follows, trying to catch up with her. She does not want him to catch up—she does not want him here.

She gets into the Fiat Uno and drives away. Don gets into his Saab and follows the Uno, which tears angrily through Ontdekkers Road without regard to traffic. She stops at a BP Garage and buys Afrikaans Sunday newspapers, some meat pies and a litre of Coca-Cola. Don follows her and buys himself the *Sunday Times* and *City Press*. Once more she speeds to Weltevreden Park and he snaps at her heels like a hound after quarry.

As soon as they have both parked outside the house and jumped out of their cars, they face each other like fighting cocks. She with an angry face, and he with the continuing self-satisfied smirk which infuriates her even more.

'You embarrassed me,' she says.

'Serves you right. You see, if you were cooperating with me, I would have changed into a nice black suit like the *volk* in the church, and I would have stayed in the car and waited until you came out. As long as you don't cooperate with me, I'll be wherever you are. And I mean everywhere. No more Mr Nice Guy.'

'Mr Nice Guy?'

She seems to find this funny and almost chuckles. Almost.

'Ja, no more Mr Nice Guy,' repeats Don, laughing now and unlocking the security grille for her.

'That's stupid,' she says, and walks into the house.

She goes straight into her bedroom with her newspapers, meat pies and Coke. She remains there for the rest of the day. Don spends the day reading his newspapers. He daydreams of the Sunday lunch he would be eating in Soweto and of the banter and political debates he would be having with Fontyo and Bova at Wezile's.

He orders a pizza from Debonair Pizza, who deliver it in black tie, as is their style. He meets the delivery man at the gate and tips him generously. He, too, is his brother's keeper, even if his brother wears a tuxedo.

When Don wakes up the next morning the magistrate has already left the house. She must have stolen away at dawn in order to ensure that he does not follow her.

Why bother? He goes back to bed and stays there reading yesterday's papers and masturbating to a fantasy of Tumi. But the magistrate creeps into the fantasy. He wonders how she would be in bed. There is an old adage that a cat cannot stay in the same room as a saucer of milk without lapping it up. But then, on second thoughts, he does not imagine any right-thinking male would see her as milk. Although he must admit that she is not bad looking under that cloak of dowdiness, especially if you establish in your mind that she is the girl in *Scope*. But, my, what a cold, distant bitch she has turned out to be. He'd better not even think about her. She is not worth wasting his imagination on. Tumi is the girl for him. There is no place for anyone in his life but Tumi. Not that he has never been unfaithful to her. Once or twice, he has met a drunken girl at Wezile's and has used Bova's backyard shack as a stadium. But those were one-night stands when Tumi was travelling overseas. They did not mean anything. Tumi is for ever.

The whole masturbation exercise is futile, so he gives it up, wakes up and takes a shower. He does not bother to trim his moustache, which normally is his daily ritual. Instead, he cleans the living room, kitchen and his bedroom. And then he goes to the pool and tries to clean it as well. The pump is faulty but he is able to fix it. One of the pipes of the Kreepy Krauly has a hole, so he walks to the pool store at Palm Court Shopping Centre, which is just down the street on J. G. Strijdom Road. He also buys chlorinators. Then he buys fried chicken and bread rolls for lunch. He returns to clean the pool. It takes him longer than he envisaged because it has not been cleaned for a long time and the slime is thick on the walls. But the Kreepy Krauly is still very powerful and after a while, it has vacuumed most of the dirt.

He has his lunch by the pool and relaxes with a cold drink. He will let the chemicals take effect before he takes a dip. Maybe tomorrow it will be ready.

He phones Tumi's office but the secretary tells him that she has not come to work yet. He tries her cellphone. She is at Three Oaks, nursing the blues, as she puts it. She feels let down because the television licence bid has failed. Instead, the Independent Broadcasting Authority selected a bid presented by a trust dominated by trade-union leaders. All those meetings were in vain. All that reading at the university library. All those hours she would have used to market her models. Don tells her how sorry he is that things did not work out as planned. Things have been a bit slow on his side too. All he's been doing today is clean the house and the pool. She demands to see him immediately; she is so depressed that she does not feel like going to the model agency at all today. Don suggests that they meet at the Cresta Shopping Centre.

In less than thirty minutes, they are both at the mall having coffee and cakes at a delicatessen.

'So, how's the magistrate?' asks Tumi.

'She's a cranky old fart, but I can handle her,' says Don.

'But cleaning her house? You are her bodyguard, not her house servant.'

'I stay there, Tumi, and you know that I can't live in a pigsty.'

'How long is this assignment anyway? You've been there a number of days and nothing has happened to her.'

He knows what is coming next, so he steers her away from the subject by asking her about the television bid. How did her partners take the sad news?

'We haven't discussed it yet,' she says. 'We're meeting tomorrow night.'

But, for her part, she has decided to move on and focus on her model agency. Although she had had great hopes for the television station, which undoubtedly would be a money spinner judging from the projections that their consultants had made, there will be other opportunities. Of course she would be lying if she told anyone that the loss of the bid has not taken its toll on her emotions. Everyone seemed so certain that they would win it. No one expressed the slightest doubt. After all, the Mabanjwa Trust is composed of people who made sacrifices for the country in the prisons of apartheid. And some key government officials and cabinet ministers are also members of the trust. How could they ever doubt that they would be granted the only free-to-air licence that will be allowed for a number of years to come?

She tells him how she and her two buddies, Nomsa and Maki, were already plotting the role they would insist on playing in the running of the station and how they were already boasting to their colleagues, relatives and neighbours that very soon they would be owners of a television station. Now, how are they going to face these people?

'You must come home, Don,' she says all of a sudden. 'I need you back home.'

'I've got to stick it out for as long as it takes, Tumi. Maybe after a week or two when they see nothing is happening, they will call it off.'

'A week or two? What about me, Don? What about us?'

'What about us? There's nothing wrong with us.'

'There's nothing wrong when you have to spend all your nights with her?'

'With her?' he asks disgustedly.

'You know what I mean, Don,' she says giggling. 'At her house. At her pigsty.'

'You are the one who wants me to be a Black Diamond, Tumi. And I'll only become one if I pass this test. So, let me stick with it.'

'I need some loving, Don,' she says. 'I need lots and lots of loving. You know I can't do without it.'

This, of course, is enough to send the fires of hell blazing through his body. Only this morning he was fantasizing about her. Now here she is. In the flesh. And she needs lots of loving. Without another word he goes to the till and pays the bill.

'Come on,' he says. 'I must be back before the magistrate returns from work.'

He almost lifts her to her feet and they hurry out of the mall to the parking lot. They get into their different cars and speed down Beyers Naudé Drive to their North Riding townhouse.

They do not waste any time on niceties. They strip naked as soon as they enter the door, almost tearing to pieces those stubborn garments that want to cling to the body. In a situation like this, even a La Perla gets no respect. If it insists on gentleness then it will be ripped off without ceremony. The garments leave a trail that follows the man and the woman through the living room to the bedroom. Their bodies are glued to each other as they kiss passionately. She assists him into his trusty Rough Rider. Even in this giddy haste they never forget that they are not ready to deal with either a baby or a devastating disease. He kisses her ears, her neck and lingers on her breasts as he suckles on the nipples like a hungry baby. She begs him not to waste time—she is wet and ready. Even here on the bed there is no gentleness, which is exactly how she wants it today. Some nights she pleads, 'Be gentle, Don. Please, be gentle.' But not today. She urges him to move faster and with more vigour. He does not need any encouragement in that direction, he has been too hungry for her for too long. And when it's her turn to be on top she rides him so roughly that he sobs like a child who is being spanked for getting into some mischief. Her long smooth thighs hold his waist in a tight grip. He dances to the rhythm of her soft moans. She dances to the rhythm of his dance. They both scream as they come at the same time, not giving a shit if the thin walls carry the sounds to the rest of Three Oaks.

They are utterly exhausted and both fall into a deep sleep in each other's arms.

It is dusk and the street lights are shining through the window when they are startled by the Dave Brubeck *Take Five* ringtone of Don's cellphone.

'You should have switched your damn cellphone off, Don,' says Tumi as he reaches for it.

'I knew you would bail out on me sooner or later,' says the voice of the magistrate.

'Who says I have bailed out?'

'Where were you when this happened?'

This worries Don. What if something terrible has happened and he was not there? The magistrate would not be calling him for nothing—not when she has been trying to get rid of him all this time.

'When what happened?'

'You were supposed to be here, looking after my house.'

'I just came to my apartment to check on a few things. I took a nap and overslept. That's all. What happened?'

Tumi is tickling him naughtily. She whispers in his ear while biting it, 'Why lie to the old fogey? Why not tell her you came home for a good fuck.'

He jumps out of bed. He is still on his cellphone.

'What the hell happened there?' he asks. 'Are you OK?'

But she has hung up. He dresses quickly. As soon as he opens the bedroom door his cat rushes in meowing. It follows him into the kitchenette. He gets some cat food from the cupboard and feeds it.

'You've not been feeding Snowy properly, Tumi,' he says. 'She's lost some weight.'

'As a matter of fact I've been looking around for an animal shelter that will take it,' says Tumi from the bedroom. She is very unhappy that he has to leave and he knows that she'll take it out on the cat. Sending it to an animal shelter is not just an empty threat. She will certainly do it. Sooner or later she will do it. He must find a way of saving his Snowy.

North Riding is only fifteen minutes away from Weltevreden Park. Or ten if you are racing on the highway like a lunatic, which is what Don is doing. As soon as he enters the gate he sees the writing on the front wall. Big, ugly, red letters dripping like blood sprayed above the door—*Death to the Bitch*! More spraying on the cast-iron security grille and on the steps. On the double doors of the garage as well—*The bitch must die*!

As soon as he enters the magistrate yells at him, 'What good is your presence here? What kind of a bodyguard are you?'

'Calm down,' says Don. 'You don't have to get hysterical about it. Remember, you're the one who told me you don't need a bodyguard.'

'*Ja*, man, but you're supposed to look after my house.'

'That's not my brief, Ms Uys. I'm supposed to be your bodyguard, to see to it that nothing harms *you*. From now on I'm going to guard you and not your damn house. And if you play the kind of trick you played this morning, stealing away from the house, I'll go to that courthouse and sit right next to you on that bench.'

'Oh, no, I'll not have you follow me around.'

'I'm not asking for your permission. If something happens to you on the way to and from work, they're going to ask me why. No one will ask you anything 'cause you'll be dead. And guess what—from now on I'm not going to sit here and wait for things to happen. I'm going after those Visagie Brothers. I'm going to confront the one who is not in jail. He must know something about this.'

The magistrate is relieved to hear this. At least that is better than following her around like a puppy.

11

WIDOWS' LONG MARCH TO FREEDOM

For the first time the magistrate and the bodyguard sit down to discuss how they are going to work together. Of course, she makes it obvious that if it were up to her, she would have nothing to do with the bodyguard. He is someone who has invaded her private world. But until Stevo Visagie is put in his place, and is forced to stop his childish games, she has no choice but to tolerate the impudent presence of this man in her house.

This morning she will go to work and he will stay at home and organize the removal of the red paint on the wall. He can only hope nothing will happen to her on the way to or from Roodepoort.

'If you see anything suspicious, such as a car following you, call me on my cellphone immediately,' he says.

He orders three guards from VIP Protection Services and in no time they have cleaned the walls and the garage doors with a solution of turpentine. Before they get into their armoured vehicle and return to the office, he asks them to help him move the furniture. He is able to vacuum places that have not been cleaned for a long time.

Obviously the so-called maid who is supposed to come once a week has not been doing a proper job of cleaning the house. And the magistrate has not bothered to inspect her handiwork. This week she didn't come at all, so Don has not met her. The magistrate doesn't know if she came last week. Or the week before. She vaguely remembers getting a call from someone about a grand-mother's funeral in the Eastern Cape or something like that. It is not one of the important things in her life; she shouldn't be expected to remember anything about it.

It is not that Don enjoys taking on the responsibility of keeping the house clean. He just cannot live in a filthy environment. If he has to stay here then he must clean at least his room, the living room and the kitchen—the spaces that he uses. Today there is help from the guards, so he might as well get the whole house cleaned, beginning with the magistrate's bedroom.

It is locked. There are two other bedrooms and they are locked too. Well, he cannot blame her. He is, after all, a stranger and there is no reason why she should trust him. He cannot deny that had the rooms been unlocked he would surely snoop around. He is intrigued by this woman, especially after reading all those things about her in the magazines and newspapers. There is more to her austere life than she is letting on.

He thanks the guards, gives them a tip and releases them to their more important duty—that of guarding the lives and property of affluent Johannesburgers. And of protecting their social events, private parties and music festivals so that they may celebrate the new South Africa without let or hindrance.

He is doing the finishing touches to the cleaning. Everything is now spick and span and the living-room furniture has been rearranged. The piles of dusty papers and files on the coffee table and on every flat surface have been packed neatly in boxes that he has stacked near the bookcase. While he is removing the final specks of dust on the display cabinet with a feather duster the magistrate arrives.

She is alarmed at what has been done to her living room. For a while she is open-mouthed. Don stands there like a showman who has just rendered a bravura performance, waiting for applause. But instead of showing approval, the magistrate's face displays anger.

'Who said you could touch my things?'

Don looks amused. He is trying to understand why she is angry. He just cannot take her seriously.

'A simple "thank you" would have been in order, Ms Uys,' he says, still smiling.

'You have no right to mess with my stuff.'

'Mess? You call what I have done a mess?'

Once more the magistrate surveys the room. It no longer looks like her living room. It no longer feels like the space she has known for years. The space over which she had dominion. Her life is no longer her own but the stranger's.

'Put it back the way it was,' she commands.

'What? Are you serious?'

'I want it exactly as it was.'

'Tell you what, Ms Uys, you put it back the way it was yourself. I'm not touching that stuff. If you want your mess the way it was, then you do it yourself. I can't live in a messy house.'

'Then don't live in it. Go back to wherever you came from.'

Don is really amused now.

'I'm paid to look after you, Ms Uys. And I'm going to do it whether you like it or not. You're not going to get rid of me that easily.'

She goes to her room in frustration. She is used to having her orders obeyed. She does not know how to handle this new situation. If she were in her court she would know exactly what to do—cite the impertinent upstart for contempt and summarily sentence him to a term of imprisonment. No one has ever tried any bullshit in her court. Until Stevo Visagie. And look where he is now.

In the evening she returns to the living room to watch the news on SABC 3. Don is already watching the news and occupying the sofa. He shifts to one side, creating space for her, but she ignores him and goes to the sideboard for her room-temperature bottle of wine. She also gets one glass from the display cabinet and sits in an easy chair away from Don. She pours herself a glass of wine. There is an uneasy silence between them.

After a while Don says, 'I do drink wine too, you know.'

'You are my bodyguard, not my friend,' she says sternly. 'I have no obligation to accord you any hospitality.'

'Accord me?' Don asks, mocking her accent. 'Well, I never! Anyway, Ms Uys, I would not touch that wine if you begged me to. I like mine chilled. And certainly not from a bottle of plonk.'

She was going to respond but her attention is suddenly drawn to the screen. The Society of Widows, led by Aunt Magda and Ma Visagie, is demonstrating at the gates of Diepkloof Prison. Although this is a small ragtag group of women, it has attracted the attention of the media because Sun City is an odd place to demonstrate when one has a grievance against any arm of the government. No one remembers anyone demonstrating outside the gates of the prison because that is not where the authorities who run the justice system, or even the prison system, are located.

Aunt Magda tells the television reporter that it was her strategy to take the mass action, as she continues to call it even though no masses are involved, to the gates of Sun City because it is in that very hell that an innocent man is being held. A man who is a friend of the widows and all the suffering masses of South Africa.

'We have a petition that has been signed by a hundred people,' says Aunt Magda. 'People who have benefited from the generosity of the Visagie family.'

'So, what do you intend to do with your petition?' asks the reporter.

'Give it to the man who runs this prison, of course,' she says, as if the reporter has asked the dumbest question ever.

'But he's not the person who has the power to free Mr Visagie.'

'He's not?' This is news to Aunt Magda. 'No. It cannot be. He is the man who is holding Stevo Visagie.'

'Anyway, why is there so much interest in the release of Mr Visagie? Some might say he's just a petty criminal who deserves to be in jail.'

'They said that about Nelson Mandela too, didn't they? Yet he was fighting for the rights of the people. The Visagie Brothers feed the poor. They are our Nelson Mandela.'

Ma Visagie is not pleased that all the attention is on Aunt Magda. It is Aunt Magda that people will be watching on television that evening, yet she is the one who carried the hero in question in her womb. She will not allow her to hog all the limelight. She grabs the microphone from the reporter.

'That's right,' she says. 'And that magistrate who sent my innocent baby to jail, she's waging a war against the Visagie family. She's not satisfied that she sent my little baby to jail for nothing—she went there to attack him while he was in chains.'

'Are you saying the magistrate is waging some kind of a vendetta against the Visagies? Why?'

'A vend what? Whatever you call it, she's not gonna get away with it. My little boy is gonna come out of that jail one day.'

The magistrate has heard enough. Her face displays nothing but contempt. She reaches for the remote and switches the television off. Once more there is an awkward silence between her and Don for some time. After a while he breaks it.

'What are you going to do about it?' he asks.

She will do nothing. She is the magistrate. Magistrates are not allowed to take pre-emptive action. They are effective only after a crime has been committed.

'But a crime *has* been committed. They vandalized your walls and broke into your house and cooked rotten tripe in your precious pot. That should be illegal, shouldn't it?'

'We don't know who did that,' she says.

'You should have called the police to investigate.'

'Well, I didn't.'

'Both you and I know that the Visagie boy, the one who's not in jail, has something to do with it. He either did it himself or got his henchmen to do it. The cops would have made him sing like a bird. They have their ways, even though torture is now illegal in South Africa.'

'How stupid of me not to figure that out!' Of course, Don is aware that she is being sarcastic.

Just now she looks so vulnerable. Don feels sorry for her. He undertakes to do his own detective work. He is going to do his damnedest to get new evidence of the Visagie Brothers' criminal activities, so that both Stevo and Shortie face new charges before Stevo's contempt of court sentence is over. In that way he will stay in jail for much longer and will give up on his mission to make the magistrate's life a living hell.

The magistrate smiles despite herself. She obviously approves of this plan of action, although she is too proud to say so.

'Why do you want to do all that?' she asks. 'What's in it for you?'

'So that I can go back home to my clean apartment,' he says and laughs.

But she does not see the joke. She has become the ice queen again, after the brief moment of weakness evidenced by the smile.

'We are going to crush those Visagies once and for all,' says Don as he leaves for his room. 'I'm going to start with that Shortie Visagie. He's obviously Stevo's evil hand in all this. I'm going to squeeze . . . well, if you were not a lady I would tell you exactly what part of him I am going to squeeze. This madness will come to an end.'

At that moment Shortie wouldn't have been fazed by Don Mateza's Delphic pronouncements even if he knew of them. He is sitting at the kitchen table surrounded by the people he loves and who love him, in the form of Ma

Visagie, Aunt Magda and three other women who are members of the Society of Widows. This is Aunt Magda's war cabinet, and they are 'strategizing the way forward', as she calls it. They have just watched the news and Aunt Magda is telling them how satisfied she is with the way she appeared on television. Of course, she would have worn more make-up if she had known for sure that television cameras would be present at the demonstration. More shimmer blusher in flame. Vivid violet eyeshadow. Hot rouge lipstick instead of the earthy brown she is wearing today. The rouge makes her lips look more sensuous, which is important for a woman who is now a television star, even if her face is etched with the deep furrows of age.

When she phoned the news tip line of the television station at Auckland Park asking them to send a reporter to Sun City because an earth-shattering event was going to take place there, she had not reckoned that they would take her seriously, although she hoped they would. One never knows with news people. Sometimes they just send a radio reporter, in which case it becomes a futile exercise to look beautiful. But this is a good lesson for all of them. And by all of them, she emphasizes, she means the leaders of the movement. The rest of the members of the Society of Widows must look destitute to prove the point that without Stevo Visagie there is a lot of suffering in Roodepoort. But it is imperative for her as a leader to look presentable.

As far as Ma Visagie is concerned Aunt Magda has overstayed her welcome. The matriarch does not like the idea of someone else calling the shots in her territory. A quiet storm is raging in her as she sits at the kitchen table listening to Aunt Magda prattling on about a long march to freedom that the Society of Widows must undertake. A long march is the only thing that will top their demonstration at the gates of Sun City in so far as attracting the media is concerned. Yes, they are going to march to Pretoria, fifty-five kilometres away, straight to the Union Buildings, and demand to see the president of the republic.

'I'm not going to walk to Pretoria,' Ma Visagie bursts out. 'I'm not that crazy. If we must go to Pretoria at all why not take a taxi?'

'That's the whole idea, Ma Visagie,' says Aunt Magda condescendingly. 'The march is what is important in this whole thing. Not just reaching Pretoria.'

Actually, Aunt Magda is beginning to get on Shortie's nerves too.

'I think we must find out from Krish Naidoo first if this is the right thing to do,' he says.

Aunt Magda has nothing but contempt for such reactionary thinking. She dismisses the idea out of hand. After all, Naidoo is a lawyer and like all lawyers, he is interested in making as much money as possible from Stevo's incarceration. The more the matter drags on and Stevo remains in jail, the more money Naidoo will make since lawyers are paid by the hour. For every hour that Stevo is in jail Naidoo is making money.

Shortie is not sure about this. It sounds rather strange to him. He must find out from Krish Naidoo because if it is true it will mean their bill by the time Stevo is released will be so big that they will have to sell their scrapyard business to pay him. And that's not what the lawyer told Ma Visagie when she first approached him to defend her sons.

'I'm still not walking to Pretoria,' says Ma Visagie.

'Those who want to see Stevo out of jail will walk,' says Aunt Magda with the finality of the revolutionary general she imagines she is.

Now, this is not the smartest thing to come out of Aunt Magda's mouth. Ma Visagie lets her know that she will not tolerate anyone talking to her like that, especially in her own house. Although Aunt Magda apologizes, tension remains between the two of them.

After the meeting, mother and son confer. They both take a resolution that Aunt Magda must go. Tomorrow, when they visit Stevo at Sun City, they will tell him that they are sending Aunt Magda back to Athlone, even though they know already that he won't be pleased with that.

They are right. Stevo Visagie objects.

'Leave the poor *bushie* alone,' he says. 'She's just having fun.'

Although *bushie* is a derogatory word for the coloured people of South Africa, when they use it among themselves it is acceptable. Although Stevo himself is not coloured but a *boertjie*, as Aunt Magda used to call him, he has always called her a *bushie*, and both of them accepted *boertjie* and *bushie* as terms of endearment.

Shortie is not surprised to hear this. He knows how attached Stevo has always been to Aunt Magda, ever since she broke his virginity when he was only slightly older than a tyke.

'But, Stevo, she's getting on my nerves,' says Shortie.

'Get on her nerves too, my china, and leave her alone,' says Stevo.

'She's getting on Ma's nerves too.'

Stevo finds this funny. So Ma has at last met her match? It seems after all these years Aunt Magda has returned from the Mother City a changed woman. Stevo remembers that when she was their maid, Ma Visagie used to boss her around no end, and she would confide her frustrations to little Stevo. The two of them would plot how they would kill Ma Visagie one day.

'But as you can see,' says Stevo still laughing, 'we never got to kill her.'

'It's not funny, Stevo. Ma is serious about it. Aunt Magda must go.'

'Listen, Shortie, instead of bothering with a poor *bushie* from Cape Town who never did nothing bad to you except raise you, you should be doing what I asked you to do. You know? About you-know-who?'

'But I *am* doing something, Stevo.'

'Writing threats on her wall? That helps, I suppose. That keeps her on her toes. It reminds her that we are still there and we are not going nowhere. But threats alone are not enough for a woman like that. I need action, china. The cat! The cat!'

After this prison visit Shortie is rather loose with his tongue and Aunt Magda gets to know that there is a plot to get rid of her. She feels betrayed by the family she has worked for all these years, the family for which she left her own in Athlone to come all the way to Johannesburg to help them deal with a crisis they couldn't handle on their own.

'You want to get rid of me after I have helped your sons with mass action?' she asks Ma Visagie with a wounded look.

The march of the widows must nevertheless go on. Aunt Magda gathers her troops. She boosts the small group that has formed the core demonstrators so far— joined by onlookers and layabouts who would participate in any demonstration irrespective of the cause—with a number of retired prostitutes. She has managed to track down the ageing women who used to work for Ma Visagie when she was still one of the top madams in the city, and has promised them great rewards in future since mass action will expand to deal with fund-raising to fight the poverty of the 'widows' of South Africa as soon as they win their first battle—that of freeing Stevo Visagie.

On the N1 highway to Pretoria commuters' attention is drawn to a motley band of about fifty women in black, marching with placards that read *We Demand Justice for the Visagie Family . . . Free Stevo Visagie! . . .* and other messages to that effect. Some motorists honk and make thumbs-up signs, even though they don't know what the protest is about. A protest is a protest and it must be supported. People are fascinated by the composition of this group. Whoever thought that one day one would witness protesters representing the racial make-up of South Africa, including white women? These are some of the wonders of the new South Africa. Like white women who beg for alms at traffic lights.

The taxis, however, are impatient with the protesters. They also honk, not in encouragement but in anger, because the protesters are marching in the emergency lane, which taxis to and from Pretoria seem to think is meant for them instead of genuine emergencies. They hurl insults and make rude gestures at the women. This is the busiest highway in Africa and at any hour of the day or night, there are thousands of cars in the multiple lanes. It is worse at peak times in the mornings and afternoons when people who live in Johannesburg travel to work in Pretoria and vice versa. Cars move at such a slow pace that a journey that would normally be thirty minutes takes more than two hours. That is why the patience of the taxi drivers is tested to the limit by the

demonstrators. After a few kilometres, two traffic policemen on motorcycles are sent to make sure that the
women are not marching in the emergency lane but on
the side of the road. One rides behind the women and
another in front. A police escort, of course, lends dignity
to the protest march and makes Aunt Magda feel very
important.

The women are busy singing their garbled protests
songs and do not notice that for some time now a Saab
convertible has been following them, right behind the
traffic cop on his motorcycle.

It is Don Mateza.

He has negotiated his way through the lanes until he
reached the women. Now he drives slowly parallel to the
marchers and waves at them. They wave back, thinking
he is one of their supporters, and they walk on.

He learnt about this march when he was following
the magistrate's Fiat Uno from her Weltevreden Park
home to the Roodepoort magistrate's court. He was listening to Radio 702 and there was Aki Anastasiou with
the traffic report. The traffic to Pretoria was even slower
than usual because of what looked like a demonstration
of women, he reported. Their leader was carrying a plac-
ard that declared them to be the Society of Widows and
the other women's placards were about some Visagie
family that had been treated unjustly. By the look of
things from the traffic helicopter, they were determined
to march to Pretoria, but some of them were beginning

to straggle a bit, even though they were hardly halfway to their destination.

Don knew immediately that they were the protesters he saw on television a few days before. Even then, he had been intrigued by their leader who seemed to love the limelight and he wondered what she hoped to gain from the protest. He decided to find this woman. Who knew? There may be a chance of recruiting her to spy on the Visagies. Of course, he would first have to determine her commitment to the family and what drives it. And then, he would size her up to see if she was the kind of person who could be bought.

As soon as the magistrate got to court Don went to his office across Dieperink Street to catch up on urgent messages and to submit a progress report to Jim Baxter. Fortunately he was not at work yet, so he wouldn't delay him with questions. He left the report on his desk and rushed back to his car. He tore back to Ontdekkers Road and then joined the N1 on 14th Avenue.

He patiently weaved his way through the slow traffic, forcing his car from lane to lane whenever there was the smallest opening. Drivers honked at him and gave him the middle finger. He returned the favour and drove on until he caught sight of the protesters. It was only then that he moved to the emergency lane so that other cars would not force him to drive past his quarry.

He waves again and opens the window. After catching Aunt Magda's attention he yells, 'I want to talk to you.'

'Who are you?' she asks.

He has to think fast. He has to lie.

'I am a reporter,' he says.

'For what?'

'A newspaper.'

'I only talk to TV.'

'I know TV people too. I work with them. I can get you interviews on all the channels in South Africa. But I've got to talk to you first.'

'*Ja*, but we can't talk now. We are on the march.'

'Listen, there's a Shell garage a few kilometres ahead. Please stop there just for a few minutes. I'll buy you all drinks and then we can arrange when my television friends can interview you.'

'Why would you want to do that?'

'Because I like you, and support what you stand for.'

He has slowed the traffic to walking pace in his lane and the drivers behind him are all honking impatiently. South Africa is famous for its road-rage incidents, so he speeds up before someone gets the idea of getting out of his car and blowing his head off with a gun or, if he is lucky, shattering his side window with a jack and leaving his head bleeding. He can only hope that when the women get to the garage, they will take a detour for refreshments.

He seems to wait for ever at the garage. The traffic has thinned out on the highway and cars are racing by at high speed. But there is no sign of the women. He hopes nothing bad has happened to them. Perhaps they got tired. But there would be no point in turning back. Not unless someone came to pick them up in a bus.

It is afternoon already and Jenny Crwys-Williams is talking about the contents of her handbag on Radio 702. He loves her irreverence and her laughter that is so full-bodied you can touch it. Just like Tumi's naughty giggles. He remembers the kind of junk Tumi always keeps in her handbag—things she would never use, that have accu-mulated over the years. Yet she transfers them from handbag to handbag.

Tumi. He wonders where she is at this moment and what she is doing. He hasn't seen her since the last time they made love, though they talk on the phone every day. He dreads her calls because she wants him to come back home. There must be other ways of getting a promotion. Don't allow them to humiliate you any further. Come home, Ma-Don-za, come home!

He is about to give up on the women and drive back to the Roodepoort magistrate's court when he sees them straggling along in the distance. And, indeed, they branch off to the garage where he is waiting.

All their enthusiasm has fizzled out and they are complaining loudly of exhaustion.

'Perhaps we should have listened to Ma Visagie,' some are saying.

Aunt Magda is worried that her leadership is fast losing credibility with this deflated lot.

'What is wrong with you?' she yells in Afrikaans. 'Do you think the *swart mense* would be the rulers today if they had given up their struggle? Mass action is not for the faint-hearted, I tell you. But the rewards will be great. Look at people like Molotov Mbungane who you see on television every day. Do you think they would be billionaires today if they had given up on their mass action?'

But the pep talk doesn't seem to help. The women insist that they cannot walk any further. There must be other ways of joining the ranks of Mr Mbungane than to suffer in the sun like this. Aunt Magda does not argue. She herself is bushed.

She admits to Don that they underestimated the long walk and the state of their fitness to accomplish it. They are giving up and will phone Shortie Visagie to fetch them in a lorry, though she doubts Ma Visagie will let him do so since she was against the march in the first place. But Shortie has a heart. He will not abandon them in the wilderness of Midrand. He will come for them even if he has to make two trips.

Don learns that she genuinely loves the Visagie boys—after all, she brought them up as if they were her own children—though she is bitter at the treatment she is receiving from Ma Visagie who has been plotting to kick her out of the house.

He sees an opportunity here. If she is so aggrieved with Ma Visagie, she may easily be used against the family. She is obviously a mine of information about the criminal goings-on there. A person like her, who depends

solely on her government old-age pension for her livelihood, will surely welcome the extra cash in exchange for
some titbits of information.

He buys everyone cold drinks and Marie biscuits on
a VIP Protection Services credit card. After swearing Aunt
Magda to secrecy, they exchange telephone numbers and
arrange to meet soon.

He drives back to the Roodepoort magistrate's court
quite satisfied that he is on his way to nailing the Visagie
Brothers once and for all.

12

BLONDE BOMBSHELL

The magistrate is at her desk drafting her judgement for a stock-theft case. A man stole a neighbour's goat and slaughtered it for a Sunday *braai*. What complicates the case is that the neighbour was not supposed to be keeping livestock within the city limits in any event. He insists the goat was a pet and not livestock, even though evidence was presented that in fact the neighbour has been keeping a number of goats from time to time, which he sells to township residents in Dobsonville for ancestral sacrifices.

The magistrate shakes her head in wonderment at how 'these people' still practise all this 'superstitious mumbo-jumbo' in the twenty-first century. Nevertheless, it is not her place to pass judgement on that particular aspect of the case. Hers is to examine the evidence from both sides and determine whether the man is guilty of stock theft or not. She never thought that one day she would be dealing with a stock-theft case in the middle of Roodepoort.

Such cases are a waste of her time. As are the petty civil matters over which she has to preside. She would rather be hitting her gavel hard on the heads of the degenerates that have broken families and destroyed the moral fibre of the community—the sex trade in all its forms: the sleazy brothels and strip joints and so-called escort services that have changed the face of Johannesburg and its satellite towns, such as Roodepoort.

The phone rings and she reaches for it.

'Hi, honey,' says a strange voice on the line.

'And . . . who are you?' asks the magistrate.

'Is that the Blonde Bombshell?'

She has never been called anything like that before; she is not certain if she heard correctly.

'Blonde what?'

The voice becomes hesitant.

'Is that not the escort service?'

The voice has lost its honey-coated slickness. It is a bit embarrassed.

'This is the office of the Roodepoort magistrate,' says the magistrate, 'and I am the magistrate.'

'Oh, my gosh!' cries the voice—it has now become panicky. 'Sorry. Wrong number.'

She puts the phone back and ponders what has just happened. Perhaps there is nothing to it. Just a misdialled number. Men! And the bastard may be someone's husband too. The wife thinks he is at work when he is busy calling escort agencies.

The phone rings again. At first she hesitates to answer it. After a few rings she reaches for it. It is a different caller asking for the Blonde Bombshell, breathing heavily and promising to give her such a great time she will never want to be fucked by anyone else ever again.

A cold sweat runs down her spine. She can feel the presence of the callers as if they are in the room with her. They have invaded her space, just like it has been invaded at her home but in a different manner. The office had become the only refuge where she could feel in control. Now the calls are infringing this sacred space. She feels so violated she wants to take a bath—wash away the slime that has dripped from the voices on to her body. OK, OK . . . she must calm down now . . . regain her composure. This may just be a mistake. Perhaps a typo in an escort-agency advertisement in some tabloid or pornographic magazine.

She is not going to answer the phone again. But what if it's important court business? What if it's the chief magistrate? She decides to leave it off the hook and continues writing the judgement.

After a while her cellphone rings. It is Krish Naidoo.

'Where are you? I have been calling your office.'

'I'm in the office. I left the phone off the hook.'

'What on earth for, Kristin?'

'Because it is my phone and I am busy.'

'We've got to talk, Kristin.'

The last thing she wants to do is talk to Krish Naidoo. It can only be about the Visagie case. She does not want to be explaining to him why she hasn't touched that file since the last time they discussed the matter. But she herself needs to talk to someone. And Krish Naidoo is the only one left of the people who knew her in the past and with whom she and her husband used to socialize—well, at least at those events that had something to do with the legal profession. Since her divorce she has pushed everyone away. He is the only one who could not be totally pushed away because his practice is in Roodepoort and he occasionally has to appear before her.

They arrange to meet for coffee at Mugg & Bean. The nearest is located a number of kilometres away at the Town Square Mall in Weltevreden Park. The whole of Roodepoort is so run-down and is now so downmarket that there is not a single Seattle Coffee Shop or Mugg & Bean in the whole town. Only fish and chips cafes and stores that sell cheap clothes, mostly factory rejects, and the ubiquitous furniture stores. And, of course, the sleazy sex joints. But there is no place for a decent person to relax with a latte and a muffin as there are in the suburbs. It is the same story with all inner-city districts on the Rand. Life has migrated to the suburbs.

They drive in separate cars because from Town Square she will go home, which is just three streets away.

Krish Naidoo is already waiting at the table for two in the coffee house. As soon as she takes her seat, even before the waiter takes their orders, Kristin tells him about the calls she has been getting this morning and accuses Stevo Visagie of being behind them.

'My client is in jail, Kristin,' says Krish Naidoo. 'Why are you blaming him for this?'

'He has people outside. I will get to the bottom of this,' she says. 'And if I find that the Visagies have anything to do with it, someone will be very sorry, Krish.'

'I still don't understand why you won't involve the police. I'm sure they would have caught whoever is harassing you by now.'

'I don't want the publicity, Krish. That should be clear by now. I don't want every scumbag in Johannesburg thinking that they can intimidate me in my fight against prostitutes, their pimps, their madams and their brothels.'

This exasperates Krish Naidoo. He pounds the table with both hands, which startles both Kristin Uys and the waiter who is waiting patiently to take their orders. The white men and women in the cafe look askance at the lovers' quarrel between a white woman and an Indian man. Old South Africa finds it difficult to rest in peace in places like Weltevreden Park. Sometimes it rears its head in the guise of the old white-haired woman who looks at the couple with disgust and hisses, 'Sies!'

The waiter takes their orders. He will have an espresso and she a mocha.

'Give it up, Kristin, will you?' says Krish Naidoo, but softly now. 'Your problem is that you don't want to forget the past.'

'I know that you qualified as an attorney, Krish,' she says. 'But I didn't know you also qualified as a shrink.'

'Your sarcasm doesn't impress anyone but you, Kristin. All I'm saying is just because Barend fell into disgrace is no reason for you to go out on a moral crusade.'

'A poor excuse for a shrink, I must add. I divorced Barend. We went our bloody separate ways. Why do you want to make him an issue in my life?'

'And it's no reason to push your old friends away.'

Barend left town a broken man. The scandal with prostitutes destroyed his career as a local government politician who had been so highly respected that he was slated to be the next mayor of Roodepoort that year. He was also stripped of his position as an elder of the church and later the Law Society struck him off the roll after it was discovered that he had used funds from his trust account to service his addiction to prostitutes. Whatever one may say about him, Krish Naidoo is certain that he moved on. He did not push away those who wanted to help. He picked up the pieces, as the cliché goes, and glued them together. He was not deterred by the fact that the cracks could still be seen. Instead he got himself a clerical job at a platinum mine in Rustenburg and immersed himself in a new life. Ordinary and less prestigious, but a new life all the same. Kristin should move on too. She must not be afraid to get involved with people on a personal level. That's not the way to protect herself from being hurt again. She should move on.

'Who says I haven't moved on, Krish?'

'No, you haven't. You used to be a nice person.'

At this he chuckles. She breaks into guarded laughter.

'So I'm not a nice person just because I'm strict in the courtroom and I rule without fear or favour? I've always been like that, even when I was still married to Barend. He has nothing to do with that.'

'I'm not talking about the courtroom, and you know it. You used to be outgoing.'

'A social butterfly, hey? Well, tough luck, Krish Naidoo, I grew up.'

Indeed she was one of the popular socialites at university. After graduating from the University of Pretoria with a BIuris she went on to do an LLB at Wits Law School against the wishes of her parents and other relatives who couldn't understand why a girl from a good Afrikaans family would want to study at an English university. That was where she met Krish Naidoo, who was there for a BProc degree. They shared some classes and got to be friends, to the extent that when Krish Naidoo got married she was one of his special guests at a Hindu ceremony and occasionally was invited for the Indian dishes that his wife cooked. That was an extremely liberal gesture for a woman brought up with strict Calvinistic values. After she married the more conservative Barend, Kristin and Krish didn't see much of each other, except when they appeared on opposite sides in some civil matter (she was still an attorney then) and would then meet for lunch and a drink afterwards.

'Now I keep to myself by choice,' she says defiantly.

'Because you think your former society friends are laughing at you? Well, I have news for you—they have their own problems.'

For the first time we see the magistrate getting emotional, with glassy eyes and a teary voice.

'Do you know how it felt when I saw on television that a brothel had been raided by the Hillbrow police . . . and there was my husband . . . my childhood sweetheart . . . among the regular patrons who were caught with their pants down . . . right there on the TV screen . . . handcuffed to a whore!'

Krish Naidoo holds both of her hands to his chest. He would like to give her a warm hug and tell her everything will be all right, but he knows that she would find that humiliating. She hates to display any sign of weakness if she can help it. She is ashamed of herself for breaking down like this as it is and tries to brush everything aside by changing the subject.

'So, Krish, what did you want to discuss with me? We didn't come here to talk about my marriage to Barend, did we?'

He wanted to talk about the Visagie case, to find out why it is taking so long for the judges of the high court to review her summary judgement. He also wanted to tell her that if he does not hear from the judges within the next seven days, he will lodge his complaint directly with the chief justice. But this is not the time.

'Never mind,' says Krish Naidoo. 'It can wait.'

Back at the magistrate's house Don Mateza is in an apron and is busy cooking in the kitchen. In the morning he followed the magistrate to work, went to his office to check on things and then was struck by the brilliant idea of surprising her with a candlelight dinner. So, he drove to the supermarket at Palm Court to buy a few ingredients and then back to the house to transform them into a samp-and-beans wonder that sings in the mouth in a completely different tune from that of the traditional Xhosa dish. His is cooked with shoulder mutton and an aromatic mixture of cardamoms, mixed masala, cinnamon, fennel seeds, bay leaves, curry powder, crushed garlic, crushed ginger root and fresh coriander. If this does not melt her heart, then nothing on earth will ever do so.

One thing wonderful about this dish is that you cook everything in one pot.

He plans on returning to the courthouse at about four-thirty to accompany the magistrate back home. He will set the table before he leaves for Roodepoort.

The dish still has to simmer for a few more minutes. It would have been ready by now if it were not for the calls he had to answer as he was beginning to chop the mutton into tiny pieces. When the phone rang for the first time he rushed for it hoping it was Tumi but then remembered that Tumi has never called him on the magistrate's landline. She calls him only on his cellphone.

It was a strange voice.

'Hi, Blonde Bombshell, I need your services,' it said chirpily.

'You need my services, hey?' responded Don, just as chirpily. 'What exactly do you want me to do?'

'Hey, is that not the escort service?'

'Where do you get that idea?'

'In the newspaper,' said the voice. Now it had lost its cheeriness. It named the newspaper and the date and continued, 'In the personal classifieds. *Blonde Bombshell will give you the time of your life*. And there are two telephone numbers.'

'Are you sure one of them is this number?'

'*Ja*, man,' said the voice impatiently. 'It must be a sick joke. I called the first number and they told me it's a magistrate's office.'

Don broke out laughing.

'Yeah, it *is* a sick joke,' he said. 'I suggest you try another escort agency, my friend.'

After this he went to the BP Garage at Palm Court and bought the tabloid. And indeed the advertisement was there. He immediately phoned the classified section and took them to task for publishing the telephone numbers of the magistrate. He demanded to know who had placed the classified ad but the woman at the end of the line was not forthcoming with that information. When he threatened her and her sleazy paper with the full force of the law, she asked him to hold while she checked the files. A minute or so later she came back with some name and address, which were obviously false. There were no other details on record. Not even a telephone number. The advertiser paid in cash for only one insertion.

'Don't you verify the identity of whoever places a classified ad with you?'

'We have no way of verifying identities,' said the woman.

'So you are just happy to grab the money and run? If you ever publish that advertisement again my client, who happens to be the magistrate of Roodepoort, will sue your pants off. I want you to publish a retraction or whatever you call it. The magistrate must not receive dirty calls again from your sleazy readers.'

After fielding a few more calls from horny men, he decided to leave the phone off the hook.

He is laying the table and Vivaldi's *Four Seasons* is playing on the stereo. He has observed that's what the magistrate plays when she returns home, bushed after work, and relaxes with a glass of warm wine and a therapeutic caress of the cat. Suddenly she arrives. He did not expect her so early. She stands at the door and sniffs at the aroma. She has a puzzled look on her face.

'You didn't tell me you run an escort agency on the side,' says Don jokingly from the dining room.

'So they phoned here as well?' she says as she unloads some documents from her briefcase on to the coffee table.

Don joins her in the living room and winces at the thought that she is again messing up the place he has tidied. He doesn't say anything about it though, but shows her the classified in the tabloid.

'Oh, yes, Blonde Bombshell owns both your home and office numbers.'

As he returns to the dining room he tells her not to worry, he has handled the matter quite effectively. The paper won't publish the trashy advertisement with her telephone numbers again. She follows him to the dining room and tells him he shouldn't have taken it upon himself to meddle in her business. It is however very obvious that she is relieved that he took the trouble to protect her, but she must pretend otherwise if only to show that she is still in control.

She stops in her tracks when she sees the table set with candles and all.

'And what is this all about?' she asks.

'A peace offering. I want us to be friends.'

At this he goes to the kitchen and returns with a steaming serving bowl of samp and beans. He gingerly puts it in the middle of the table, and waits for the accolades with a broad smile. None are forthcoming. Only the snarl of a wounded cat.

'I don't need friends, OK? Just be a bodyguard. That's all you are paid to do.'

She leaves in a huff and he follows her to the kitchen. She explodes in anger when she sees a pot simmering on the stove.

'You used my special crockery without permission, and now my pots.'

'I had to cook the food in something,' says Don calmly.

'These are very special pots, damn it! They are waterless pots, and that means you don't use water in them.'

Don finally loses his patience.

'Hey, I used only one pot! And you can't cook the great dish that I busted my ass cooking for you without water. So, there, sue me!'

'Well, I'll take the food to my homeless people.'

'You even own homeless people? And you're going to feed them with my food?'

'They'll enjoy it, I'm sure. It does smell good. Very good, in fact.'

'You know what? I'm done with you. I'm not used to this kind of shit.'

He storms out of the kitchen to his bedroom. He takes his bags down from the top shelf of the built-in wardrobe. He quickly shoves his clothes into the bags. Even his neatly pressed Versace suits are stuffed roughly into the suitcase. He is fuming. He has been insulted enough by this white bitch and will not take it any more. Those Visagies can do whatever they want with her for all he cares. She deserves every bit of it. Tumi was right. This was a very humiliating assignment. Promotion or no promotion, he will never take such an assignment again. Never!

He walks to the living room with his bags and looks for the magistrate. She is not in the kitchen. Maybe she is in her bedroom. Why should he bother even to say goodbye to her? Why doesn't he just take his bags and leave? After all, he owes her nothing.

Then he hears her voice coming from the dining room: 'Mmmmh! This is good.'

He walks to the dining room and to his utter amazement there she is, sitting at the table and munching away on the food he has cooked.

'You're a hell of a cook,' she says as she chews with an enthusiasm that he has not seen in her before.

He hesitates. He does not know how to respond to this belated compliment.

'Come, sit down,' says the magistrate. 'This is good, you know? Very few men can cook like this.'

'What the hell do you mean, man?' asks Don, without any anger because it has been dissipated by the compliment. 'The best chefs in the world are men.'

He is about to sit down but then he remembers that he is still angry with her.

'I refuse to be treated like dirt any more,' he says and walks to the door.

She is too occupied with the food to stand up and watch him leave. Instead she calls after him, 'What's this dish called?'

'*Umngqusho*,' says Don as he struggles to the door with his bags. 'Don't forget to feed some to your cat before you take the rest to your hoboes.'

He bangs the door after him, leaving her with his aromatic dish and her Vivaldi's *Four Seasons*. He locks the door and the security grille and then loads his bags into the boot and the backseat of his Saab. He opens the gate and drives away. He will never see the bitch again. Not if he can help it. He is going back to his beloved Tumi. For sure, she will be very happy he gave up this silly assignment. Maybe he should phone her. No, he will surprise her. She hates surprises but this one is so special that she will just be grateful to receive it. And oh, will she be so grateful! But what if she is not there when he arrives? Perhaps at a photo shoot or fashion show or business meeting? It doesn't really matter. She'll definitely be grateful when she returns late and finds her bed warm. And she will demonstrate her gratitude the best way she knows how. He does not even want to imagine what she will do to him. Or how he will pump all his anger and frustration and longing into her body until she explodes.

He is waiting for the traffic lights to change at Jim Fouché Road when his cellphone rings. It is Tumi.

'Guess what, lover boy?' she says.

There is a lot of noise in the background. The traffic light turns green—he joins Beyers Naudé Drive and tears away towards North Riding.

'Guess what yourself?' says Don. 'I'm on my way home.'

'Oh no! I'm at the airport.'

'A photo shoot at the airport?'

'No, silly! I'm on my way to London.'

She is at the check-in counter at O. R. Tambo Airport and the clerk is processing her ticket as she speaks. Something urgent came up. He is crestfallen. He is not getting it tonight.

'An emergency?' he asks.

'No, no! Nothing bad. Great news, in fact. Marabella Glamour is signing up two of my models. I've got to close the deal.'

He knows about these deals that take Tumi away, sometimes for days on end. She is known as a fighter in her industry. She fights for black models who are being sidelined for editorials and runways. When she goes to London or Paris or New York to sign an exclusive contract for her models with one of the big fashion or cosmetic houses she does not come home immediately, even after the deal has been clinched, signed and sealed. She takes advantage of being in that city to host cocktail parties at her hotel to introduce her models to casting directors. Who knows when she'll come back from London? The thought depresses Don. He can only hope that on this trip she is not accompanied by some models she hopes to display at the parties. That would mean a prolonged stay of up to a fortnight. And what with all the shopping that she loves to do on these trips . . .

'I left that damn assignment, Tumi,' he says, quite pitifully.

'You did what?'

He is not sure whether she is asking because she didn't quite hear what he said or she was just expressing her surprise.

'She's full of shit, Tumi, that damn magistrate. I can't stand it any more.'

'Listen, baby, we'll talk about it when I get back. I'll only be away for a week. Ten days tops. Gotta go now.'

'The cat!' he screams frantically. 'What have you done with Snowy?'

'That's all you're ever concerned about. I left your stupid cat with the old lady at Number 37, Don. You know how she likes it. I promised her that you are likely to let her have it for keeps. Now I must go. Love you, baby.'

And she hangs up.

What would be the point of going to Three Oaks if neither Tumi nor Snowy is there? Of course, Snowy is at Three Oaks, but he cannot wake up the old lady at Number 37 to get his cat back. And he needs to talk to someone. He needs to be in the company of sanity. At the gate of Three Oaks he turns back and returns to Beyers

Naudé Drive. Then he branches off to join the N1 South. He takes the Maraisburg off-ramp, drives past the former coloured suburb of Bosmont and speeds through New Canada and Noordgesig to Orlando West.

There is a party at Wezile's Restaurant. Bongo Maffin's 'Bongolution' is blaring and men and women are dancing. There are some white girls too, most probably American tourists, since they are much more adventurous than white South Africans who are still dead scared of Soweto. Don enters and his eyes search for his friends. They've got to be somewhere here. He remembers that the dance floor is the wrong place to look for them. Well, Fontyo does dance, especially when he is soused, but Bova is a consummate bloviator who will never be caught kicking his legs and shaking his bum on anyone's dance floor. The drunker he gets the more argumentative he becomes, polemicizing about the great betrayal of the comrades who fought for the liberation of this country by opportunists and capitalists and sundry scoundrels who never in their lives touched an AK-47 or a grenade with their soft clean hands.

And indeed Don finds his friends in a room reserved for the folks who would rather debate the state of the world economy than dance to *kwaito* music, or any other music for that matter. Even here there are two white guys; probably they came with the white girls who are busy 'shaking what your mama gave you'—as the dancers keep hollering. The men sitting on sofas round a coffee table laden with beer and brandy are listening to Bova attentively as

he narrates some of his adventures in the wars of freedom. Fontyo, on the other hand, is paying more attention
to the skinny girl he is fondling. She, like both Bova and
Fontyo, has a *phuza* face—which is what a face that has
been ravaged by alcohol is called.

The guys are happy to see Don and the drinks begin
to flow. He feels much better with himself. You cannot
but feel better when you are in Soweto. It is a place of nostalgia, and nostalgia does have a healing effect. Nostalgia
is analgesic—it numbs you into a world where things
were better, even though no one realized it at the time.

Soon the beer takes effect and Don is as loud as his
comrades. When the white tourists hear that he is a
mantshingilane, as his friends keep on calling him, and
when the meaning of the word is translated for them by
Fontyo's girlfriend, they are amazed how articulate South
African security guards can be, and how well dressed.
They themselves are in jeans and T-shirts whereas the
security guard is in a lemon Versace suit. Of course, it is
unlikely that they would identify it as a Versace suit without reading the label. Only the Sowetan lovers of *jewish*
(to the older generation) and *threads* (to the younger)
would know at once just by looking at the suit.

A beautiful young woman is tired of listening to politics. She invites Don to the next room for a dance. He
obliges and dances for a while but soon gives up. He is
either too drunk or is just not in the mood. The girl is disappointed; something could have developed here. Don

has similar thoughts. Tumi is flying up the African continent and she would never know if he took the young woman to Three Oaks for a quick one and then dispatched her back to Soweto. But he is not in the mood for that kind of adventure. Not tonight.

So he bids his friends goodbye and drives back to North Riding. In his state of inebriation he is not supposed to be on the road, but he will risk it. After all, the lazy traffic cops aren't working at this time. And if they are, he can always bribe them with a few banknotes, as a lot of people do.

He drives very slowly and erratically until he arrives at Three Oaks. The security guard opens the gate for him and he drives into the complex and parks at his regular spot next to Tumi's. At first he wonders why Tumi's Jaguar is not there but then he remembers that Tumi is on her way to London and her car must be at the long-term parking lot at the airport. If Tumi is floating in the clouds there is no need to go into the house. His legs will not carry him there anyway. His joints have turned into jelly and his head is buzzing with strange sounds. He does not get out of the car. His last thought before he falls asleep on the steering wheel is of the stone-cold white bitch he left at Weltevreden Park. The hell with her. He never wants to see her ever again.

Kristin Uys never wants to see the impudent black bastard ever again either. She pours herself a drink in an elegant wine glass and takes one swift sip after another.

And then she pours more wine into the glass, again and again.

She feels liberated. It is as if her body had been imprisoned for a long time, like a bat trapped in a bottle. Her body needs to breathe out. Even blow out. She is going to reconquer her space. She is going to flap her wings and fly out of the bottle to a faraway place, somewhere in the middle of Sandton private clubland. Not one of your cheap skanky clubs but a very classy one. No one will know who she is as she sneaks in, wearing a red wig, high heels and a long black coat. She will find an empty seat. There'll be men drinking expensive-looking drinks and smoking cigars. They'll give her a nod and continue with their conversation as they drool over a stripper who is pole-dancing. She will take in everything as long-legged women in dark-toned underwear strut their stuff, serving drinks. A man will try to chat her up but she will ignore him. He will depart with a sour-grapes smirk. He will then go to put some banknotes in the G-string of a lap dancing stripper, making sure that Kristin sees what she has missed.

She will get sloshed sipping from her elegant glass of wine but will still be able to study the stripper's moves closely. A voluptuous stripper with an ample bosom will dance on the stage, discarding her garments one by one, while fondling her own boobs. But soon the stripper will morph into her. Into Kristin Uys. A distraught Kristin Uys in her pink and black bedroom. Dressed in the regular clothes she was wearing when she stuffed herself full of samp and beans after the bodyguard upped and left. Kristin Uys with a trusty bottle of wine, a second one, and an elegant long-stemmed wine glass.

She looks at herself in the mirror on the wall. She undresses very slowly and deliberately. She stands naked and examines her body, paying particular attention to her tiny breasts. The cat comes meowing and she caresses it. Soon she transforms herself into a 'whore'. She is in a skimpy black dress, fishnet stockings and stilettos. She wears an oversized stuffed bra, and makes herself up quite garishly, exactly like the prostitutes we once saw at the trial of the Visagie Brothers.

She stands in the middle of the room like a glorious dominatrix, her cat curled next to her feet. She caresses her bosom but her fingers sink in the soft padding of the bra. She struts around wielding her whip. The cat escapes to her bed. It knows what will follow. It has seen this routine many times before. Every time she is stressed.

She claps her hands three times in a regular rhythm, and The Clapper switches on the CD player, the strobe and other flashing disco lights. The music is the kind that used to be popular at techno raves. She begins to dance, wielding her whip. She is now very happy as she dances up a storm, occasionally drinking directly from the bottle of wine instead of using her elegant wine glass. After a while her dance loses the elation and becomes pathetic. The more she drinks the more pathetic her dance becomes.

The music is so loud and she is so engrossed in her dance that she does not hear the gate opening outside and

Don's Saab driving in and parking next to her Fiat Uno in front of the garage. He was woken by the cold in the middle of the night and decided to swallow his pride and return to the magistrate's house. After all, his promotion depended on it and Tumi was not there and he was feeling very bad and useless and a failure who couldn't even handle an assignment that was only made unpleasant by a difficult woman when he has handled tougher situations in his life. All this rationalizing saw him drive down Beyers Naudé back to Weltevreden Park in the wee hours of the morning. He thought he would just sneak into the house and sleep, and the magistrate would be surprised to see him in the morning. He is glad that he did not return the keys when he left last night and she did not remind him about them either.

He is greeted by loud techno rave music as he enters, carrying his bags. He stands there for a while, wondering what it is all about. He leaves the bags on the living room floor and walks to the door of the magistrate's bedroom. He stands there and listens for a while. He knocks at the door but there is no response.

Kristin Uys continues her pathetic dance. She does not hear the knock since at this point nothing else in the world exists. Don enters quietly and stands near the door. He is astounded to see the magistrate in her whore get-up dancing like a stripper. With her voluptuous boobs she is a parody of the Blonde Bombshell of the *Scope* magazines of old. She is oblivious of him. He looks on for a while, dumbfounded, now and then having to duck her flying whip. To avoid the whip he is forced to move against the wall, further away from the door. He wants to escape but now the dance is very close to the door. She is gyrating and moaning as if she is in sexual ecstasy. When she moves towards the centre of the room, Don sees it as his chance to make for the door. But she can now sense that there is someone else in the room. She stops dancing, and claps her hands four times. The Clapper switches off the CD player and the disco lights. At the same time the 'house lights' rise. The room is a flood of brightness and she stands there with her defences down. She breaks down and cries. He holds her in his arms.

She is messing up her make-up, smudging it with tears. They sit on the bed while she continues to sob quietly. She looks so vulnerable, and something stirs in him. He holds her tightly and she submits. They remain like that for a long time.

But as soon as she regains her composure she pushes him away from her and from her bed. She is now livid.

'You had no business entering my room without permission,' she cries. 'You had no business spying on me. You had no business seeing this.'

Without a word Don Mateza walks out of the bedroom.

13

SHOOTOUT

Don Mateza is in the kitchen frying eggs. Kristin Uys enters, all dressed up for work. The moment she sees Don she turns away and tries to sneak out shamefacedly. Don leaves the pan on the stove and goes after her. They face each other, although in fact she does not look him in the eye. Things are awkward between them.

'Come on,' says Don, 'we can't avoid each other for ever.'

She turns and walks out of the house. He just stands there in exasperation. Smoke comes out of the kitchen—the eggs are burning. He runs back to save them. But it is too late. After removing the pan from the stove, he returns to confront Kristin but she has left the house. She is already in her Fiat Uno and is waiting for the gate as it slowly opens. He gets into his Saab ready to follow her.

She hollers at him, 'What's the fuck with you, man?'

'Whoa! That's wonderful! I didn't know you knew that kind of language.'

'You shouldn't have come back. I hate you! I hate you!'

She speeds away. He follows closely at first but slows down later. He maintains a discreet distance as they cruise on J. G. Strijdom Road and then up the steep hill at Golf Club Terrace. Before she rolls down the hill, an old grey Mercedes Benz tipper truck and trailer speeds past Don's car and forces itself between the Saab and the Fiat Uno. It has no number plates. Don can no longer see the magistrate's car but his instincts tell him that something is not right because the face of the truck driver is hidden in a woollen balaclava. In this hot weather no one covers his face in that kind of headgear just for the heck of it.

He steps on the accelerator hoping to overtake the truck but stops trying when he realizes that he can't see if there is oncoming traffic or not. Just before the Ontdekkers Road traffic lights, the truck swings towards the Fiat Uno, pushing the small car off the road and squashing it against the railings. The magistrate is trapped in the smashed car. The man in the balaclava fires some shots at her car from the cab window. Don jumps out of his car and returns the fire as the truck speeds away into Ontdekkers.

He rushes to the aid of the trapped magistrate and tries to open the door. It is stuck. He phones 10111, but even as he is dialling tow trucks swoop like vultures from all directions. How on earth they knew of this accident remains a mystery to Don. But each one wants to tow the car away, without even finding out if anyone is injured or even dead. All they are interested in is towing the car to wherever the owner wants it towed for a hefty fee.

'You've got to get her out of there before you can even think of towing the car away,' says Don. 'And then wait for the police.'

It doesn't take them much time to prise the door open. The magistrate is quite shaken but fortunately she doesn't have any visible injuries.

A few moments later Netcare 911 paramedics arrive on the scene and insist on taking her to the hospital. Even in this state she is still stubborn, although it has dawned on her that she is no longer dealing with what she thought were petty thugs but dangerous criminals who are prepared to murder her to make a point.

She is shivering and Don puts his jacket over her shoulders and holds her in his arms. She clings to him. Her body is so warm, so soft and supple it makes his mind roam to forbidden places. He feels guilty that he should have such ungodly thoughts about a woman who was almost murdered. But she looks so vulnerable right now, and therefore so in need of love and protection that it gives him a shameful hard-on. If only the moment could be frozen for a while longer—not in ice though, for that would make her revert to being the ice queen she usually is, but in some warm and snug freezing substance that is yet to be invented.

The police arrive on the scene to spoil the moment. She is suddenly self-conscious and pulls away from his embrace. They are two young white guys and she doesn't want them to get the wrong idea about her. But they are more concerned about the accident and take statements from both of them. They cannot buy it when Don insists that it was an attempted murder, until he mentions that there was a shootout. They ask him to go to the Honeydew police station immediately, and call a detective who will attend to him there.

Don contracts one of the tow trucks, the burly guy who prised the door open, to take the Fiat Uno to a panel beater he knows in Strijdom Park—the panel-beating capital of South Africa. He is not sure if the car is a total write-off or if something of it can be salvaged.

He manages to persuade the magistrate to go with the paramedics to Flora Clinic, just to make sure that everything is fine with her, that she has no internal injuries that may give her problems later.

'Call me when they're done with you and I'll come pick you up,' he assures her.

As he drives to the Honeydew police station he decides that he will reveal everything to the police, including the past harassment, such as the telephone calls that the magistrate has been receiving. If she won't let the police handle the Visagies, he will drag them into taking action against the brothers, whether she likes it or not. This has gone beyond a joke now, beyond a few telephone pranks. She could have been killed. If she wants to continue playing her childish game of standing up to what she considers cheap bullies, he will not be part of that. The bullies have now become killers. Or, at least, prospective killers. They won't give up. They are going to try again.

A uniformed policeman ushers him into an office where a detective is waiting for him. He is playing patience and seems annoyed that his card game is being interrupted just when he was winning against himself. The uniformed policeman also takes a seat and jots down some notes as Don speaks.

The policemen don't seem to take the harassment of the magistrate too seriously. If the magistrate is being threatened by criminals why haven't they received such a report from the magistrate's office? Why would a magistrate, a senior official of the court, want to keep such a thing to herself? As for the so-called attempted murder, did Don see the truck driver's face?

'No,' says Don. 'He was wearing a balaclava.'

'Then how do you know it's the Visagie boy?' asks the detective.

'Who else?'

'Maybe it was just an accident. A hit and run.'

'And the shootout? An accident too?'

'*Ja*. You got a point there.'

'Get that Shortie Visagie and squeeze his balls until he talks.'

'We no longer work that way,' says the detective in a cynical voice. 'Not in the new South Africa. We respect people's human rights. We must find the grey Mercedes

Benz tipper truck with a trailer. That will solve all our problems.'

However he will not assign anyone to the case until he has spoken to the magistrate. She is the one who must lay a charge. When told that she may be reluctant to do so, the detective says that without her they cannot proceed with the case. Don cannot be the complainant in a case that only involves him peripherally as a bodyguard.

As he drives to Flora Clinic he wonders if Kristin Uys will finally lay a charge. He has his doubts. She is such a stubborn bitch, although perhaps the experience this morning will bring her to her senses.

She is not at Flora. She took a metered taxi back home as soon as the doctor had finished examining her and assured her that, apart from a few bruises, she was fine. He is really mad at her and phones her house. She is not there. What if something happened to her and he was not there to protect her? Not only would he never forgive himself for letting her out of his sight soon after some maniac attempted to kill her, but his company would see him as a failure and he would surely not get the promotion. Without the promotion he will never gain Tumi's respect.

He calls her cellphone. She is at a car-rental company in Randburg and seems to be going on with her life as if nothing has happened. This infuriates Don.

'What the heck are you doing there?' he shouts.

'I am renting a car. I must have a car.'

'But you promised to wait for me at Flora Clinic. You were not supposed to leave Flora Clinic without me, damn it!'

'Don't yell at me, damn it!' she says and switches her cellphone off.

He dials her again. He wants to ask her the address of the car-rental company so that he can go there immediately to protect her, willy-nilly. But her phone is on voicemail. The bitch! She is going to be the death of him.

He decides to confront Shortie Visagie personally at his home. He may be fortunate enough to find the tipper truck there. He phones the secretary at VIP Protection Services for the address, since they have it in the file on the magistrate's case. Then he drives straight to the Visagie home in Strubensvallei.

He stops in the street near an open gate, gets out of the car and walks into the yard. Shortie, in greasy overalls, is under a car that has been lifted up with a hydraulic jack. His back is supported by a skateboard.

'Hey, Shortie Visagie,' calls Don.

'Who are you?' asks Shortie.

He slides out from under the car.

'What did you do with the truck, Shortie?'

'How the shit do you know it was me in that damn truck?'

Don chuckles at the *dof*-ness of the question.

'Because you just told me.'

'I don't know what you are talking about,' says Shortie, trying to display an innocent mien. But he is not a good actor. And he is jittery.

'You'll tell that to the judge. The cops are going to catch up with you, Shortie. We know all about you. We know Stevo has been using you to create shit for the magistrate, and if you don't stop you'll have me to deal with.'

Shortie tries to look menacing but it doesn't suit him. Instead he looks ridiculous.

'You think you can scare me, china? We are the Visagies—we are not afraid of nothing.'

Ma Visagie appears round the corner, bringing her son a steaming mug of coffee. She stops in her tracks when she sees this strange man confronting her boy. Neither man sees her as they glare at each other aggressively.

'You are going to join your brother in jail, Shortie,' says Don. 'He's not coming out any time soon. Instead you're going to join him there, and you'll stay there for a long time. Attempted murder is not a small matter, Shortie. And we are getting more evidence of your other criminal activities. And of your brother's too.'

Shortie's bravado has disappeared. He is scared now and cannot hide it. Ma Visagie disappears round the corner.

'You'll regret you ever tried to kill the magistrate. I am going to squeeze your balls until you tell me where you have hidden that tipper truck.'

At this he walks threateningly towards Shortie and Shortie reverses towards the house until he finds himself against the wall.

Shortie leaps at him. Don is taken by surprise and before he can duck Shortie punches him in the stomach. Don falls down. We see that Shortie can be very dangerous when he is cornered. He is about to kick Don in the face with his huge boots, but Don rolls on the ground, grabs Shortie's leg and throws him down. Don is quick on his feet and kicks Shortie in the stomach. Shortie screams, 'Eina! Ma! Ma!' Don is about to kick him again when Ma Visagie appears armed with a shotgun.

'Out of my yard or I'll blow your brains out!' she yells.

Don jumps back, away from Shortie, who is writhing on the ground. He has an amused expression on his face as the woman points the gun at him.

'Hey, you can't do that, Ma Visagie,' he says, as he raises his hands in surrender.

'Try me. Just try me,' says Ma Visagie.

Don thinks this whole scenario is funny. He just stands there and laughs. His hands are still up though. Ma Visagie blasts the ground in front of his feet. His amused expression turns into a horrified one—he realizes that Ma Visagie means business. He jumps on the spot as two or three bullets raise dust in front of him, and then he runs like a scared rabbit to his car, while Shortie—who is now standing up and enjoying the whole show—and Ma Visagie laugh their lungs out.

Ma Visagie shouts after him, 'My boy will be out of prison soon and you're all going to *kak*!'

It was not very smart of him to invade the Visagies, he admonishes himself as he drives away. Instead he should have tackled the problem from the magistrate's side, persuaded her to lay a charge. He can't get anywhere without her cooperation. Then he suddenly remembers Aunt Magda. He just might discover the Visagies' weak spot from her. One never knows unless one tries.

He still has her cellphone number so he calls her.

She is not at the Visagies' house in Strubensvallei but at an Irish pub in the Florida suburb of Roodepoort where she has been holding a meeting with some of the members of the Society of Widows. She does not seem to remember who Don is, but the mention of publicity for her society is good enough for her to promise she will wait for him at the pub, even though her meeting is over and the other members of the society are leaving.

Don knows that Irish pub. He has been there before with Tumi after she met with a visiting casting agent at a nearby hotel. It is only fifteen minutes away, so he goes straight there.

Aunt Magda is sitting alone at the bar nursing a glass of wine. As soon as she sees Don she gives him a broad toothless grin.

'Now I remember you,' she says. 'You're the open-coupe newspaperman who's going to get his friends to put me on TV.'

'*Ja*, but first I've got something serious to discuss with you.'

'What can be more serious than getting me on TV?'

'Were you at the Visagie house this morning? You live there, don't you?'

She begins to sniffle pitifully. She no longer lives there, she says. Ma Visagie kicked her out. After all she has done for that family with her mass action. Ma Visagie was jealous because the women of the Society of Widows, which she founded with her sweat and blood, believe in her and not in Ma Visagie. It is the very society that put pressure on the magistrate to release Shortie Visagie through its mass action. The very society that will continue to put pressure on the magistrate until Stevo Visagie is also free. And now when Ma Visagie sees that they are on the verge of success she kicks her out of her house without Stevo's knowledge. Stevo would never have allowed that. Stevo is a good boy, unlike Shortie who did not even raise a finger to stop Ma Visagie from kicking her out. Shortie is a traitor. The magistrate released the wrong brother. Shortie is the one who should have stayed in jail instead of Stevo. It is clear to her now that Shortie also wanted her out of the Visagie home. And she doesn't even have money to go back to Cape Town. She is grateful to one of the sisters of the society who has given her temporary accommodation. She may have to return to Cape Town before Stevo is free, thanks to the ingratitude of Ma Visagie and Shortie. Sniffle. Sniffle.

Don buys her more wine. The barmaid gives him a coquettish smile and wants to know what he will drink. He will have a beer just for appearances. He is uncomfortable about drinking during the week, especially so early in the day. He is one of those types who are not casual drinkers. When he drinks he drinks to get drunk, and only on weekends when he is in the familiar surroundings of Soweto.

'Do you know the grey Mercedes Benz tipper truck that Shortie drives?' he asks.

'What's Stevo's truck got to do with it?' she asks, suddenly becoming alert.

'I just want to know where I can find it. There's money in it for you.'

'What do you want with Stevo's truck?'

'I want to rent it,' he says.

She looks at him suspiciously.

'How do you know about the truck? No one ever uses it. Where did you see it? What is this all about?'

But before he can respond she asks to be excused while she goes to 'powder her nose', as she puts it. The barmaid thinks it is her chance to get close and personal with him. She leans close to his face, her cleavage hovering over his beer.

'So, where is your *modlara* girlfriend now that you go out with a toothless *magogo* like that?' she asks with an impish smile.

'Who says I'm going out with her? We are talking business here.'

'I know . . . I know . . . you want to hire her son's truck. I was just joking, man.'

'You have no business listening to other people's conversations.'

'I am a barman. That's what we do.'

Well, if she is a barman at all she is a very beautiful one, without a single trace of 'man' in her. And she is forward too. Now Don remembers her from the last time he visited the bar with Tumi. She is the girl who said to Tumi, 'Girlfriend, you must take me to the places you go to so that I can also find a beautiful man like that.' Tumi answered curtly, 'You don't *find* a guy like this—you create him for yourself.' Though she was annoyed at being addressed as 'girlfriend' by a mere barmaid, who was also ogling her man, she was obviously flattered that the barmaid recognized her fine taste in men. He always looks so good and well groomed and handsome. That is why Tumi likes to show him off at her functions and parties. He is her arm-candy.

'And I am free after ten if you have the time,' the barmaid adds.

Aunt Magda returns to save him from this maneater. Any other day he would not want to be saved, especially with Tumi away in London. But today his mind is full of more important things than wanton pleasures.

'I don't see any powder on your nose,' he says. OK, it is a lame joke and Aunt Magda doesn't get it. But she seems to be mad about something.

'You lied to me,' she says. 'You went to Strubensvallei to attack Shortie.'

It turns out instead of powdering her nose, she phoned the Visagies, trying to ingratiate herself back into their fold, and told them about this guy who was making enquiries about Stevo's truck. Although Ma Visagie refused to speak to her, Shortie told her about the confrontation.

'Do you know what your Shortie did with that truck?' Don asks her. 'He nearly killed the magistrate. That truck is an attempted-murder weapon.'

'*Ag tog*, the magistrate who sent his brother to jail? Not Shortie. He may be a *dofkop* but he is no killer. I'm sure it was an accident.'

'An accident? He fired shots at her car,' says Don. 'Listen. Those people don't care about you. They kicked you out of their house.'

'Stevo cares. Stevo always cares,' she says with emphasis, as if she is not only trying to convince Don but herself as well. 'I'm not going to sell Stevo out. I'm not *impimpi-ya-mabhulu*.'

Don cannot help laughing. She is getting her isiXhosa vocabulary from one of the freedom songs that used to be sung during apartheid, and the words mean 'a police informer' or 'spy of the Boers'.

'Listen, I'll pay for any information that you give me. I'll pay you well too. Your friends have left you high and dry. I'll look after you.'

He gives her a fifty rand note. At first she is reluctant to take it but greed or hunger gets the better of her.

'Now, I want you to tell me where I can find that truck.'

'It's always parked outside the yard in Strubensvallei.'

'It was not there. Do you think they hid it in the backyard?'

'It can't be in the backyard. The gate to the backyard is too small and there's no way you can park a truck there. It's just a swimming pool and stuff there. Did you look at the Visagie scrapyard at Strijdom Park?'

'That's where it must be. Don't tell anyone you spoke to me about this.'

'I'm not a fool, mister. I love life too much to do that. It's you I'm worried about. Sooner or later when you don't need me no more you gonna rat on me.'

'I give you my word. I am going to call you again. We need to talk some more.'

He is pleased with himself as he drives back to Weltevreden Park.

A red Volkswagen Golf is parked where the Fiat Uno used to be. It is the magistrate's rental car.

As soon as he enters, Kristin Uys—who is sitting in front of the television with a glass of wine—says, 'What took you so long? I was worried sick.'

'About me or about you?' asks Don.

'You are supposed to be my bodyguard.'

'Listen, Ms Uys, I want you to go to the Honeydew police station right away and make a statement about all the threats and harassment you have been receiving.'

'You cannot give me orders,' she says.

'Don't you see this has become very dangerous now? You nearly died this morning. These guys mean business. They won't stop until you are dead. We know who did this, but the police won't even investigate unless you yourself lay a charge.'

'OK, OK, I'll do it.'

'I am taking you to the police station now.'

'Oh no, you're not taking me there. I am the magistrate. I'll call the detective to my office tomorrow and make a statement.'

14

THE CURSE OF THE ZARA MAN

Tumi is unpacking very expensive designer dresses, pants, tops, shoes and underwear from a number of leather suitcases. After admiring each item, and holding it against her body to estimate how it fits, she arranges them neatly in the closet and in the drawers of her dresser. The closet is overflowing already and she has to press some dresses and coats together in order to create more space. She needs a bigger house just for the clothes, she thinks, or at least a bigger bedroom with a walk-in closet. If things continue to go the way they did in London she will be able afford a mansion in Sandton soon. However, she is not in any hurry to move out of this love nest that has given her and Don such memorable moments.

She is exhausted after the long trip, but as soon as she hears the door open she brightens up. She knows it is Don because she called him when she was at the airport and he said he would come immediately as his charge is at work.

'Tumza!' calls Don from the living room.

'I'm here, baby,' she responds.

He dashes in and sweeps her into his arms. They kiss passionately for a long time.

'I really missed you, Don,' she says breathlessly, and then breaks away excitedly.

'Guess what I brought you,' she says.

She rummages through one of the suitcases and brings out an orange jersey.

'A jersey?'

'It's a Zara Man, baby. You can't get it in South Africa. You're going to look like a real Black Diamond in that.'

Black Diamond. He hasn't heard those two words for days. Maybe weeks. It is strange how they make him feel very uncomfortable now. As if Tumi has uttered curse words. He does not understand why he should feel this way because he does want to be a Black Diamond one day. He badly wants to live up to her expectations. He knows very well that he represents Tumi's long-term aspirations and he doesn't want to let her down. So, it is quite silly to get the heebie-jeebies at the mere mention of such beautiful words.

He takes the Zara Man, feigning enthusiasm, and holds it close to his chest. It is a beautiful jersey. You can see it is great quality just by looking at it. But orange is not his colour. He will get used to it though. After all, he got used to lemon and violet and pink Versace suits when all his life he wore dark-coloured clothes—black, navy blue and brown. The lightest colour he ever wore was grey. He was not a suit-man either. But Tumi changed all that. She said she didn't want him to look as if he was going to a funeral every day. Bright clothes make for a bright disposition, she said. And a bright disposition makes for a bright future. And now he loves his Versace suits—they are part of his image. Eager gazes from the ladies made him realize that indeed Tumi was on to something with those pastel-coloured suits.

Tumi knows best.

'Wear it, baby,' she says.

But before he can put it on the doorbell rings. He rushes to open the door. It is the old lady from Number 37 and she has brought the cat.

'I saw Tumi arrive and then you and I thought you'd want your cat back,' she says. 'Snowy is such a dear. Tumi tells me you're looking for a home for her. I just want you to know that I'm ready and willing.'

'Not yet, ma'am. Tumi didn't quite get it right.'

She is disappointed. She says if ever he changes his mind he should remember that Snowy already knows her and is quite comfortable at her home. He promises to remember that and thanks her profusely for looking after the cat.

When he returns to the bedroom he is cuddling the cat. He has missed it while he has been away. There is a cat at the magistrate's house but, let's face it, it is not Snowy. It has got used to him now and likes playing with him but it is also given to wild habits. It often disappears through the cat flap and spends the whole day chasing birds outside. One night it dragged a live rodent into the house and played with it in a most sadistic manner, tearing at it with its claws and teeth, bit by bit, until it died. And the magistrate enjoyed the whole spectacle and stopped Don from intervening. Snowy is much too civilized for that kind of behaviour.

'You made me into a liar to the old lady,' says Tumi.

'We didn't agree on anything like that, Tumi,' says Don. 'You made that decision without me.'

'I want to see you in the Zara Man, baby,' she says, regaining her earlier zest.

Don puts the cat down. But it struggles against being placed on the floor. It is as if it suspects that this guy will desert it again.

He wears the Zara Man and it looks good on him. He was hoping it would be too big or too small, but it is the right size. Tumi never gets it wrong when it comes to the size of his clothes or his shoes. She stands there, arms akimbo, admiring her man.

'Just the right colour for you,' she says with a broad smile. 'You look good in it, my beautiful Black Diamond.'

But the cat spoils her joy. It leaps at Don and claws its way up his left arm, ripping the Zara Man in the process. Tumi shrieks in horror.

'This is the last straw, Don,' she screeches. 'The cat must go. Now!'

'Surely it was an accident, Tumi.'

'This is a Zara Man, Don. A Zara Man! The cat must go.'

'If my cat goes, I go too, Tumi,' he says sulkily.

Of course, it is an idle threat. Where would he go? He would not be so stupid as to leave a beautiful woman like Tumi for a cat.

'You go too then. You go with your damn cat.'

He takes Snowy to Number 37. The old lady thanks her lucky stars, thinking that Tumi was right after all— they are looking for a good home for the cat. She is disappointed when he disabuses her of that notion but agrees to look after Snowy for a little while longer.

He does not go back to the apartment to say goodbye to Tumi but gets into his car and leaves. It's too early to fetch the magistrate from the Roodepoort magistrate's court, so he's got to kill time somewhere. He had budgeted a few hours for cuddling the cat and making love to Tumi but now the Zara Man has spoilt everything. That silly Zara Man was nothing but a curse!

He is very close to the Honeydew police station so he might as well go find out what is happening with the magistrate's case since she finally did call the police to her office and made a statement. She warned them very strongly though, that she did not want any publicity about this as it would make the thugs think that their threats were having the desired effect on her.

The detective handling the case is out but a uniformed officer tells Don that they did bring Shortie Visagie in for questioning.

Shortie was quite adamant during the interrogation that he had nothing to do with harassing the magistrate or attempting to kill her. He was busy at the scrapyard at the time and his labourers could vouch for that. The police pressed as hard as they could but he was just as stubborn. He stood his ground even when they threatened him with violence or with locking him up until he confessed.

'I told you I don't know nothing,' he said. 'You can keep me here for the whole night I'll still know nothing. For the whole year, I'll still know bugger all.'

They glared at him angrily. He glared back unflinchingly. The stand-off continued for some time, until the police gave up and let him go. It is not the end of the matter though. They promised him that they would be watching him.

'What about the truck?' asks Don. 'That should be the evidence you need.'

'We searched the scrapyard in Strijdom Park,' says the officer. 'There was no truck. We even took the liberty of searching neighbouring panel-beating places. There is not even any record that the Visagie brothers or their mother have a truck registered in their name.'

As he drives to the Roodepoort magistrate's court he tries to figure out how he will get the necessary evidence to nail the Visagie Brothers so that Stevo stays in jail for a longer period and Shortie is charged with a new crime. Aunt Magda is his only hope.

Although it's only a few minutes past three o'clock, the magistrate is standing outside on the steps anxiously waiting for Don.

'What happened to you?' she asks. 'I should have been home a long time ago.'

'You have my number. You should have called me if you knew you were going to finish work early.'

'You are supposed to be my bodyguard. You're supposed to be here.'

'And it's a damn good thing you think so,' he says. 'I'm glad you're now aware that you're in a dangerous situation and you need me. The old Kristin Uys would just have driven home without bothering to wait for me.'

'It's only temporary. Just until they catch the criminals.'

She walks haughtily to her Volkswagen Golf.

Don follows her closely. He has learnt his lesson. He will not allow any vehicle to cut in and insert itself between them. He would have been more comfortable if they both rode in the same car. But Kristin Uys is still Kristin Uys, even with the minor softening up that has obviously been brought about by her frightening experience.

Don plays with the cat in the living room while the magistrate hibernates in her room. He has changed into shorts and a T-shirt and is dangling some newfangled toy mouse in front of the cat. It jumps up excitedly and wrestles with the toy. Don finds this hilarious and laughs.

He talks to the cat in a loving and caring tone, as if he is talking to a baby.

'I knew this was just the toy for you,' he says.

The magistrate opens her door and comes into the living room, curious to see who Don is talking to. She stands there for a while, amazed at the way in which Don is getting along with her cat.

'I knew you'd like it,' says Don. 'I knew it . . . I knew, kitty . . . I knew it.'

The magistrate watches for some time and her face melts. It breaks into a smile. A guarded smile, yes, but a smile all the same. When Don rolls on the floor with the cat all over him he sees the magistrate and pulls himself together. He is embarrassed that he has been caught at this silly game with a cat.

'You're a black man,' says the magistrate. 'You're not supposed to love cats.'

He jumps to his feet and faces her.

'You're a white woman. You're not supposed to smile at a black man.'

The smile dies on her lips.

'It's a joke,' says Don.

'I know it's a joke,' she says. 'I'm not stupid.'

Don gives her a huge boyish grin.

'You should smile more often,' he says. 'You are beautiful when you smile.'

Her face softens once more.

'Only when I smile?'

'You're beautiful, full stop. But anger hides your beauty.'

They face each other awkwardly. Then she turns her back on him and walks to her ultimate refuge, the bottle of wine.

'You have a way with cats,' she says as she pours herself a glass of wine. 'I've never been able to make it behave in such a carefree manner since I found it as a stray.'

Don notices that she is pouring a second glass. She is actually pouring wine into two long-stemmed glasses and she has never done that before. She gives one to Don. Quite shyly. He likes his chilled but he is grateful for small mercies. At least now she is being sociable.

'It's because you're not carefree yourself,' says Don. 'The cat takes your mood. You gotta let your hair down sometimes. And I'm not just talking about the privacy of your bedroom with loud music playing.'

The reminder of her private dance embarrasses her. Perhaps this was not the right time to bring up the subject. It may spoil the new spirit of peace and friendship and brotherhood/sisterhood to all humanity that was evidently brewing in their midst. But what the heck—he has been dying to know exactly what gives with her sexy night dance and there is no better time than now to find out.

'You have the temerity,' she yells, but then controls herself and continues softly, 'You had no business to spy on me like that. You were supposed to have left . . . for good.'

'A good thing that I came back too . . . considering the Visagies are now trying to kill you.'

'You were not supposed to see that,' she says sadly.

She gets up to go but he stops her by standing in front of her.

'We've got to talk about it some time, Kristin,' he says. He is surprised at the tenderness in his voice. Once more there is an awkward silence between them as they face each other. He notices that she is trembling a bit. He does not know why. She notices his breathing has acquired a faster rhythm. She does not know why. The cat is impatient for the game that was interrupted by the magistrate to resume. It does not know why Don suddenly takes refuge in squatting next to it and stroking its fur. Nevertheless it doesn't complain but purrs with satisfaction.

'I've one of my own,' he says.

'What?' asks the magistrate.

'A cat. But my girlfriend wants to kill it.'

'She hates cats?'

'Like the plague. Right now it is a refugee at a neighbour's house.'

'You can bring it here, you know,' she says, with a strange combination of hesitancy and earnestness. 'As long as you live here, your cat is welcome as well.'

Once more he shoots her that boyish grin. She smiles back. Self-consciously. Then she runs back to her bedroom and locks herself in there for the rest of the day. She thinks she has made a fool of herself. He, on the other hand, is happy that her resentment of him seems to be breaking down.

He is tempted to phone Tumi but decides against it. Maybe she's still mad about the Zara Man. And for sure he's still mad about her implied ultimatum—either the cat goes or you both go. Rather, he will go and fetch his cat from Number 37.

But at that moment both the Zara Man and Don are the least of Tumi's concerns. She knows that Don will come back after his brief rebellion, simply because he loves her and she loves him. Their relationship is rock solid and the tiff will add even more vigour to their lovemaking. What is paramount at this time is the praise she is getting from her two friends, Maki and Nomsa, for her refined taste in haute couture.

There is a lot of giggling and teasing when the women get together, but Tumi observes that Maki is a bit reserved today. It is as if something is worrying her. She first noticed this when they were gossiping about Don, after Nomsa wanted to find out how he was doing at work and if Tumi thought he would get the promotion. Then Nomsa said, jokingly, 'Even if he doesn't get the promotion he still has a great ass.' Tumi rejoined, 'He's endowed with more than just the ass.' Both Tumi and Nomsa laughed naughtily. But Maki just stared at them as if she was fed up with the petty banter. Ordinarily she would have been part of it, with even more explicit descriptions of the male anatomy. That's when Tumi realized that something was eating Maki. Why, she wasn't even having any of the wine and cheese that Tumi has served. She just nibbled a little on the Gouda and that was it.

Tumi brings out the new shoes for their admiration.

'I tell you, girlfriend, you're going to kill them with that shoe,' Nomsa says. 'What do you think, Maki?'

'They're nice,' says Maki coldly.

Tumi is beginning to get it now. Maybe Maki is jealous. That must be the reason. She must be jealous of her and to some extent of Nomsa, because both women are more successful than she is, are more established in their careers and make good money, while she is struggling serving articles with a firm of lawyers, and they drive better cars than her tiny BMW 3-series. But they have never given her any reason to be jealous. They have always shown her genuine respect because soon she will be practising as an attorney and they are going to be her clients. Even now, she is the one who scrutinizes their documents, including contracts, and gives them legal advice on complicated corporate-law issues.

Tumi feels the need to defend her shoes. They can't just be *nice*.

'This is a Givenchy, Maki. Straight from the Shoe Box in London,' she says, emphasizing every syllable.

Maki doesn't respond, while Nomsa drools over Tumi's jewellery.

'And what about the Mikimoto pearls, girlfriend? You look like a million dollars in them.'

'Like the million dollars Tumi promised we would earn in no time if we joined the television licence bid?' asks Maki, with a sneer in her voice.

Oh, so that's what this is all about!

'Are you blaming me for the failure of the bid, Maki?'

Yes, she is. Tumi dragged them into a futile venture where they wasted their precious time.

'But that's how business is done, Maki,' explains Tumi. 'You win some, you lose some. You guys told me that at the report-back meeting Kenny Meno said there will be other bids. You don't give up just because you lose one bid.'

But Maki's issue is not whether they won or lost the bid. She says she was seething inside when, at the report-back meeting that Tumi did not attend because she was in London, Kenny Meno revealed for the first time that he and his executive committee knew even as they went to defend the bid before the Independent Broadcasting Authority that they were not going to get it. Kenny Meno was not even ashamed to tell the meeting that the deputy president of the republic called him to let him know that this time the bid would be won by the trade-union empowerment group, and that the Meno ex-prisoners empowerment group would get their opportunity next time. If these people had this sort of information then why did they proceed with the bid? She feels that she was being used to window-dress a system that is inherently undemocratic. There was all this pretence that all bids were equal, and that the bidders would all be given the opportunity to defend their bids before an independent committee, yet all this was nothing but managed democracy because the political leaders—no less a figure than the deputy president of the country—had already decided which bid was going to win. And the bid that won was nothing but some form of reward for cronies. Hence the need to assure other cronies that they should not think they have been forgotten because their chance will come next time, there is another trough in which the chosen can bury their snouts.

Both Nomsa and Tumi are taken aback by Maki's rant.

'Although I also learnt after defending the bid before the committee that Kenny Meno knew that we were not going to get it, that didn't bother me because that's how business is done, Maki,' Tumi explains once more, trying very hard not to lose her patience with her. 'I would not have walked out of that bid. People like Kenny Meno are good to have on our side. They have the deputy president's ear and even the president's. They will involve us in another bid. Soon they'll be inviting bids for the third cellphone provider, and guess who will win that bid.'

'Leave me out of that one,' says Maki.

Tumi never realized that Maki was such a stupid ass. Instead of being grateful that through her tireless networking Tumi had brought them into contact with influential business leaders like Kenny Meno, and therefore to billionaires like Molotov Mbungane, she is complaining about being used.

Nomsa supports Tumi. After all she is a beneficiary of a contract for the construction of low-income housing that must have been decided in a similar manner—only in her case it was not political patronage but her white business partner was savvy enough to pay discreet kickbacks to individual ruling-party cadres who had been deployed to the tender board.

'Do you think a fledgling construction company like mine that had never built a single house in its short life— I had never even seen a house being built, let alone built one—would have won the tender if we had not worked through the insiders in the ruling party or if we had not paid a percentage into someone's Swiss bank account?'

'If that's how the game is played, count me out. It goes against everything I stand for. Fair play and justice. That's why I went to study law.'

At this she takes her handbag and leaves.

'She'll never be a millionaire, that one,' says Nomsa and laughs.

But for Tumi it is not a laughing matter. She really does value Maki's friendship.

Maki meets Don at the door as she walks out. She returns his greeting in an icy tone and he stands there looking at her, wondering what went wrong in the house. He enters and Tumi is very happy to see him. He is carrying Snowy in a cat carrier bag.

'You're not bringing it back here, are you?' asks Tumi.

'I'm taking Snowy with me,' says Don as he bends to give Tumi a quick peck. But she grabs his neck, pulls him back to herself and kisses him passionately. Don is happy that perhaps she has now forgotten about the Zara Man. Unless of course she is just showing off to her friend, not wanting her to know that they are in the middle of a lover's spat. He responds to the kiss just as passionately.

Nomsa ogles him as he walks to the bedroom where he says he is going to get some of his clothes.

'Hey, bitch, he's out of bounds,' says Tumi.

And they both laugh.

'At last he found a home for that damn cat.'

'Yeah! I can't imagine sharing a man with a cat,' says Nomsa.

Once more they fall over each other laughing. But a tinge of sadness lingers in Tumi. She will miss Maki. And what about Don? He is in the bedroom packing more of his clothes. When will this assignment end? She misses him. She hopes he will be smart enough to leave his cat at the magistrate's when the time comes for him to come back home. Otherwise there will be no peace.

In Weltevreden Park, Kristin Uys is cooking at the stove. Her cat is curled up in the corner. She has not cooked for ages, not since Don Mateza invaded her space. But today she just felt the urge to cook. And to cook a lot of food too, so she can take some to her homeless people. They must have missed her cooking and are sure to be wondering what happened to her since she just stopped going to the park without any warning.

She is not cooking anything elaborate—just chicken curry. She suddenly feels inadequate when she remembers the last cooked meal that she ate in this house. It was the samp and beans cooked with mutton by Don, the day that he left her with the potful that she had to deep-freeze. She forgot all about it in her anger at his unexpected return and at his witnessing her secret dance.

She takes the food out of the freezer and warms it in another pot. She is going to surprise him with his own cooking. For the first time since he invaded her space—and she will continue to see it as an invasion because she no longer has her privacy and cannot relieve the tensions of life with her secret dance as long as he is here—she will invite him to sit down at the table with her. They will break bread together in the form of chicken curry. She will serve him his samp and beans, which he never got to eat that night, and will pretend that she cooked it herself. She can't wait to see if he knows enough about his cooking to recognize it as his own dish.

Don enters with his snow-white Himalayan cat. The magistrate is struck by its beauty.

'It's a pedigreed cat!' she says.

'Of course it is pedigreed,' says Don.

'Are you trying to shame me or what?' she asks jokingly. 'Mine is a stray mongrel.'

'Only dogs are mongrels, not cats. Yours is beautiful too, in its own way.'

'Don't patronize my cat,' she says. 'Any animal that's a result of interbreeding is a mongrel. My cat is proud of its mongrelity.'

'Mongrelity?'

They both laugh at this accidental invention.

He crawls on his knees to introduce his cat to the magistrate's.

'Snowy, meet . . . I never got to know your cat's name.'

'I never got around to giving it a name,' says the magistrate.

'Snowy,' says Don ceremoniously, 'meet Mr No-Name. Or is it Ms No-Name?'

'I have no idea,' she says.

'It has no name and you don't know what sex it is?'

'Well, I never checked. How do you know?'

'The same way you know with people,' says Don.

They both laugh. Don lifts the tail of the magistrate's cat and inspects it.

'It's a girl,' he says. 'I hope it's spayed.'

'Yours is a boy, is it?' she asks.

'It's a girl too. A spayed girl. They will make a great lesbian couple.'

Once again they laugh.

There is a lot of laughter today.

15

SMART OKES USE PSYCHOLOGY

Diepkloof Prison. Shortie Visagie is waiting anxiously for his brother. He knows he has heard already of his brave act and he can't wait to bathe in his praise. Stevo is rather stingy with praise, especially when it comes to his brother, but this time he will have no choice but to admire Shortie's resourcefulness. At last he will win Stevo's respect, even though his mother thinks it was a dumb thing that he did, trying to kill the magistrate. Stevo knows what is at stake here and will be highly appreciative of Shortie's final attempt at a solution. Much more effective than just boiling a cat.

When Stevo is led into the visiting area, Shortie observes that he is no longer in handcuffs and leg irons as before. He is walking side by side with the warder and they are chatting like old friends. Even though the warder is a darkie. Stevo's orange jumpsuit prison uniform is well pressed and he looks fresh and clean-shaven. Prison must be doing strange things to him because Stevo never used to be fresh as long as Shortie has known him, which is Shortie's whole life. He was always in greasy jeans, just like Shortie. It was never the tradition of the Visagies to be fresh and clean-shaven. And to smell of Old Spice cologne. The Visagies are men's men with prickly stubbles and manly scents emanating directly from their rich sweat glands.

'Hey, this place agrees with you, Stevo. You look so beautiful I could have mistaken you for a girl,' says Shortie.

A woman visiting a convict boyfriend overhears this comment and remarks to another woman sitting next to her that it is an insensitive joke to make to a man who is in prison where some men do actually become girls.

'And you don't have your bracelets,' adds Shortie. 'They must be treating you nice here, my china.'

'It's no thanks to you, Shortie. It's no thanks to you at all, my china,' says Stevo glaring at him. 'I have to pay for these comforts with hard cash, which has not been coming from you lately. Do you know they will take my microwave away if I don't pop out some money? And my TV? And all you and Ma ever do is complain that business is slow and there's no money coming in. The only thing you and Ma know how to do is to kick a poor *bushie* woman out of the house.'

Shortie did expect Stevo to bring up Aunt Magda at some stage, seeing he has always been her favourite and all. But he did not expect her to top the agenda. After all, what he did for his brother surpasses Aunt Magda's woes by far.

In any event discussing Aunt Magda is a futile exercise. Ma Visagie lays down the law and the law is that Aunt Magda is a nuisance who tried to control everyone's life with her cockamamie Society of Widows. Ma Visagie wouldn't have minded if she kept her busybody self to her area of expertise, namely mass action. But when she tried to run the Visagie home, giving orders on how Stevo's food that is sent to the prison whenever anyone visits him should be cooked, as if she knew more about Stevo than Stevo's mother, that was the last straw for Ma Visagie. There can only be one alpha female in the Visagie household and that is Ma Visagie herself. Not some coloured woman from Cape Town. Not even Stevo can be an alpha anything, though he fancies himself as some sort of boss.

'You and Ma spend years without coming to see me,' moans Stevo.

'You've not been here for years, Stevo,' Shortie says.

'And do you know who comes to see me? Aunt Magda. Do you know who gives me money to pay for my TV and microwave? Aunt Magda. Do you know who brings me Old Spice so I can smell good? Aunt Magda. Do you know who will be with me at my side when I become a big-time syndicate boss . . . who will be my henchman . . . my sidekick, like they say in the movies? Aunt Magda.'

'What about me and Ma? We are family, Stevo. You can't leave us out of it all. Me, I've even done more than Aunt Magda ever did. I almost killed the bitch for you.

And you say fuck all about it. No thank you, no nothing. All you want is to talk about Aunt Magda this and Aunt Magda that. What about me, Stevo? What about what I've done for you?'

Stevo smiles slyly at his brother and says, *'Jy's 'n skelm,* my china. I didn't know you had it in you.'

Ja, at last the man is coming to his senses! Shortie is pleased with himself for being called a crook by his brother and his face is beaming for all the world to see. Praise doesn't come easily from Stevo, especially towards members of his family.

'You didn't think I could do it, hey, Stevo?' says Shortie. 'You always thought I was a coward.'

He realizes too late that he is too loud and his excitement has invited the attention of the other prisoners and their visitors, and even of the solitary warder who is pacing the floor pretending not to be interested in the various conversations that are taking place, so he places both hands on his mouth.

'I didn't think you could be so stupid, Shortie,' says Stevo.

'I just got excited, Stevo. Sorry.'

Shortie hopes he is misreading the contempt in Stevo's smile.

'I'm not talking about that, you *dofkop.* I am talking about killing the bitch. That's the dumbest thing you've ever done in your life.'

Shortie thinks that perhaps he did not hear his brother well. He came here for accolades, not for this.

'It's a good thing she didn't die—we'd all be in shit now,' adds Stevo.

'What has become of you, Stevo? What has jail done to you? You've become too soft, Stevo. It's not like you to talk like this.'

Maybe it's not the jail at all. Maybe Stevo is just becoming himself—his irrational and jealous self. Maybe he is jealous because Shortie has done something great, something he himself has never achieved—running a magistrate off the road and almost killing her. Stevo has always been jealous of him. It's like the thing with Elsa which Shortie can't forget even though it happened many years ago when they were primary-school boys. Stevo fancied Elsa but was afraid to approach her because Elsa was the most popular girl in the whole of Roodepoort. So he asked his little brother, who was even then much bigger than the older brother, to write her a letter on his behalf expressing his feelings. Shortie was best suited for this task because he was the more literate of the brothers and his handwriting had big loops and curves that Stevo reckoned would be very attractive to girls. When he didn't need Shortie's help and wanted to piss him off he called it girly handwriting.

After Shortie wrote the letter, Stevo forced him to deliver it to Elsa, even though he knew that Shortie was dead scared of girls. He would rather have died but Stevo had such a stranglehold on him that he had no choice but to obey. He just dropped it in her hands during recess and ran for dear life. Elsa read the letter and then ran after the scared boy to give him the reply, which was, of course, yes, she would be honoured to be Stevo's girlfriend.

But their thing didn't last. Elsa wanted to follow Stevo everywhere he went, which was rather annoying to him. And she had this irritating habit of asking him if he missed her even when she had only gone to the bathroom for two minutes. He blamed Shortie for the whole irksome mess. If Shortie had not written the ill-fated letter, he would not be in this predicament.

'Writing that letter was the dumbest thing you've ever done in your life,' he said.

That was the irrational Stevo. Blame your mess on someone else, especially if he is your little brother who hero-worshipped you to the extent that he would follow you down a precipice.

After Stevo had wriggled his way out of the relationship with Elsa, she began to follow Shortie, if only to make Stevo jealous. Shortie was just happy that a popular girl like Elsa was interested in him for whatever reason, and he in turn followed Elsa like a puppy. He didn't mind her annoying habits, and indeed, whenever she asked if he missed her he answered quite positively that whenever she was out of sight he found life quite unbearable. He in turn asked her the same question, which in the long run she found irritating.

Elsa was his first girlfriend ever and he spoke about her all the time to the annoyance of Stevo.

'Falling for that girl is the dumbest thing you've ever done in your life,' said Stevo.

That was when Shortie knew that his big brother was jealous of him.

Like now.

'*Jy's 'n plank*, Shortie,' says Stevo.

Being called a *plank*, which means that he is an idiot, finally makes him lose his patience with his ungrateful brother.

'You're just jealous, Stevo, that's all. You're just jealous because you've never ever tried to kill a magistrate in your life,' he says.

'I've never tried to kill nobody because I'm not *'n brood*,' says Stevo. 'If I wanted to kill her I would not have bungled it like you did. She would be dead by now. But we are the Visagies, man. We don't kill nobody.'

Another insult! Being called *bread*. It means that he is an imbecile, although no one has ever explained why bread should be associated with that state of mind.

Shortie complains that he did not come here to be called names and he would rather go back to his scrapyard if Stevo continues to be rude and ungrateful. But Stevo tells him to calm down and listen why it was a lousy idea to attempt to kill the magistrate. The police will find the truck and will trace it back to the Visagies. Shortie tells him that he was smart enough to take care of that.

The police will never find the truck because Fingers Matatu is hiding it in Soweto. He also reminds his brother that he removed the number plates before committing the act, and in any event the truck is not registered in anyone's name since it had been scrapped many years ago and he never got to register it after rebuilding it.

'So, you see, *my broer*, we are safe,' he says, with the knowing wink of someone who has covered all the bases.

But still this does not satisfy Stevo. He must find another reason to be mad at him. He says that now he will lose his truck. He will never be able to hire it out again because the police will be looking high and low for it. He won't be able to sell it even after he has bribed traffic officials for new registration documents. The police will be relentless. They stop at nothing to hunt down cop killers. What more will they do for magistrate killers?

'We'll just strip it for parts,' says Shortie.

'Since when do you have an answer for everything, my china?'

'I always have an answer, Stevo, 'cause I'm smart. You just don't see it 'cause it's me who's smart this time and not you.'

'There's nothing smart about spoiling my plan for the bitch. I tell you, my china, you don't punish nobody by killing them. We don't kill, we Visagies. We are smart *okes*. We use psychology. You know what that is, Shortie?'

It seems that jail has taught Stevo some big words. Big English words, *nogal*, instead of the good old homely

Afrikaans. Maybe Stevo has been reading books in jail. That can be the only reason. Maybe that's why he's all so messed up and angry and clean-looking—it's the books.

'No, I don't know no psychology, Stevo,' says Shortie resignedly.

'It's when you mess somebody's brains up . . . mess them up to nobody's business.'

'But that's exactly what I was trying to do with the truck, Stevo. I wanted to crack her head and mess her brains out all over the street. She was never gonna bother us again.'

'Oh, our Shortie!' says Stevo in exasperation. 'He can be so *dof*.'

He makes his brother promise that he will not attempt anything silly again. Instead he must kill the cat, as per his instructions, and cook it in the magistrate's kitchen. Just as he did with the rotten tripe. That's what psychology means. The cat will be a masterpiece. It will break her down and it will make her run mad.

'She will shit her pants out of her wits before she knows it,' says Stevo.

'There are two cats now, Stevo,' says Shortie.

'How do you know there are two cats?'

'I watch that house like you said I should. I saw the bodyguard play with two cats on the front lawn.'

'Kill them both,' says Stevo firmly.

'Two cats? I can't kill two cats, Stevo,' says Shortie, almost pleading.

'You are a Visagie, my china,' says Stevo, almost cajoling. 'Remember what Ma always says—we Visagies are not afraid of nothing. A Visagie can kill two cats. A Visagie can kill a hundred cats.'

'I don't mind killing her any time, Stevo, especially as she pissed me off sending you to jail and all. But a cat is another story. I can't kill a little pussy cat. I don't think it's gonna work no ways, Stevo.'

It's going to work all right, Stevo insists. Even though the magistrate has changed the locks Shortie can get Fingers Matatu from Soweto to pick them. Fingers Matatu can pick any lock, even though he has now grown so old and arthritic.

'And don't steal nothing, my china,' says Stevo. 'Just cook the cats and leave.'

'Jeez, Stevo,' protests Shortie. 'I'm not a thief.'

'I was just saying, Shortie—in case you get tempted. I don't want it to look like robbery. We are decent folks, my china, we don't steal nothing. Plus, it's going to spook her like hell when everything in the house is intact but there are two fat cats simmering on the stove.'

He breaks out laughing. Obviously he is enjoying the scenario he has created in his imagination. Shortie just stares stupidly. He doesn't see anything funny.

He is still sitting there staring into empty space when a warder comes and yells, 'Time up!' and leads Stevo away. Still laughing.

In the magistrate's kitchen something is simmering in the pot. Take it easy, it's not the two fat cats. Don and Kristin are enjoying themselves at the stove. Don is cooking a chicken *breyani*. He is very sentimental about this dish because, apart from the traditional Xhosa *umngqusho*, this used to be his mother's favourite. She learnt it from an Indian colleague from Lenasia. She would cook it for Sunday dinner, and Don remembers how he hoped to feast on it for the whole week after school. But alas, within a day the leftovers would fill the four-roomed house with the stench of decay. Very few people had fridges in Soweto those days and his mother was not one of them, even though she was a staff nurse at Baragwanath Hospital. In any event, even in a fridge *breyani* spoils too quickly and too easily.

Don is truly a chef manqué and Kristin hopes to learn a few tricks from him. She has a notebook and writes down every detail as he chops the onion and fries it until it is brown and then adds grated ginger root, tumeric, curry powder, cayenne pepper, *breyani* masala that he bought ready mixed, bay leaves, cinnamon sticks, chopped tomatoes, nutmeg and crushed garlic. Then he adds pieces of deboned chicken. After a while he adds basmati rice and some water.

What frustrates her is that he does not measure any of the ingredients.

'How am I going to know how much to use when I cook this for myself?' she asks.

'We never use measurements when we cook,' he says with pride. 'Just use your hand and your head to estimate the right amount.'

While the pot simmers slowly she offers him some wine. When they began there was some awkwardness between them but the dollops of wine have released them from the bondage of shyness. By the time he adds potatoes and pre-cooked brown lentils, which is after almost an hour, they are like two kids playing house.

She insists on displaying her culinary skills too by contributing her favourite dish *bobotie*. She uses some of the ingredients that Don bought for his *breyani*, particularly the turmeric, crushed garlic, bay leaves and curry powder. But she needs other items that are not in the house. She says she will go to Palm Court, which is less than five minutes down the street, to buy dried apricots, Granny Smith apples, minced lamb, sultanas and almonds.

'You can't go alone,' says Don. 'It's not safe.'

'Hey, I'm not a child,' she says.

'I'll go with you,' he insists.

'OK, you go,' she says. 'I'll look after things here.'

He chuckles to himself. He can see through her—she does not want the neighbourhood to see her traipsing down the street in a state of inebriation with a black man. She writes out a list for him. In no time he is back with a plastic bag of the ingredients, including eggs which she forgot to write but are essential for the dish. He knows a thing or two about cooking *bobotie*, although he pretends he has barely heard of the dish—it is important to him that she must believe he has learnt something from her as well. It is a sensitive situation and he must nurse it.

They lay the table with the best silver and china in the house—the same that is normally used by her homeless people. She takes the *bobotie* from the oven and brings it steaming to the table, which is already laden with the *breyani* and a simple lettuce-and-tomato salad.

'Smells good,' he says as he cuts the *bobotie* into slices.

'It's a traditional Afrikaner dish,' she says.

'Cape Malay,' says Don, and immediately wishes he could take back the comment—he forgot that he was pretending not to know anything about the dish.

'Afrikaner, Cape Malay, same dishes mostly. Cross-pollination,' she says, without noticing what he regards as a faux pas. 'Normally we eat it with yellow rice. But what the heck, we might as well eat it with your *breyani* and have an overdose of meat once and for all.'

They eat with relish, while guzzling more wine. This time it is not her cheap room-temperature wine but a chilled Boschendal Chardonnay that he bought specially for this dinner.

'I didn't know you cooked,' he says.

'I used to love it . . . when there was someone to enjoy my cooking,' she says with wistfulness in her voice. 'But I can learn a thing or two from you. There's something sexy about a man who knows his way round the pots.'

Don cannot hide his surprise at this. She is embarrassed. She wishes she hadn't said that. It came out the wrong way. She hopes Don won't misinterpret it.

'Did I say something wrong?'

'No, no, no. You said something nice. It's a wonderful sentiment. My girlfriend doesn't see things that way though. She thinks my interest in cooking disgraces all African men. Just like my love for my cat.'

It is Friday and the magistrate is not going to work tomorrow. Don suggests that they go to a nightclub in Melville. They are already tipsy enough to be reckless and without any reticence at all she jumps at the idea.

'I'll change quickly,' she says.

'I'll wait in the Saab,' he says.

'Saab?'

He forgot that she leads an unbranded life and would possibly not know what a Saab is.

'My car,' he says.

'Oh, why didn't you just say so? Fancy names mean a lot to you people.'

'You people?'

'Come on! You know I don't mean it that way.'

Don takes her to a cigar club, a place that he has only visited as a bodyguard to some businessman. Today, courtesy of his VIP Protection Services expense account, he will be one of the patrons. He can be lavish because his company will charge the whole expense to the Department of Justice—it is part of protecting the magistrate from the criminals who are threatening her.

Cigar clubs are not Tumi's scene; otherwise he would have been a patron here years ago since once in a while, when she wants to unwind, they do pub-crawl and even go to some of the nightclubs in Rosebank and jazz clubs in Sandton. Don has observed that cigar clubs are discreet places and Kristin will not feel out of place here. But also there is no chance of Tumi walking in on them.

Kristin is, however, ill at ease as they sit at the bar. Most of the patrons here are the pretentious nouveau riche of the new South Africa—mostly black, but with a few white hangers-on. She looks beautiful with her blonde tresses hanging to her shoulders instead of her usual old-fashioned bun, and he is not ashamed to be seen with her. Her dress is formal and conservative though—more like something a woman executive would wear to a business meeting.

'I never come to places like this,' she says.

'There's always the first time,' says Don.

She becomes more relaxed after two fast whiskies, one after the other. He is amazed at how she can hold her liquor, especially after all the wine during dinner. He is determined to ply her with more drink while he takes it easy.

'First time? I used to be a socialite, you know? They didn't have multiracial clubs like this then but I used to be at all the good society parties.'

'Then what happened?'

She shakes her head sadly; she does not want to talk about it. He is a bit disappointed. He was hoping that at last she was beginning to open up. After an awkward silence accompanied by a few gulps of whisky, Don says, 'It was him, wasn't it? The man who used to like your *bobotie?* It was him who did this to you?'

She giggles nervously.

His cellphone plays Dave Brubeck. He switches it off quickly as soon as he sees Tumi's name on the screen. He does not want to speak with her, not when he is at a cigar club with another woman.

Shortie watches Don drive out with the magistrate. He has been biding his time, waiting in the street in a service van, hoping that the magistrate and her bodyguard would leave the house. But they never did. They seemed to spend all their lives indoors. He wondered what the hell they were doing there all this time. He has established a routine. He watches the house for a few hours on the off-chance that she and the bodyguard will leave. And then he drives home. He returns the next day in a different car and parks outside a neighbouring wall and watches the magistrate's house. After two hours or so he goes back home.

He should be doing his mischief during the day when the magistrate is at work, as he did with the rotten tripe. The bodyguard often goes with her to Roodepoort and comes back only later. Some days he stays away from the house and only returns with the magistrate after work. That would have been the opportunity to get the cats. But he came with Fingers Matatu once, and he tried the new locks but failed to pick them. He needed more time to figure them out, he said.

Daytime is not safe. Not only will passers-by see him while he tries to entice the cats, but one never knows when the bodyguard will return.

Shortie's plan is a simple one. Kidnap the cats and take them home with him. That will drive the magistrate and her precious bodyguard crazy. That's what Stevo called psychology. Then on a later date, when Fingers Matatu has consulted his comrades on how to pick the newfangled locks that were invented long after he had retired from his cat-burglar business, he will come back and cook the cats. After putting them to sleep, of course. Stevo will never know that he sedated them before cooking them. He needs to find out about chloroform or something like that.

It will be double psychology when the magistrate and her bodyguard find the cats cooking after they have been missing for days.

He climbs the wall into the yard and walks boldly to the door. He is carrying a small black bag. He goes straight to the cat flap, opens it and makes cat sounds.

'Miaow! Miaow! Kitty! Kitty! Miaow!'

He takes out some catnip from the bag and places it near the cat flap while continuing with the cat sounds. Soon the magistrate's cat waggles its way out of the cat flap. Snowy is much too smart to be attracted by aromatic smells and silly sounds pretending to be a cat. But the no-name cat has always been adventurous and is an outdoorsy type that always jumps out of the cat flap at the slightest provocation, leaving Snowy slumbering in the kitchen near the stove.

Shortie tries to catch the cat but it snarls and charges at him. He retreats and takes out a butcher knife from the bag. He wants to take it alive but if it is full of fight he might have to kill it. He charges towards the cat but it runs in circles on the lawn. Then it stops and looks at him as if sizing him up. He stares at it too. He is considering his next move. He leaps at the cat with his butcher knife at the ready but the cat fights back. He screams as it claws him, his knife dropping to the ground.

'Voetsak! Voetsak!' he screams.

That's dog-language for 'scram!' and cats don't understand it. So, the magistrate's cat pays no heed to his command.

He manages to escape with a few scratches and stands at a distance. He inspects his bleeding arm and is mad at himself for allowing this to happen to him. The cat is arching its back, gearing for a fight. Shortie and the cat contemplate each other. He is struck by a great idea. He looks for his bag and finds it near the door. He came prepared, so he gets some dry cat food from it, and entices the cat with it. The cat is suspicious at first but when he throws it one bit, and another one, it eats it without hesitation and loves the taste. He gives it more of the food and it surrenders. He has his knife ready to stab it. But he cannot bring himself to kill it. He cannot bring himself to capture it and put it in the bag either. Instead he pets it and it purrs with satisfaction.

He takes it in his arms, opens the flap door and puts it back inside.

As he drives back to Strubensvallei he decides—to hell with Stevo. He is not going to kill anyone's cat. From now on, if Stevo wants to do his psychology he'd better do it himself. He is done with harassing the magistrate, once and for all.

At her suggestion Kristin and Don have transferred to a nightclub in Rosebank. She wants to experience the nightlife of Johannesburg that she only reads about in the papers or hears about in court when she is presiding over a case that involves some skulduggery that took place at an entertainment venue. He made a point of not choosing one of the classier nightclubs where someone who knows

Tumi would be bound to spot him. Or where some mysterious tabloid press gossip columnist is likely to hang out—one who might have seen him often in the company of the model-agency boss and would be sure to expose the fact that he has been seen at some nightspot with a blonde. Gossip columnists have eyes everywhere and every rag has one who tries to out-scoop others with some juicy piece of scandal. They don't give a damn if they destroy lives in the process. This, however, is not one of your seedy places. It's just not upmarket enough to be frequented by the A-listers, as the press calls them, who are worthy of being gossiped about.

A jazz quartet is playing and couples are dancing. Don and Kristin take the floor in a slow dance. She is comfortably resting in his arms without any hang-up at all. By now they are both quite intoxicated, so their dance is only lumbering along.

He drags her back to the bar. She is very carefree now. The barman serves them two shots of tequila, salt and slices of lemon after Don suggests they try something different from the whisky they have been drinking all along. He teaches her how to drink tequila. She copies him as he licks the skin between the thumb and the forefinger, sprinkles a pinch of salt on the area, licks the salt, gulps the tequila and squeezes lemon juice into his mouth. She squirts the lemon all over her face.

'Ag, *man!*' she says. 'Why should these Mexicans make it so complicated?'

She giggles as he cleans her chin with a paper towel. He's thinking, *I should be doing it with my tongue.*

'It's simple really,' says Don. 'Just remember the three steps—lick it, slam it, suck it!'

'What?' exclaims Kristin.

They both laugh when they realize that the three steps really sound like something much naughtier.

It is the small hours of the morning when they drive home. And a good thing too, because the car is moving at twenty kilometres an hour on the winding streets and would surely have attracted the attention of the traffic cops had this been happening earlier in the evening or later in the morning. Imagine the magistrate of Roodepoort appearing at the Randburg magistrate's court as a witness in a drunken driving case and the revelation as the evidence is led that she herself was sloshed to pieces.

She is undoubtedly more drunk than he is. He was smart enough to nurse his drinks while she guzzled hers, one after another. Don thought it was a sign that she was getting more comfortable with him. It also indicated that she was beginning to trust him and felt safe in his company. And he had thought she had issues with trust. Maybe this is the time to bring up her past, at this unguarded moment, when she is still so carefree, before sobriety brings back her magisterial self-consciousness.

'The man who loved your *bobotie*,' begins Don.

Without even waiting for him to complete the sentence she says, '*Ja!* He was a whoring bastard. I discovered too late that he was sleeping with prostitutes.'

'Don't take it out on the poor hookers,' says Don lightly.

'And guess what? He blamed me for it. It was all my fault. I was too reserved to engage in adventurous sex, he said. I kicked him out. Oh yes, I kicked the whoring bastard out, yes, siree.'

'And you lived a happily celibate life ever after.'

'You haven't heard me complain, have you?'

'Not at all. But I have seen you dress and dance like the whores you detest. The very whores you aim to punish with stiff sentences in your court.'

'Tell you what?'

'What?'

'Fuck you!'

Don enjoys this no end. He could kiss her. He would try if he were not driving. Perhaps she would react by slapping his face. Perhaps she would kiss him back. Perhaps this is not the time to entertain such thoughts.

'You are a magistrate, man,' he says. 'A lady, *nogal*. A respectable member of the NG Kerk. You're not supposed to use that kind of language.'

She laughs drunkenly and says, 'You've corrupted me, you bastard.' And promptly falls asleep on his shoulder. He nurses the car along Beyers Naudé Drive, staying in the extreme left lane so that fast cars may zoom past him without hindrance. He is not so drunk as not to be mindful of the consequences of an accident. Or of the chance that Tumi might just be driving by on her way from some late function. How would he account for this?

He should have called her before he left for their big *jol*. He should have invented some urgent meeting that he had to attend. It was a dumb thing not to call her.

They are already in the yard when she wakes up. Don parks next to her Volkswagen Golf and the drunken pair get out of the car and walk to the door. Before they open the security grille they notice the magistrate's cat is waiting outside. It got out of the cat flap as soon as Shortie pushed it in, hoping to get more of his goodies. But he had already jumped the garden wall to his vehicle.

'Hey, what's your cat doing outside?' asked Don.

'Your pedigree Himalayan cat kicked my mongrel cat out of the house.'

'You're hurting its feelings, Kristin,' says Don reaching for her cat and stroking its fur. 'Cats are people too—they have feelings.'

In the house Don shoots straight for the toilet. He sits on the seat and phones Tumi.

'What happened to you, Don?' she says frantically. 'I've been calling you all night. I've been worried sick about you.'

'I was in a meeting,' he says. 'I had to accompany the magistrate to an important convention of magistrates.'

'At this time? And you're drunk too. I can hear it in your voice.'

He is not a good liar. Tumi can sense that something is wrong. A woman always knows—especially if that woman is Tumi Molefhe.

'I'm going to kill you, Don Mateza. I'm going to kill you with my bare hands.'

Kristin Uys is knocking at the toilet door and asking why he is taking so long.

'What did you do with that Boschendal? Surely we didn't drink it all before we left,' she is yelling.

Don switches off the phone, just when Tumi is asking what the heck is happening. From now on it will have to stay off. He will answer to Tumi tomorrow. Or next time he sees her.

'Forget the Boschendal, Kristin,' calls Don as he zips up his pants and fastens his belt. 'We've drunk enough, don't you think?'

Kristin has found the bottle which was on the dining room table where they had left it. She grabs it and runs to her bedroom, with Don chasing her.

'Give it back, Kristin,' he says.

They horse around drunkenly in her bedroom. He discovers her skimpy 'whore' skirt and fishnet stockings on the floor and waves them around as he dances towards her. He is re-enacting the sexy dance he once caught her performing. But this is too much for Kristin. She almost becomes hysterical.

'Stop it! Stop it, you bastard!' she screams.

He holds her in his arms. Her body is shaking violently with sobs. He undresses her, taking off her blouse first. She is not wearing a bra because her tiny breasts don't need it. She instinctively hides them with her hands.

'Don't hide them,' says Don. 'They're beautiful.'

'Don't lie to me,' says Kristin. 'They're like a little girl's.'

'They're sexy. Who says men only go for big boobs?'

'He hated them.'

He tries to bring some levity into the moment by asking, 'The man who loved your *bobotie* hated your breasts?'

She pushes him away from her with both hands and sits on the bed.

'You think it's funny?' she asks.

'No, no, no! Of course not!'

She can see him now. Barend Uys. Standing in the middle of this very room. He has bought her a Valentine present. A padded bra. Now she will look like Dolly Parton, he says. He loves Dolly Parton and her tarty look. He wants his wife to dress like her. Tartish. Short sequined dress and an oversized bosom. Just for him. In the privacy of their home. In public she will continue to dress like all decent Afrikaner society ladies in sunny dresses and big fruity or flowery hats. But the padded bra is good for all occasions. It makes her look good, doesn't she think? It makes her look more desirable. She wears it, yes. She wears it to work. She is ill at ease in it. All the time. When she is defending clients as an attorney she is self-conscious about it. It is not her. It's just not her.

Barend. He wants her to dress like a whore for them to be intimate. He goes to sex shops and buys her whorish make-up and underwear because he says it turns him on. She wears it to please him. But she feels dirty and humiliated.

He gets carried away and instals strobes and other types of flashing disco lights in the bedroom and wants her to dance like a disco queen. At first. And then like a stripper. He teaches her the moves. He knows them because he has secretly visited strip joints. He buys a video on lap dancing. What next? Will he be forcing her to watch pornographic movies before they make love? He never does. He hates pornography. He just wants her to dance like a whore and then bend over in all sorts of obscene positions. She is his pornography. She is full of shame—she is a well-brought up Afrikaner *meisie* with Old Testament values. Leviticus values. She prays in church to be forgiven and regrets she is not a Catholic; otherwise she would be buying better forgiveness with her confession to the priest.

It becomes worse when he buys her a whip and wants her to use it on him. Still she goes along with it. Barend is her first love. Her only love. She must sacrifice for him even if it kills her inside. After all, it is in the privacy of their bedroom. No one will ever know about it. She whips him. Gently. But he wants to be whipped real hard until he bleeds. This becomes too much for her. She will not do it. She will just have to put a stop to everything.

He is disappointed and for a long time they don't speak. About it. About anything.

That's when he starts going for the real stuff out there in the high-class gentlemen's clubs of Sandton. To a professional dominatrix. And that's when he gets caught. Not in Sandton but in the dives of Hillbrow. For he had gravitated to Hillbrow. He had sunk that low.

For a long time she blames herself. She should have been more accommodating. He gave her the chance to be accommodating before he went to brothels. She should have been more flexible. Couples play sex games all the time, don't they? They play doctor-nurse and are not ashamed of it. You read about these things in women's magazines and you know that in the privacy of their bedrooms upright citizens spice up their sex life that way. She shouldn't have been so stiff, she tells herself. But that's just how she was brought up. She knows she shouldn't be blaming herself, but she still does.

After the divorce she is all alone. Empty and angry. One consolation is that the new South Africa arrives and she is appointed a magistrate. As part of redressing the white-male-dominated apartheid past, black men and women of all races and people of every sexual orientation are appointed to the judiciary and she is one of the beneficiaries. Yet she is still empty and angry. Until she takes to wearing the whore costume that Barend bought her. It is a way of punishing herself. Her body desperately needs the humiliation that comes with the costume.

Her body is shaking with sobs and sighs and sniffles. Don Mateza holds her tightly to him.

'When I saw you dance I didn't see any humiliation,' he says. 'I saw joy. It was glorious.'

She gives him a teary but knowing smile.

'Ah, I see,' he says. 'Instead of humiliation you found that you actually got some thrill from it.'

'It has become a habit,' she says, her voice full of shame, 'especially when the day has been stressful.'

Don kisses her all over, which at first she tries to resist.

'You won't need it any more,' he says. 'I promise, you won't need it any more.'

She responds to the kisses and submits completely. They kiss passionately. Then he peels the remaining garments off her body. She is sprawled on the bed helplessly. In the courtroom surrender is not an option, but here on this bed she wants to be taken. He kicks his shoes off and cannot rip his clothes fast enough from his body. He notices that she has closed her eyes tightly, as if she does not want to see what will be happening to her.

He dons his studded latex.

He spreads her golden tresses on the pillow and they frame her oval face like the rays of the sun. He is between her open thighs and they are hot like the fires of hell. He inserts himself in her. She is ready for him. She has been ready for a long time, although she did not know it. He slides in and out her trembling body and in no time muscles stiffen and angels sing hallelujah!

Or could it be demonic voices?

The next morning Kristin Uys is attacked by pangs of remorse when she wakes up, not only in the same bed as Don, but in his arms.

'What did we do?' she asks, pushing him away.

'Was it that forgettable?'

'You took advantage of me in my moment of weakness,' she says. 'We shouldn't have done this.'

But Don silences her with a long kiss. Once more she submits. Once more they make furious love.

Shortie has his share of remorse as well. He is at the kitchen table with Ma Visagie and a maid in pink and white overalls is serving them breakfast of bacon, eggs and toast. Although Ma Visagie doesn't care that much for breakfast, her son begged her to sit with him because they need to discuss Stevo's case.

'From now on I've stopped harassing that magistrate,' he says. 'I'm gonna be killing no cats, Ma.'

'Tell that to Stevo,' says Ma Visagie.

This does not feature as one of the most important things in her life. She thought it was a silly game anyway that the boys were playing with the magistrate, and if Shortie now wants to stop, it is his business.

'You tell him, Ma,' pleads Shortie. 'Please tell him. He always listens to you.'

'I'm not gonna tell him nothing. It's between you and Stevo.'

'It's wrong, Ma,' says Shortie emphatically, as if someone has argued that killing cats is the right thing to do. 'We are the Visagies. We don't go around killing nobody's cats. Not so, Ma?'

Ma Visagie does not answer. Her mind is occupied with more important things—how to make a livelihood without the resourcefulness of Stevo, especially now that the police are watching the family like hawks and they have to lie low with their pimping activities. Her silence worries Shortie. He really wants his mother's approval.

'Come on, Ma! We are the Visagies!'

'Of course we are the Visagies, boy,' says Ma Visagie impatiently. 'Who else can we be?'

'So you must tell Stevo.'

'You don't think he knows that?'

'It helps no one to kill cats,' says Shortie, as if to convince himself. 'We must leave everything in the hands of Krish Naidoo. He's a good lawyer. Stevo will surely be out of jail before Don Mateza . . .'

'Don who?'

'That bodyguard who came to threaten me here, Ma. Before he gets the evidence to keep Stevo in jail for ever. That's what he promised to do. Get more evidence to keep Stevo in jail. But Krish Naidoo is gonna get him out of jail before you know it. And when Stevo is out of jail he will deal with that magistrate himself. And with that bodyguard. You can make Stevo understand that, Ma, can't you?'

'Don't let Stevo force you to do things. Stand up to him. Use your head, boy.'

Doesn't Ma know that Stevo is a stubborn little bastard and that when he has made up his mind about something nothing can change it—except Ma's orders? If Shortie goes to Diepkloof Prison and announces that he is no longer part of psychology, Stevo will just find another way of persuading him. Stevo has a powerful mind which overwhelms Shortie altogether. Ma knows that very well. Stevo will only stop his psychology if Ma orders him to. Can't Ma understand that?

'OK, Ma,' says Shortie as a last resort. 'If you don't want to talk to Stevo then I won't tell you something big that's happening over there at Diepkloof Prison.'

'Are you trying to blackmail me, boy?'

'And it's big, Ma,' says Shortie, hoping that he now has his mother where he wants her. 'And it's about Stevo and someone else that you know very well and don't like very much.'

Ma Visagie stands up to leave. She has no time for this nonsense. Or so she pretends. She knows Shortie too well and will call his bluff. He will blurt it out sooner or later if she acts as if she has no interest in the so-called big thing that is happening with Stevo in jail.

And sure enough he blurts it out.

'He's gone all clean and perfumed,' he says.

This stops his mother in her tracks. From her experience of the world as a madam who has been in prison a few times and knows what the score is even in the men's section, this can mean only one thing.

'You don't have to lie about your brother, boy, just because he is forcing you to kill a cat. Stevo is a man. And he's tough. Nobody can do nothing like that to him in jail.'

''Strue's God, it's not a lie. And do you know where he gets all the money and the perfume and roast chicken? From Aunt Magda.'

That Magda is as beyond the pale as anyone can get.

'Where does she get the money to do all these things?'

Shortie does not know.

Ma Visagie is certain that Magda is trying to destroy her son to get even with her for kicking her out of her house. Why is she still here and not back in Cape Town anyway? She must go to that Diepkloof Prison and talk sense into Stevo. The sooner she gets her little boy out of that jail, and out of Magda's claws, the better. Why hasn't that stupid Indian lawyer reported back to the family, after she paid him such heavy fees? Could it be true that he has been bought by the magistrate?

She calls Krish Naidoo.

It is a radiant Kristin Uys who walks to the park at midday on Saturday. It is an exhausted but fulfilled Don Mateza who follows her carrying a box of cutlery and china wrapped in a tablecloth. She is holding a pot of *breyani* in both her hands. Under the lid slices of *bobotie* rest on the *breyani*. The food spent the night on the dining room table instead of the fridge and she fears it will soon spoil. She is taking it to her homeless people; her first visit since Don gatecrashed into her life.

Plastic bags litter the grass in the park and debris of various sorts is scattered all over the place. Municipal workers do clean every week but they can't keep up. The denizens of the park don't care for their surroundings and don't seem to know what rubbish bins were made for. Even as they populate broken swings and merry-go-rounds they discard plastic containers of milk or glue in front of them. This disturbs Don. Nothing gets to him as much as a disorderly environment. That's one thing he and Tumi have in common—they are both neatness freaks.

Tumi. She called this morning when he was still in bed with the magistrate. After another bout of hectic love-making. Tumi was already up and about in Sandton, even on a Saturday. She was having breakfast at a coffee shop with Nomsa at the time, after a meeting with a team of young South African fashion designers who are planning to showcase their creations at the Johannesburg Fashion Week to be held at the Sandton Convention Centre later in the year.

'You've not been returning my calls, Don. What's up?' she asked.

'Oh, Tumi, you know . . . eh, things have been hectic.'

Kristin opened her sleepy eyes. After figuring out what was happening she covered her head with the duvet, as if she wanted to hide herself from Tumi.

'I have got to see you today, Don. I have never heard of a job where one doesn't get a day off. I need to see you. That bloody Jim Baxter can post another guard there. I need to spend this weekend with you. Do you hear me?'

Tumi. As usual, she laid down the law.

'Things are hectic, Tumi,' repeated Don. 'You know, I've got to look after the magistrate.'

'Is there something wrong, Don? I can hear it in your voice when you lie to me.'

'Listen, Tumi,' he said really panicking now, 'we'll talk some other time, baby. I'm a bit tied up now.'

He cut her off.

As he follows Kristin, avoiding broken glass on the grass, he feels very bad about Tumi. He hates lying to her. But what can a man do?

The homeless greet the magistrate with much enthusiasm. They bombard her with questions: Where was she all this time? Did something terrible happen to her? Professor, the hobo who reads newspapers instead of just sleeping in them, claimed that he read in *Sowetan* that she was involved in a very suspicious car accident—is that true? She answers none of their questions. The cynic in Don thinks that they were more worried about their stomachs than about the magistrate's safety. However, he does not vocalize these thoughts.

Don is in denim jeans and *takkies*, and the hoboes think he must be the magistrate's gardener. He doesn't correct them; he stands aloof and watches Kristin as she silently spreads the tablecloth on the grass and serves the food on the precious crockery. He watches them as they eat—some are lying on the grass while others sit on the swings and merry-go-rounds. She sits on a bench and also eats. Don will have none of the food but stands behind her bench as if on guard duty.

Professor notices the bulge under Don's T-shirt and knows immediately that it is a gun in a holster. He deduces from the way the guy is just standing there, hawk-eyed, and the fact that his designer jeans are clean and well-pressed and his sneakers are the expensive-leather type, that the man cannot be anyone's gardener.

'He's not a gardener,' he tells his mates. 'He's a body-guard. Gardeners don't carry guns. You see, it's like I told you. They nearly killed her, so now she has a bodyguard.'

After the meal Don helps her carry the stuff once more and they leave the park. Throughout the whole ritual she hasn't uttered a word to Don or to her homeless people, Don observes. She did not greet them when she arrived, nor does she say goodbye to them when she leaves.

'What was that about?' Don asks at last.

'Feeding the homeless,' she says curtly.

'Why?'

'Because they're hungry and they've got to eat.'

'This is just like your dance,' says Don. 'It's for you, not them. All this guilt-salving liberal nonsense. Those hoboes should go to work but they won't. You know why? Because they know that somebody will come on Saturdays and feed them.'

'Ja,' she says sarcastically. 'Like, if someone fed *you* once a week you would decide not to work for the rest of your life. Like one meal on Saturdays satisfies all *your* human needs for the whole week.'

He decides not to argue about it. But if they are going to be together at all he will have to put an end to such odd behaviour. If they are going to be together at all? Where did that come from? Is he reading too much into their relationship after just one night of steamy sex? As these questions race through his mind he makes a resolution to stop being presumptuous and to focus on mending bridges with Tumi. Tumi is the woman for him. Tumi has always been the woman for him, *van toeka af*. Way, way back.

But the following fortnight Kristin Uys becomes his intoxicant. He finds that he can't get enough of her. She can't get enough of him either. To the extent that she takes leave from work, postponing a number of cases.

Mr Bangani Mbona, the chief magistrate, cannot refuse her leave even though there is a heavy backlog on the roll because she has not taken any for a number of years. She needs a rest, she tells him, and deserves one, otherwise she will have a breakdown. Mr Mbona would rather have a backlog than a magistrate who is a nervous wreck.

The first order of business for Kristin and Don—all cellphones switched off and the landline is unplugged. But not before Don sends a text message to Tumi that he will be away for a while on a secret mission and will have no access to any means of communication. She must not worry though, he adds, all is well—he will explain when he returns. And he calls Jim Baxter to inform him that the magistrate is taking a brief holiday and needs him to protect her. So, Baxter must not be alarmed if for the next two weeks or so he does not report at the office.

Kristin and Don spend the first few days of the fortnight at her house which they convert into a love nest. They sit by the pool and have a *braai*. Once again they are like kids playing house. Don feels so liberated but also feels guilty about feeling liberated. Especially for feeling liberated with a white woman. Kristin, on the other hand, feels dirty. But it is the kind of dirt that she wants to wallow in at this time. It is dirt that is more fulfilling than her night dance, which also used to leave her with a tinge of grubbiness. She feels squalid and wicked and loves every moment of it.

The following week a letter arrives from the Roodepoort magistrate's court. Mr Mbona says he has been calling her home number and has left numerous messages on her voicemail. He wants her to report to his office, not for duty, but to handle just one matter, the Visagie case. There have been new developments that she needs to address.

'I'm not ready for this,' she says. 'Not yet. The Visagies will have to wait.'

'If you don't reply to that letter Mr Mbona will come here looking for you. Maybe you should go and dispose of the matter once and for all.'

'We'll have to escape to Cape Town. Just for one week. Or maybe two.'

Don thinks it is a great idea, although he has no money for this unplanned holiday. Kristin says she will foot the bill. After all, she has not been on holiday for ages and has saved quite a bundle because her needs have always been meagre. Don sees this as a chance to escape from Tumi. At least for a while. When he returns from Cape Town he will go back to her and concoct some story about having to hide from drug lords who are bent on killing him and the magistrate. He will then beg for her forgiveness. Tumi loves him and will certainly forgive him. In any event, Tumi needs to learn a lesson. Isn't she the one who got so worked up about a mere jersey, and who said he must choose between her and his cat?

'What do we do with the cats if we go to Cape Town?'

'Take them to a cattery,' she says. 'I know a good one in Honeydew—the Cat's Whiskers.'

In the South African Airways business class Kristin and Don are in adjacent seats huddled up under a blanket. He suggested that she should buy economy-class tickets even though he normally travels business or first class, courtesy of the important people whose bodies he guards on domestic flights, but she insisted that she wanted to spoil him and herself—she has not travelled by air since she was a young attorney married to Barend Uys and attending a mercantile law convention in Port Elizabeth. Those were the days she still thought she would end up as a corporate lawyer for one of the large parastatals like Eskom or Sasol, which guaranteed sheltered employment for young Afrikaners like herself. It was before her life crashed round her when Barend betrayed her, before she resigned herself to being a small-town attorney, and before Mandela's South Africa gave her another chance, that of joining the judiciary.

In Cape Town, they book into a luxury self-catering apartment at the water's edge in the Victoria and Alfred Waterfront Residential Marina.

In the evenings they walk among buskers and tourists at the waterfront and explore seafood restaurants. In the first few days he is quite jittery, fearful that someone from Johannesburg who knows him and Tumi may spot him. Fortunately, it is not holiday season and most of the tourists are from America and Europe rather than the Gautengers who normally invade the place in December. But one can't relax completely.

As days go by he decides to chill and enjoy life and everything else be damned.

'You know, I used to dance,' she says out of the blue one day.

'Of course, I saw your dance,' he says.

'I'm not talking about that, silly,' she says.

Silly? That's what Tumi calls him when she thinks he said something stupid.

'I'm talking about ballroom dancing. I think we should look for a dance studio and go ballroom dancing.'

And sure enough there is an Arthur Murray Dance Studio in nearby Green Point.

Don and Kristin slide on the shiny floor to a waltz. They both move with great flair, as if they have been dance partners for years. She is a changed woman. She no longer has her schoolmarmish bun, and her golden locks are flowing as carefreely as she seems to be. Her mature beauty has blossomed—she glows.

The next day they tackle the walks and the trails at the Cape of Good Hope Nature Reserve at Cape Point. She is amazed at the diversity of the wild flowers that are in full bloom in different colours; he doesn't care much for nature, perhaps a result of his ghetto upbringing in Soweto, or of the years he spent in the bush fighting her people's armies. It was no picnic there and he had enough of the bush to last him a lifetime. But at Cape Point they have a picnic on the high cliffs with a view of the ocean waves down below. She has a basket full of sandwiches, fried chicken, cooldrinks and potato crisps, and he is trying to spread a tablecloth on a rock. But the wind blows it away. She laughs at him as he runs after it. It has blown over the edge and he says goodbye to it.

They walk on the white sands of Clifton Beach hand in hand for the first time. It just happens and they are not aware of it. And they walk for some time swinging their arms. She is the first to be conscious of the interlocked fingers and she pulls away. She breaks into a run and he chases her. He catches up with her and holds her to himself. He is about to kiss her but she pushes him away. She is not one for public displays of affection. There is a little bit of the old South Africa still lingering in the environment: What will all these people who are staring at them think?

By the end of the fortnight they have graduated as seasoned Cape Town tourists. They know which places to revisit and which to avoid. They ride repeatedly on the Table Mountain aerial cable car and picnic on Signal Hill.

And he accompanies her to the malls where she shops for a new, brighter wardrobe. Again Don observes that she just buys something she likes without giving a hoot about what label it is. And yet her taste is good even though she goes for the less expensive items. He does not see any difference between the designer clothes she avoids and the less expensive ones she chooses. She feels the cloth with her fingers and knows at once that it is good quality. When they get back to the apartment she tries on the clothes and models them for him. Like Tumi loves to model for him whenever she has bought something new. But Kristin is not tall and busty like Tumi. She is quite petite, in fact. But my, she does look good in these dresses and skirts and blouses and jackets!

Unfortunately, Don and Kristin can't be refugees in Cape Town for ever. They have to return to Johannesburg. Each has to face his or her own music. For her it is Mbona, Naidoo and the new Visagie developments, whatever they are. For him it is Tumi.

A few days after their return from Cape Town Kristin brings up Tumi. He is in the kitchen feeding the cats and she is just standing there looking at him. He senses that some change has come over her. She is not the carefree Kristin of Cape Town. A new tenseness can be seen in her posture. He dismisses it at first as the tension of having to return to work—the return she has been postponing to the next day every morning.

But it is not about work. It is about them. So this morning she brings it up.

'What about her, Don?' she asks.

He knows at once that she is asking about Tumi.

'What about her?' he asks.

'I feel bad about her,' she says.

'Things will work themselves out, Kristin.'

'I think so too,' she says. 'Maybe that's why you should leave, go back to your apartment.'

This, of course, takes him by surprise. It must be a joke. She can't mean it. Not when things are going so well. Not when they have spent fourteen glorious days in Cape Town hiding away from the world in plain view.

'Hey, I'm still your bodyguard, am I not? Doesn't mean just because we share a bed you no longer need my protection.'

'Stevo's harassment has stopped,' she says. 'It's been a while now since there's been anything. There's no longer any threat to my life, Don, so you must go.'

Now he sees that she is serious about this. They should have buried themselves in Cape Town for ever. Johannesburg has a bad effect on people. It is such an intense place it gets into you. That's why there are more road-rage incidents here than anywhere else in the country.

'You don't really mean it, Kristin,' he says. 'You're just getting cold feet about us.'

'No, I'm not. I just want us to take it one step at a time. Give each other space.'

'I don't take that much space.'

His attempt to introduce some levity is futile. Her face does not crack into a smile.

'You know what I mean,' she says.

'I know exactly what you mean. You are discarding me like a piece of chewing gum.'

'We'll still see each other,' she says, her voice acquiring a new imploring tone. 'But we need to be apart. Only then will I know I have triumphed over my own hangups. Only then can we be sure we are serious about each other. And there's Tumi. I don't want to be the cause of your break-up with her.'

The next morning he takes Kristin to work in his Saab. Then he goes to report to the VIP Protection Services office across the street. Jim Baxter is eager to find out what his mission away from Johannesburg was all about. The magistrate had to give some courses in Cape Town, some kind of in-service training that she was conducting for new magistrates. So, he went along to protect her because he thought the gangsters might take the opportunity to assassinate her there. So, it was not really a holiday as he had previously told him. Baxter praises him for his dedication and assures him that this will count in his favour when the board considers the promotion, which could be any day now.

Don is pleased that at least he will derive some benefit from the whole sorry affair with Kristin. 'Sorry affair' because he might have lost Tumi over it and now Kristin doesn't need him any more.

There is not much work for him at the office, so he decides to return to Weltevreden Park. He knows exactly what he will do when he gets there.

In the afternoon he is back at the Roodepoort magistrate's court waiting for her. He is sitting in his convertible with the top down. The engine is running impatiently. Kristin appears from the courthouse and minces down the steps. Although she is carrying her magisterial briefcase and gown, Don cannot help marvelling at how different she looks from the dour and dowdy figure he first knew. There has been a glowing transformation both in her dress sense and her hairdo—it is now in a fashionable bob. She would not be out of place in a fashion magazine that specializes in sensible understated dress devoid of bells and whistles.

Just at that moment Tumi walks out of the VIP Protection Services building across the street. She came to confront Jim Baxter, to find out exactly where he sent Don, and what kind of an assignment this is that does not allow him to contact her, or even to have his cellphone switched on. She got no joy from Baxter because men are scoundrels and will always protect each other. At least that was her conclusion, although Baxter, for his part, did his best to confirm that Don was indeed on a mission with the magistrate but is now back, and indeed he came to report at work this morning.

As she walks towards her Jaguar which is parked on Dieperink Street she spots Don sitting in his car, and a blonde opening the door and taking a seat next to him.

He says something in her ear and they break into laughter. He pecks her on the cheek before he pulls out of the parking lot. Tumi waves frantically at them to stop and runs towards Don's car. But they don't see her. The Saab speeds away.

Tumi gets into her Jaguar but does not drive away. She just sits there, stunned.

'So, what did the chief magistrate want to see you about?' asks Don as he negotiates the peak hour traffic in the town.

'He was not there,' says Kristin. 'His secretary made an appointment for me for tomorrow.'

Don tells her about his own meeting with Jim Baxter. He is in line for promotion, and Baxter seemed confident that he will get it. He does not tell her though, how great a role the vacation in Cape Town has played in tilting things in his favour. Instead he exuberantly outlines his plans. The same plans he used to discuss with Tumi— how his position as the chief executive will make it possible for him to access BEE opportunities and that one day he will take over the company and other companies and become a millionaire or even a billionaire like Comrade Molotov Mbungane.

Kristin doesn't seem impressed. All she says is: 'That's how you people gauge the success of the new South Africa . . . by the number of millionaires you create?'

There's that 'you people' again!

Don stops at a traffic light and a sunburnt white woman comes to beg. Don looks the other way and the woman runs to Kristin's side and relates her woeful tale of hungry children. Kristin rummages in her purse and hands her some money. But the traffic lights turn green and Don pulls off. The woman runs after the car and fortunately is able to grab the money from Kristin's hand.

'That was not very nice,' says Kristin.

Just like it is not very nice to dismiss with contempt my enthusiasm about my bright future. But he does not voice these thoughts. Instead he expresses his lack of sympathy for white beggars in general because they squandered all their opportunities during apartheid when all the benefits of wealth, health and education were skewed in their favour.

'She could not have been more than ten when apartheid came to an end. Why should she pay for the sins of her fathers?' asks Kristin.

Before he can rebut that his cellphone rings. He forgot to switch it off this morning after talking to Jim Baxter to inform him he would be reporting at the office.

'Surely you're not going to answer that,' says Kristin. 'Not only is it dangerous but it is also against the law.'

He answers it nonetheless. Because he is driving he can't read the name on the screen but hopes it is Jim Baxter with the good news. He said it could be any time now.

'I've just seen you with a white bitch,' Tumi screeches into his ear.

'Where are you?' he wonders.

'I went to VIP to ask your boss for your address at that magistrate's house and the bastard said he can't give it to me for security reasons. And then when I was leaving I saw you.'

'I'm coming home tonight, Tumi. We'll talk about it.'

'I don't ever want to see you back there, Don,' she says. 'Who is that bitch?'

'That's the magistrate I am supposed to protect, Tumi.'

'You lie to me! That was no old white woman. And do you always kiss the people you guard?'

'I never said she was old,' says Don. 'You did.'

Kristin looks at him questioningly and disapprovingly.

'You've been sleeping with her, you son of a bitch!' screams Tumi. 'Don't come back here.'

'Tumi, please let's talk about this.'

She hangs up on him.

'Someone is in the doghouse,' observes Kristin softly.

He does not respond. They drive quietly for some time. You can feel the tension between them.

'You'll be happy to know that I'm all packed. I'm leaving tonight,' Don says as he drives through the gateway of her Weltevreden Park home.

'What makes you think I'm happy about it?' she asks, with a sob in her voice.

He parks the car in front of the garage. The tension continues as they walk away from the car. At the door they are greeted by a gory sight. A pig's head dripping with blood is stuck on one of the sharp bars of the security grille. This freaks Kristin out—she screams and finds refuge in Don's arms.

'I thought this was over,' she says. 'I thought the damn threats had come to an end.'

'Those Visagies don't give up easily,' says Don calmly, and envelops her even closer to his body. She is visibly shaken.

'This has gone too far. And you're leaving.'

'If you think I can leave you at a time like this, you have another think coming,' he assures her. 'Your life is in danger, Kristin. You'll just have to bear with my presence until this nonsense stops.'

She is relieved.

18

SEE HOW SHE GLOWS

In the boardroom of the Roodepoort magistrate's court Krish Naidoo is sitting at a big round table and is paging through a folder while he waits. A few moments later Kristin Uys enters. She looks dazzling and there is a bounce in her step. Naidoo looks up smiling, expecting a greeting from her. But she does not give him a second glance. She takes a seat a few places from him and promptly pages through her own folder. She is not really reading anything but is keeping herself occupied so that Naidoo can have no expectation of a conversation with her.

'You look different, Kristin,' says Krish Naidoo. 'Gorgeous. The way you used to look at Wits.'

'Don't pretend to be nice to me, Krish Naidoo,' she says tersely. 'Not when you have stabbed me in the back.'

Naidoo decides to let that go and returns to his folder. Kristin is miffed because she was gearing for a fight. Bangani Mbona rushes in and apologizes for keeping them waiting. He takes a seat opposite the magistrate, and his eyes betray his amazement.

'Well, Ms Uys, I wouldn't have recognized you,' he says. 'You should take more holidays.'

'With all due respect, sir, I'd appreciate it if we just get to the point,' she says.

The chief magistrate is taken aback and looks as though he may erupt into something he will later regret but common sense gets the better of him. He takes refuge in Naidoo's calm face and says, as if talking to him, 'We are quite testy today, aren't we?'

She gives the chief magistrate an apologetic smile.

'My reaction to your compliment was uncalled for,' she says. 'I am very sorry.'

'It's all right,' says the chief magistrate smiling condescendingly. 'We are all used to your little tantrums by now.'

He passes documents to the magistrate and Krish Naidoo, sliding them across the table. She knows what this is all about the moment she sees the letterhead: The High Court of South Africa—Transvaal Provincial Division.

'As you can see,' says the chief magistrate, 'the finding of the judge is that Stevo Visagie was in contempt but that the sentence was irregular. The maximum for this crime is three months.'

'But there were two incidents of contempt,' says the magistrate. 'What do they say about that?'

Instead of responding Mr Mbona points her to a paragraph in the document.

The high court finds that there was no separate contempt to warrant the extra three months. Even if the so-called second contempt was regarded as a separate incident—which it was not—the second three-month sentence would have to run concurrently with the first. Stevo Visagie has already served more than a month, and is therefore left with a few weeks or even days in jail because of the one-third remission to which he is entitled. The prison system has yet to calculate exactly when he will be free.

The magistrate is crestfallen while Naidoo is happy, although he does not want to display outright glee.

Kristin Uys does not take kindly to defeat. More than just the humiliation of having her decision reversed by a superior court, she is struck with terror when the image of the pig's head dripping with blood flashes before her eyes. If the Visagies are able to make her life a living hell when Stevo is in jail, what more will happen when he is on the loose?

Stevo, on the other hand, is savouring the moment. As soon as he receives the good news from Krish Naidoo he calls his war council, and it is gathered here today in the persons of Shortie Visagie and Ma Visagie. He would have liked Aunt Magda to be here, not only because she has been supporting him with all the goodies, but he has also bought into her story that it is as a result of her mass action that the sentence has been reduced. However, when she heard that Ma Visagie would be part of the meeting she decided to avoid a potentially dangerous confrontation. Stevo is still smarting about it.

The warder decided to waive the one-visitor-at-a-time policy for his model prisoner, who will in any case soon be released.

The only reason Ma Visagie came is to order her son to stop consorting with Aunt Magda. But Stevo is adamant that Aunt Magda is being misunderstood. She is the wronged party here and Ma Visagie should apologize. Aunt Magda looked after him when no help was forthcoming from his own family. Now he is going to be free, and it's all thanks to Aunt Magda.

'Did your Aunt Magda pay for the lawyer, Stevo?' asks Ma Visagie. She never thought she would see the day when her son stood up to her.

'She paid for no lawyer, Ma,' says Stevo. 'But she demonstrated all over the place and marched to Pretoria and created so much hell for the government that they had to free me.'

'She didn't get to no Pretoria,' says Shortie, who has been quiet all along, examining his clean-shaven and well-groomed brother closely and wondering how his once strong and manly mind got messed up in prison. 'I had to pick her and the women up in Midrand because they were tired like dogs. She lies to you if she says she talked to the government in Pretoria.'

Stevo looks at him with squinted eyes as if noticing his presence for the first time.

'That was a masterpiece, my china,' says Stevo. He is in high spirits all of a sudden. His eyes are bulging as if they are about to jump out of their sockets.

'What was?' asks Shortie, worried that he is going to be blamed for something.

'I could kiss you for it, my china.'

'I don't want you to kiss me, Stevo. I just want you to tell me what the heck you're on about.'

'Hey, don't try to play modest with me, Shortie,' says Stevo. 'You're a sly one, my china. A genius! You pretend to be stupid and all that but you're a genius!'

Ma Visagie looks at Shortie with suspicion. 'Shortie a genius? What did he do this time? What did you do, Shortie?'

'I didn't do nothing, Ma. 'S'true's God, I didn't do nothing.'

'You call a pig's head nothing?' asks Stevo.

Ma Visagie is puzzled. 'Pig's head?'

'Yes, pig's head, Ma. That's the report I got. How he thought of it without my help is still a mystery to me. But he thought of it himself, in his own head. Pig's head, it was, wasn't it, Shortie?'

'Ja. Pig's head,' says Shortie sheepishly.

'How did you think of putting a bleeding pig's head at her door?' asks Stevo, looking at his brother with belated admiration. 'How did you become such a master of psychology? She must have wet her pants when she saw that head.'

Ma Visagie is looking at Shortie accusingly. 'You didn't tell me about this.'

'He's not a man of words, our Shortie,' says Stevo. 'He's a man of action.'

No other business is discussed by the war council today because the topic of the pig's head seems to have hijacked the proceedings to the exclusion of everything else.

Shortie's masterpiece is just the beginning though. The real masterpiece, the biggest of them all, will happen when he gets out of jail, Stevo assures his family. And he will do that one himself. It's got to be Stevo personally who performs the crowning masterpiece.

'I'm not gonna sit here and listen to your silly talk, Stevo. I have work to do,' says Ma Visagie.

'Me too, I have work to do,' says Shortie.

'*Ja*, my china, because me, I don't have work to do, hey? Because I am a *bandiet* I've got no work to do? Is that it, my china? I'm coming out, man. And I will have work to do. You just wait and see. Plenty of work to do.'

Ma Visagie's parting shot is that Stevo must be careful since no one has messed with her and lived to tell the story. Both Stevo and Aunt Magda must take heed not to test her too much; otherwise there'll be a corpse in the house. She didn't bring up her children just to have some coloured woman from Cape Town putting wrong ideas into their heads. Stevo must grow up and take a good lesson from his younger brother. Shortie has publicly denounced Aunt Magda.

But it doesn't look like Stevo is listening to his mother. He is just staring at Shortie with glazed eyes and a generous smile, and he keeps repeating, '*Ja*, my china, I love your pig. I'm sure she is wetting her pants as we speak.'

Kristin Uys is not exactly wetting her pants. But she can't feign audacity any more. She and Don are in the bedroom preparing for sleep. She is sitting on the bed, deep in contemplation. Don gets into bed and invites her in. She is visibly shaken, so Don tosses off the duvet, sits with her and tries to comfort her by caressing her back. She looks like a waif, sitting there wearing only her panties.

'I don't understand this,' says Don. 'You have been brave all along.'

'I underestimated him,' she says. 'He's coming out and he is a hothead. He's capable of really hurting me.'

Don hates to see her like this. But deep down he thanks his ancestors because events are shaping themselves in a manner that makes him indispensable in her life.

'I'll see the cops again first thing tomorrow morning. I've gone a long way towards finding that truck. I haven't found it yet, but I am on the verge of a breakthrough. We'll find something that will keep Stevo in jail for a longer period, and that will also incriminate both Ma Visagie and Shortie.'

'How are you going to do that when the cops have failed?'

'Trust me, my darling. Trust me.'

This is not just idle talk on his part. He has been trying, really. For instance, when Kristin was at the office conferring with the chief magistrate on the high court decision, he was meeting with his number one spy, Aunt Magda, not at their regular bar in Florida but at a seedy tavern in the inner-city part of Roodepoort. The reason for this choice of venue was that Aunt Magda wanted to introduce him to two prostitutes who were prepared to be of great help provided he paid them well.

'You know I pay good money for good information,' said Don. 'I've paid you well too, Magda, though I haven't seen any results.'

'I'm getting there,' said Aunt Magda. 'Me and these girls, we'll finally get you more than just the truck, but lots of stuff that you can use against the Visagies. They'll regret that they ever threw me out of their house after I worked so hard for them.'

Even though it was not yet midday the place was throbbing with music and drunken dancing. The stench told Don that this had continued from the previous night and the revellers had not slept, let alone taken a bath. There were quite a few dodgy characters among the patrons smoking cigars and filling the place with smoke. No one there seemed to have heard of the law that prohibits smoking in public places, or if they had they defiled their lungs with impunity, daring the authorities to come and arrest them. Police will not bother with smokers when crime is rampant in the city.

Two women came and joined their table. Don bought them whisky and lit a cigar. His attempt to look like a hardcore gangster didn't quite cut it.

'You know Stevo will kill us if he finds out that we talked to you,' said the more mature woman with heavy make-up that hardly disguised her ravaged face.

'Then we must make sure he doesn't find out,' said Don.

'It's going to cost you, *ngamla*,' said the younger woman who should still have been someone's child carrying lunch to school packed by a loving mama. 'We don't normally rat on our friends.'

'Stevo is not your friend,' said Don. 'Aunt Magda told me he was your pimp and you fell out terribly when he refused to pay you what was due to you.'

The older woman said, 'But Mr Fingers is our friend, and that's the man you want us to get for you.'

Yes, Fingers Matatu is the man Don is gunning for. He gathered that since his retirement as cat burglar he has been freelancing for the Visagies, performing odd criminal jobs, sometimes even delivering stolen cars to the Visagie scrapyard in Strijdom Park where they are stripped for parts.

'Where do I find this Mr Fingers?' asked Don.

The girls claimed they didn't know because he didn't hang out in these parts but somewhere in Soweto. And the place being so big, they couldn't even say in which township of Soweto he spent his nights. And now that

Stevo was in the slammer the Visagie enterprise had cooled off a bit. It would therefore take a lot of trouble and expense to find out where Mr Fingers was freelancing these days.

Don placed a few notes on the table.

'Hey, people are looking,' said the younger woman.

'Doesn't matter,' said Don. 'They think I'm a john.'

The older woman counted the money surreptitiously and gave it back to Don.

'We're not cheap,' she said.

'Come on, girls,' said Don. 'You've not done any work yet. How do I know you'll fulfil your end of the deal?'

'If you want us to deliver Mr Fingers to you then you better be generous,' said the older woman.

Don placed more bank notes in her cleavage, which left her giggling. And then he playfully placed some banknotes in Aunt Magda's ample bosom as her commission for connecting him with these wonderful prostitutes who would help him nail the Visagies once and for all. As he planted the money in her blouse and then at the edge of her bra Aunt Magda flushed and sighed. He promised everyone more money if they delivered Fingers Matatu to him, and even more if they helped locate the truck.

But Don does not tell Kristin about this meeting. Just as he has never told her about previous meetings where he gave Aunt Magda money, even though to this day she has not given him any useful information. Until she produced the two prostitutes he could have sworn that she was stringing him along for some devilish reason known only to herself. But he was willing to play the game on the off chance that it bore some fruit. With the two prostitutes it looks as though now he will indeed see some results.

'I do trust you, Don,' she says. 'I have to trust you.'

She gets into bed and he follows suit. He wants some little nookie but her body language tells him he is getting none tonight. He understands that she is quite stressed. They promptly fall asleep in each other's arms.

The next morning he takes her to work. She insists that they use the hired Volkswagen Golf in case the crooks know that she now travels in his Saab. She is getting paranoid and this worries Don. It cramps their carefree life. When she is constantly looking over her shoulder she can't totally give herself to him. Now, for the first time, she wants him to be in her office with her and in the courtroom when she is conducting her cases. She does not want him to be out of sight. Fortunately he is not just a bodyguard but a lover, so he can even go to the bathroom with her.

That evening he is cooking dinner when she storms in.

'I'm not fighting the Visagies any more,' she says out of the blue. 'I'm leaving town.'

Don laughs incredulously.

'It's not a joke, Don,' says Kristin. 'I've told the chief magistrate already. He thinks I'm crazy but I've told him that I'm going to resign and leave town.'

Don loses his temper finally.

'You baulk and that's the end of us,' he says.

He forgets about the pan on the stove and reaches for Snowy who is curled up on a mat in the corner. He holds the cat in his arms and caresses its back.

'I can't stand this stress any more, Don,' she says, almost crying.

'I've invested a lot in protecting you, Kristin. I've even paid bribes to prostitutes.'

He never told her anything about meeting prostitutes to save her, she says. He is not supposed to bribe anyone on her behalf. It is illegal. She is still the magistrate and must operate within the confines of the law.

'To hell with the bloody confines of the bloody law,' yells Don. 'I've invested a lot in this relationship. I'm losing Tumi and may also lose the CEO job at VIP Protection Services once they find out what you and I have been up to.'

Kristin's cat is jealous of Snowy and tries to claw its way up his leg. He bends down to pet it too.

'You see,' she says. 'It's all about you. Everything is about you. I'm just an assignment to you.'

The food is burning on the stove and the room is full of smoke. He puts the cat down and reaches for the pan to remove it from the stove.

'Goddammit, Kristin! Now dinner is ruined.'

They repair to a seafood restaurant at Palm Court and get a table for two. They order fish and chips with hush puppies.

'Maybe it's a good thing dinner was ruined,' says Don. 'This fish is good.'

'I'm sorry it got ruined,' says Kristin. 'I always look forward to the little surprises you cook.'

He breaks a piece of fish to inspect the texture of the batter. He always does this when he eats out. He tries to figure out what ingredients were used in any dish that he likes, and then experiments with it at home.

'You don't really think you're just an assignment to me, do you?'

'Of course I don't, Don. But I'm scared. I'm concerned for your safety as much as I'm concerned for mine.'

'We'll get through this, Kristin,' he assures her. 'I'm sure we will.'

'What about Tumi?'

She is earnestly looking into his eyes, hoping for a reassuring answer. She has hardly touched her food while he chews with relish. He can taste the subtle honey and lemon juice and sherry in the batter. And the hush puppies are crunchy. Exactly the way he likes them.

'Is that the real reason you want to leave town?' he asks.

'Everything is a mess, Don,' she says. 'And I'm the cause of it all. And now you've made me fall in love with you. And yet you can't really be mine, can you?'

She has never said anything like this before. She has never defined their relationship in terms of love. The most she has said was that she cared for him. Don is suddenly overcome with emotion.

'Why not?' he asks, almost breathlessly. 'Why can't I be?'

'I feel guilty about Tumi,' she says. 'And I know that I can't compete with her. I can't see myself replacing a beautiful black woman in your life. I know you'll be happier with Tumi.'

'If I thought I'd be happier with Tumi I would be with her now.'

He wonders if he is in his right mind. Has he just made a commitment to this woman? Are his declarations not too rash? Especially his very last statement—was it not perhaps too reckless?

They eat quietly for some time. Actually, he is the one who cleans off his plate. She is only playing with her food with a fork.

'I think this Visagie thing has stressed you out,' he says. 'But there is no going back now, Kristin. We've got to see it through.'

She agrees. They have to see it through. She hopes he won't think she doesn't appreciate his sacrificing something of himself for her.

'So, no more talk of resigning?' he asks.

'No more talk of resigning,' she says.

'No more talk of leaving town?'

She giggles like a little girl. 'No more talk of leaving town.'

He kisses her. She kisses him back. She no longer cares what anyone else watching thinks. There are mostly young people at the takeaway counter and a few at the tables. They are minding their own business and don't pay attention to the mature mixed-race couple. They see a lot of this sort of thing in their ranks, especially here in the suburbs.

Just then Jim Baxter breaks their embrace with a telephone call. He wants to see Don first thing in the morning.

Don gets a doggy bag from the waitron, as they now prefer to be called, and takes Kristin's food for his lunch tomorrow.

The next morning Don goes straight to VIP Protection Services after dropping Kristin at the court-house. He is dreading what Baxter has to tell him. He hopes he is not taking him off this case. Or perhaps he wants to complain about the expense account. He has been extravagant lately, paying Aunt Magda and the prostitutes and taking Kristin to sample some of the nightlife of Johannesburg. Baxter should have no cause to complain about that because the Department of Justice will foot that entire bill—it is part of the expense of looking after the safety of the magistrate.

He rushes down the corridor anxiously to the CEO's office. He knocks timidly and enters. Jim Baxter welcomes him with a stern look. Four men are with him. Don knows that two of them are members of the board of directors, and the big white-haired man with a militaristic pose in a black suit and dark glasses is the chairman of the board.

'Mr Mateza!' says Baxter.

This worries Don even more. He has always been Don to this man, just as the man has always been Jim to him.

'You wanted to see me, *Mr Baxter*,' says Don, almost out of breath.

'We are taking you off the magistrate's case,' says Baxter confirming Don's suspicions.

'Why? What have I done?'

The men laugh. Don breathes a sigh of relief.

'I thought you'd be pleased, Mr Mateza,' says Baxter. 'Anyway, you can't be CEO of VIP Protection Services and the magistrate's bodyguard at the same time.'

Don is at a loss for words. The chairman of the board pops a bottle of champagne and another director hands out the glasses.

19

HELL HATH NO FURY

Tumi is standing at the door of her townhouse yelling for the entire neighbourhood to hear. She is in her morning gown and slippers. Don is standing outside helplessly. As she yells she throws articles of clothing on the lawn and Don scrambles to pick them up.

Hell hath no fury!

'That's always the case with you bastards,' she hollers as she hurls a shoe at him. He catches it with the dexterity of a rugby player, but before he can recover his balance another shoe hits him on the head. The head spins a bit but there is no time to nurse it because missiles are raining on him from the house.

'Once you become a Black Diamond black sisters are no longer good enough for you! Fucking a white woman is a bloody status symbol. Now that you're a bloody CEO you think you are Molotov Mbungane all of a sudden.'

He knows what she is talking about. They used to laugh about Comrade Molotov's high jinks when things were still great between them. The billionaire had a wife and two children at his home village in the Transkei before he went into exile and then to Robben Island. As soon as he was released from jail and occupied an important cabinet post he forgot all about his customary law wife and married a white woman—an Afrikaner who was a secretary at his cabinet office left over from the old regime. A white wife, according to Tumi, made him more palatable to white business. No one talks of his village wife any more. Her children grew up herding cattle and she worked as a kitchen 'girl' for the owners of the village general dealers' store.

'It has nothing to do with that, Tumi,' says Don. 'I really do care about Kristin.'

'Look at me, Don,' she says, instinctively posing like the model she used to be. 'Look at this body. You telling me you're leaving me for some old white hag? And you do this to me after all the years I have supported you, *njandini*!'

She has never called him *njandini*, you dog, before. They have never had such a public spat either. Like all lovers they have had their occasional quarrel, but always in the privacy of their bedroom. This new flaming Tumi is a revelation to him.

Hell hath no fury!

'I'm just being honest with you, Tumi. It's not working between us.'

At this another missile flies—a wicker cat basket.

'Yeah, now that you have your promotion it's not working between us. It was working all along when you were eating my money.'

'It has nothing to do with the promotion, Tumi.'

Neighbours—mostly domestic servants and house-wives since most people are at work at this time—gather to witness the row. Everyone loves free entertainment.

'Go fuck your white bitch! See if I care!'

At this she goes into the house and slams the door. Don gathers his clothes and all the other items and loads them into his car.

As he drives out of North Riding on Beyers Naudé Drive he blames himself for being a gentleman. When the thought came to him in the deep of the night with Kristin in his arms that he should face Tumi once and for all and confess his love for the magistrate, he was tempted to do so via an SMS, as text messages are called here. He actually did wake up and reach for his cellphone. But before he could even write the message he rebuked himself for being cowardly and unfeeling. He has been with Tumi for all these years and he at least owed her the decency of breaking up with her in person. Thus, after dropping the magistrate at work he went straight to Three Oaks.

He should have obeyed his first instinct.

He is at the Jim Fouché Road traffic lights when his cellphone rings. It is Tumi.

'It's just infatuation, Don,' she says.

'What is there to talk about since you threw my stuff out?' asks Don in a wounded voice as if he is the wronged party here.

'It *is* infatuation,' repeats Tumi. 'The novelty will wear off, Don. You'll come back begging, but I won't have time for you, Don. I can get any man I want, Don, and I'm going to move on. Do you hear me, Don? Don?'

Don does not respond, though he continues to hold the phone to his ear as he negotiates his way in the late morning traffic on Jim Fouché.

'OK, I forgive you, Don,' says Tumi desperately. 'We can always start afresh. I forgive you.'

'There's no starting afresh, Tumi.'

'What part of "I forgive you" don't you understand, man?'

'We'll talk later—I'm driving in heavy traffic.'

He cuts her off and puts the cellphone back in his breast pocket. It rings immediately. Again it is Tumi.

'Yes, *Tumi*,' says Don impatiently.

'I want that car back,' she says with vehemence. 'I paid the deposit for that car and I want it back.'

'I pay the instalments for it, Tumi. And I'll give you your deposit back.'

'I want it now, Don. Now! And I want that suit you are wearing back. And those Gucci shoes, and all those Versaces. I want everything back, Don, and I want it now, not tomorrow.'

He switches the cellphone off.

The next morning Kristin Uys is sitting at the dressing table making herself up. Don is in the bathroom taking a shower. A cellphone rings and she looks for it. She traces the sound to Don's clothes that are piled on the chair. She searches the pants and finds the cellphone.

'Don Mateza's phone. Hello?'

'Mrs Mateza,' says a voice with a strong Zulu accent, 'this is the Roodepoort abattoir. We are slaughtering this afternoon. Should we reserve another pig's head for you?'

'A pig's head?'

'We were wondering if you want to place another order.'

She sits dumbfounded while the man on the line prattles on in the best tradition of salesmanship about how his own family enjoys the delicacy of a pig's head, and how he thought of calling the Mateza family first before vendors came and bought everything. He realizes after a while that no one is listening on the other side, utters a curse, and hangs up.

Don walks out of the bathroom, his body naked and moist. He is drying his head with a towel. He is whistling happily to himself and is not aware that Kristin is sitting on the bed with a dazed look, like a boxer who has received one good punch which nevertheless has failed to achieve a knockout. She is still holding his cellphone.

'Don, the abattoir called,' she says finally.

'The abattoir? About what?' asks Don.

'They have another pig's head for you.' She is amazed how calm she is.

She hands him the cellphone. He extends his hand reluctantly, as if the phone is a snake that will bite him, and withdraws it again without touching the phone.

'Maybe you should call them and order it,' she says.

He snatches the phone from her hand angrily. Common wisdom tells us that the best defence is offence.

'Where do you get off answering my calls? Searching my pants?' he asks, fuming and pacing the floor.

'So, it was you all along? All this time? I have been blaming the Visagie Brothers for nothing. I have lived in fear for nothing.'

Offence cannot work here. This calls for contrition instead. He sits on the bed shamefaced and buries his face in his hands.

'Oh, no, it was them,' says Don. 'Mine was only the pig's head. The rest was truly the work of the Visagie Brothers.'

'Why, Don? Why?' Tears threaten to stream out of her eyes. But she'll be damned if this man sees her cry. Not for this. Not for him. The old Kristin Uys is back.

'I only did the pig thing,' repeats Don. 'I was afraid of losing you, Kristin. I am sorry. It was after you said we should live apart because the threats against you had stopped. It was stupid of me, but I was desperate.'

She stands up and looks at him. Her eyes are full of nothing but contempt. His nakedness worsens his shame and though he is normally a man of robust stature his body looks shrunken and pitiful, as if it wants to withdraw into itself. And hide there until the storm has passed. But Kristin's is a quiet storm. She does not rant and rave like Tumi did yesterday morning. Kristin's fury is measured. Still, it is fury.

'You must leave, Don. Now,' she says resolutely. 'I never want to have anything to do with you ever again. There is no way I can ever trust you again.'

Hell hath no fury!

Don shamefacedly grabs his clothes from the chair and some from the built-in closet. He goes to the guest room where the rest of his stuff is piled on the bed, including the items he brought from Tumi's apartment yesterday. Kristin follows him to make sure that not a single trace of him remains in her house.

'And don't forget your cat,' she says.

'I'll come back for it later,' he says.

'You just want an excuse to come back here,' she says. 'I don't want you back here, Don. Not for anything.'

'I have to find a home for it first, Kristin. I don't know where I'm going as it is.'

She doesn't have the heart to punish the cat for the sins of its master. The cat will stay. But only for a few days. She does not want anything in her house that will remind her of this unfortunate episode in her life.

She goes back to her bedroom and locks herself in there while Don packs his clothes in a suitcase. There are too many of them. He packs the rest in large garbage bags. Already there are a number of garbage bags full of clothes on the floor and on the bed.

After loading them in his car he knocks at her door to say goodbye. But she won't open the door. He can hear some sniffling. He begs her one more time to reconsider her decision to kick him out of her life. He is full of remorse, he says, and has learnt a good lesson. He truly truly loves her and has lost Tumi for her.

She shouts that he should *voetsak*, an expletive that you say only to a dog.

Don cruises on the N1 Highway in his imported Saab. He is driving against the heavy, snail-pace traffic of people who are going to work in Pretoria. He is not in a hurry to get anywhere because he has nowhere to go. The top of the car is up and he is surrounded by black garbage bags, right up to the roof.

Soweto. That's the place. That's where you go when you want to calm your spirit. That's where people who understand you are bound to be. People who know your pain because they have gone through similar pain many times over.

But today Soweto will not be Rre Molefhe's house. Not even to greet the old man and listen to his latest CD of some forgotten jazz giant. He must already know that he has betrayed his daughter. The grapevine is fast in Soweto and it works in mysterious ways.

If Soweto is not Rre Molefhe's then it must be Wezile's Restaurant. His friends are unlikely to be there because it is still too early. They are the types who sleep until midday, since they are jobless, and drink till the small hours of the morning. But he can sit there and while away time while he plans his next move. He is not completely washed-up. He is the new Chief Executive Officer of VIP Protection Services. The women who are giving him a hard time had better remember that.

Cleaners are still vacuuming and dusting the place up at Wezile's. They let him in because they know who he is. In any event a tavern, for this is what it is even though it may pretend to be a restaurant, is open for business at any hour whenever there is a customer who wants to spend his good money.

He sits in the lounge with a beer and watches the flat-screen television on the wall. He is not paying much attention to Vuyo Mbuli who is interviewing three women on his 'Morning Live' programme on SABC 2. Until he hears Tumi's voice. And Tumi's mischievous giggle. And there she is on the screen being interviewed with two of her models. One of them has been signed up by Ford Models in New York and Tumi is all effervescent about it because it means her agency is gaining more respectability internationally. Tumi has also managed to negotiate a six-figure contract for the second model to represent a beauty-soap brand exclusively. Vuyo Mbuli praises Tumi's success and hails this as a breakthrough in the South African modelling industry.

Tumi giggles once more.

Don hates her for looking so beautiful. And so happy.

He dozes on the sofa, until he is woken up by the arrival of Fontyo and Bova, who are surprised to see him in Soweto so early in the morning on a workday. They are early because there is a promotion here today and Don thinks they have come for the booze that usually flows freely on such occasions. Already Wezile is placing banners with the logos of liquor company sponsors on the street in front of the restaurant and even as far off as the end of the street in front of other people's houses. Neighbours have complained about this inconvenience and about the noise to no avail. In Soweto it is a free-for-all. There are no zoning laws.

Bova and Fontyo become quite handy in such situations. They help Wezile set plastic garden furniture and *braai* stands on the pavement. Soon the smoke is billowing and *kwaito* music is throbbing from giant speakers. No one seems to mind that there is a school only thirty metres away and the students are already streaming in. The adult patrons will look the other way when bigger boys and girls play truant and end up drunk here.

Don is hungry and they don't serve breakfast at Wezile's. The cooks are busy in the kitchen making the lunch and dinner that people will be buying during the promotion. Fontyo offers to dash to a nearby cafe to buy him breakfast, provided he gives him enough money to get food for himself and Bova as well.

As they eat *ikota*—white bread stuffed with soft chips, *atchaar*, minced meat, Russian sausages and pieces of steak—Don tells them of his woes. These are his friends, people with whom he fought a war, so he is honest with them. He tells them everything, beginning with how he got a terrible job as the magistrate's bodyguard, to how he ended up sleeping with the magistrate and how things soured between him and the two women. These are men; they will understand what he is going through. It is always a relief to unburden yourself to people with whom you share so much history; his pain is beginning to ebb away already—it is going to be their pain as well.

'What is he going to do now?' asks Bova. He is not directing the question at Don but at Fontyo. Fontyo looks at Don and asks, 'What are you going to do, comrade?'

'I don't know,' says Don. 'Maybe I can sleep at your place until I think things over. Just for a few nights while I look for an apartment or something.'

Don is surprised that Bova and Fontyo want to confer about it first. They are comrades; he expected them to offer him accommodation without his even asking. But they ask to be excused to discuss the matter privately.

When they return they say unfortunately they will not be able to accommodate Don. They are going on a very long trip. It is obvious to Don that they want to keep everything mysterious.

'Why can't I stay at your place while you are gone?' he asks.

No. That won't work. Bova tries quickly to think why not but the best he can do is come up with the feeble excuse that his relatives from some 'homeland' are visiting and therefore there will be no place for him. Don knows immediately that he is lying. Bova does not come from any homeland, nor does he have relatives in one. He was born in Soweto, as was his father before him, and his father's father. His mother, too, was a Sowetan through and through. In any event there are no places called homelands any more, not since Bova himself won the liberation struggle. There are other reasons they don't want him at their place. And this ludicrous trip, it must be a lie too. These two clowns never take a trip anywhere. Somehow they want to get rid of him.

'*Ja*, it's a trip of a lifetime,' says Bova. 'It's going to change our lives.'

Don offers them drinks but, to his utter amazement, they turn them down. They've got to stay sober for the trip. They only came here today to help Wezile set up the place for the promotion. Otherwise, for the whole day they are teetotallers. He buys himself a beer and nurses it because it is lousy to drink alone.

When Fontyo hints that they are on to something big Don feels left out. He could never imagine Fontyo and Bova keeping secrets from him.

And what has happened to their usual banter? To their teasing him about being a security guard? With this awkwardness among them he has not even told them the good news—the promotion to CEO.

'*Sies, man!*' Bova bursts out as if he has been suppressing it all along. '*Jy's 'n moegoe, jong.* You're an idiot. You leave a woman like Tumi for an old white woman!'

Fontyo laughs mockingly, '*Ulizwe kahle ikhekhe lengamla, neh?*'

So, that's what this is all about. Tumi. They are mad at him because he has betrayed their home girl. They even attribute his so-called dumping of Tumi to the fact that he 'tasted a white woman's cake', as Fontyo puts it, and it has drained him of all common sense. They don't understand. If only they walked a few yards in his shoes they would understand. He would blame their strange attitude towards him on beer but both of them are uncharacteristically sober. Or maybe they had a few puffs of *dagga* before they came here. Fontyo, particularly, is rather partial to Mary Jane, as he calls the green herb.

'He thinks a white woman's cake is the fastest way to becoming like Comrade Capitalist,' says Fontyo. 'Soon he will be looking down on us, treating us like dirt like he is doing to Tumi.'

Bova looks him straight in the eye and asks, 'Comrade AK, did we fight the liberation struggle so that we can get between the thighs of white women? Do you think our comrades died for that?'

Don is taken aback by the vehemence and the disgust in his voice.

Tumi didn't even like these guys. She didn't give a damn about them. She thought they were lazy bums who spent their time whingeing instead of getting out there and reaching for the opportunities presented by the new South Africa. Yet here they are, crucifying him for betraying her. Why are they taking his break-up with her so personally?

They leave him in the lounge nursing his beer and busy themselves with helping set up the place. In return, Wezile offers them food and a beer each but, to his surprise, they turn down the offer of beer. They will eat the *braai* meat and pap but today is not a drinking day for them.

By midday more patrons have arrived and the dancing begins. They play the crossover *kwaito* song 'Music' by Mandoza and Danny K over and over again until it gets on Don's nerves. He stands up and staggers to the dance floor in the next room. It is small because Wezile's is really just an ordinary township home converted into a restaurant. His eyes are searching for Bova and Fontyo as he dances feebly on his own. But they are nowhere to be seen. He cuts a pathetic figure and goes back to the lounge. He dozes on the sofa.

When he opens his eyes it is late in the afternoon and there are loud men and women drinking all around him. He knows some of them casually from meeting them here on previous occasions or from the days when he was a township boy.

The television is on although no one is really watching it. No one can hear the sound in any case because Mandoza and Danny K are drowning it.

Don sees a fleeting image of Aunt Magda on the screen, then the camera moves to the anchor.

'Hey *majita*, just be quiet a little bit,' he pleads. 'I just want to hear what this is all about.'

The revellers keep quiet; they are curious to see what is so important that the guy in the Versace suit wants them to stop their conversation. Don raises the volume.

'There were scenes of jubilation outside the gates of Diepkloof Prison when Stevo Visagie was released from what his followers claim was an unfair and vindictive sentence,' says the anchor.

The camera then pans to the prison gates. Members of the Society of Widows led by Aunt Magda are singing and dancing to welcome Stevo Visagie. Our prostitutes are there as well, those we once saw in court and again with Don at the tavern in Roodepoort. The very same prostitutes who were supposed to be gathering intelligence for him. Stevo walks out of the prison gates and marches among his followers holding hands with Ma Visagie, exactly as Nelson Mandela walked out of Victor Verster Prison hand in hand with Winnie Mandela. Stevo looks quite uncomfortable in a grey suit, white shirt and red tie. Shortie and the prostitutes are following closely.

When Stevo sees Aunt Magda among the dancing widows he calls out, 'Aunt Magda! Aunt Magda!' and tries to reach for her with open arms. But Ma Visagie pulls him back to her violently and the march continues to her kombi. Aunt Magda's smoky voice can be heard above everyone else's.

The denizens at Wezile's don't understand what Don's fascination is with this mundane story on television, and why they had to stop their boisterous banter, which promptly resumes even as the news item continues. One of the revellers exclaims, 'Who cares about some *boertjie* boy who was in jail?'

But Don is staring at the television screen with growing alarm. Suddenly he stands up and makes for the door.

He must get to Kristin Uys before Stevo Visagie does.

20

THE FINAL DANCE

At the Visagie home the dining-room table is heaving with a gigantic baked turkey, potatoes, rice, vegetables, sweetmeats and *koeksisters*. A topless Stevo is stuffing himself. Ma Visagie and our prostitutes are fussing over him. Shortie is quietly enjoying the meal, envying all the attention that is being showered on his brother just because he was stupid enough to insult a magistrate. He is in his greasy overalls because, while his brother was vacationing at the state's expense, he was working his butt off at the Visagie scrapyard trying to scrape a livelihood for everyone else.

Stevo is all laughter as he listens to the prostitutes. Now and then he takes a swig from a bottle of beer.

Aunt Magda is sitting timidly away from the table, almost behind the door. She is fearful of calling attention to herself by participating in the conversation. She knows that she is not welcome here by the matriarch. She came in at Stevo's insistence after she had remained outside for more than an hour with the Society of Widows who followed the Visagies to Strubensvallei and continued to sing hymns, thanking the Lord for releasing their hero from the shackles of Pharaoh. Stevo asked the prostitutes to serve the widows some drinks and invited Aunt Magda to share in their meal. Ma Visagie did not voice any objection, though her face displayed a disapproving look. She decided to shut up and indulge Stevo just for once.

One of the prostitutes is telling the table about Don Mateza—how he tried to bribe them to betray Stevo and how they made him believe they would work for him. They laugh at his credulity.

'So this bodyguard guy says he wants to get evidence that will keep you in jail for ever,' she says.

'He wanted us to get him Mr Fingers,' says the second prostitute.

This alarms Shortie.

'Fingers Matatu?' he screeches. 'How did he know about Fingers Matatu?'

'Relax, my china,' says Stevo. 'I'm here now, am I not? He's not gonna come here scaring you again. And how much did he pay for the head of Mr Fingers?'

The prostitutes are reluctant to say. Instead they blether about their difficulties when Stevo was in jail and the problem of making ends meet without their business manager, as they prefer to call the pimp. But Stevo knows what they are trying to do—take him off the subject of how much exactly they were paid by the bodyguard.

'How much, bitch?' he asks, glaring at the girls menacingly.

'It was only a few hundred,' says the prostitute.

'You think I'm gonna ask for my cut, hey, bitch? Maybe I should because you got that money at my expense.'

But Ma Visagie comes to the rescue of the prostitutes. 'Don't be hard on the girls, Stevo. They had to survive while you were enjoying a holiday at Sun City.'

Stevo breaks out laughing. 'I don't want their money, Ma. It's peanuts if you take into account what we gonna be making from now on. I have a dream, my china. We gonna be multimillionaires many times over. We gonna show them that it's not only black people who can be multimillionaires. We gonna rock this city with the biggest syndicate it has ever seen. We gonna fly in our own jet.'

All eyes are agog at Stevo's dream because it is the kind of dream that cannot be sneezed at. Unless you are Ma Visagie. She sees this as Stevo's empty talk. When the giddiness of freedom has worn off he will become normal again and will resume his regular job of pimping the girls.

Shortie is not impressed either. He knows already that his brother developed this strange habit of dreaming when he was in jail and then bursting out in excitement about the dreams.

Aunt Magda sees herself as part of the dream. Stevo would never leave her out of any dream. When she opens her mouth for the first time since taking her humble place behind the door it is to remind everyone that she spent all the money she received from Don Mateza on Stevo. She bought Stevo food and sweet-smelling colognes and a suit so that he could look like the freedom fighter he is when he walked out of prison. Even though Stevo was at first reluctant to wear a suit because he thought it made him appear a sissy, didn't everyone see how handsome he looked on television?

Perhaps Aunt Magda should have kept quiet about this. Ma Visagie begins pacing the floor and muttering something about a coloured woman from Cape Town who has no business buying her son stuff, trying to change him into a girl with colognes and suits.

Stevo tries to defend Aunt Magda. Ma should stop picking on her because she looked after him, and adds, 'Unlike some people I know who are my family but don't do nothing for me when I'm in jail.'

An unwise thing to say.

Ma Visagie demands that Aunt Magda should leave at once. Stevo stands at the door and says Aunt Magda is not going anywhere.

'If that is the case, Stevo, you can leave too,' says Ma Visagie.

'No dice, Ma,' says Stevo.

This is another example of Aunt Magda's bad influence on Stevo. He would never have tried to stand up to his mother before the Cape Flats woman came back into their lives with her mass action and fancy ideas that she claims to have learnt from what she calls The Struggle. There can be only one alpha female in the Visagie household and she is not about to abdicate that position to a woman who used to be her maid. There can be only one alpha anything, come to think of it, and Stevo is playing with fire pretending he can challenge her.

Stevo seems to understand this. At the first glare from Ma Visagie he moves his tiny frame away from the door, while Aunt Magda shifts uncomfortably towards the door.

Desperate times call for desperate measures. 'Me and Aunt Magda, we are getting married, Ma,' says Stevo.

This comes as a surprise to Aunt Magda. But she is not averse to the idea of marriage, even though she knows she is an *ouma* and at no time did the subject come up between them. She did not even know that they had that kind of relationship—maybe the poor boy is haunted by carnal memories from his early teens.

Shortie bursts out laughing. The prostitutes titter and Ma Visagie takes a long questioning look at Stevo and then at Aunt Magda.

'So there!' says Stevo triumphantly. 'She's your daughter-in-law, Ma. You can't kick her out now. She's family.'

Ma Visagie turns her back on them and walks away. Aunt Magda and Stevo breathe a sigh of relief. This is his first victory over his mother and he intends to savour it. Never again will he kowtow to her.

The prostitutes begin clearing the table, leaving only the turkey, since Shortie is still nibbling at it. He looks at his brother and Aunt Magda expectantly. His eyes are questioning them: What's next, now that you are a happy couple? But they don't seem to know what to do with each other now that they are a happy couple.

Ma Visagie saves them the agony of uncertainty. She returns armed with her shotgun which she promptly brandishes at the couple.

'If you want to leave with Magda, you can go, Stevo,' says Ma Visagie.

Everyone in Roodepoort and beyond knows that Ma Visagie's shotgun is not a toy. Aunt Magda is still keen on life, so she pushes Stevo aside and darts away as if the house has spat her out like a gob of snuff. Ma Visagie stands at the door and blasts the ground behind the hapless woman who is now yelling for help.

The last time anyone at the Visagies' sees Aunt Magda she is running for dear life down Alverstoke Avenue in the quiet and respectable suburb of Strubensvallei.

Stevo Visagie does not follow Aunt Magda. Instead he sulks and sits at the table holding his head as if he is going to cry. The women let him be and go to the kitchen to wash the dishes.

Ma Visagie, as calm as if nothing has happened, looks at Stevo briefly, shakes her head in pity, and takes her smoking gun to her bedroom. Shortie is the only one who remains with his brother in the dining room. He is calmly drinking his beer.

'So, what are you going to do now?' he asks.

Stevo suddenly becomes resolute.

'Everyone wants to shit on me, Shortie, and that has to stop,' he says. 'I have some urgent business to attend to.'

'What urgent business? What are you gonna do, Stevo?' asks Shortie, suddenly becoming nervous.

'The magistrate,' says Stevo.

Panic sets in on Shortie.

'Please forget about the damn magistrate, Stevo. It's dangerous,' pleads Shortie.

Stevo grins at him menacingly. 'Guess who didn't kill her cat, my china?'

He takes a carving knife from the table and plays with it. Then he angrily hacks at what remains of the turkey until he pulverizes it.

'Guess who messed up my plans just because he was scared of a teensy weensy cat,' he says as he walks away to their bedroom.

Shortie follows Stevo. He is worried that his hothead brother will do something very stupid. Stevo packs his gun and the carving knife.

'Guess who's trying to talk me out of taking care of the bitch who wants to stop us from becoming the best outfit since Al Capone walked the streets of Chicago?'

'I saw the movie too,' says Shortie. 'But what you want to do is stupid, Stevo. You just came from jail.'

Stevo Visagie is done with talking. He gets into the delivery van parked outside and drives away.

Darkness has descended from the sky and the city lights try to fight it back with their dull yellow glow. Don Mateza's Saab has stopped at the traffic lights. He is still surrounded by garbage bags up to the roof. He is impatient. The red light is wasting his time. But he can't risk beating it because the street is busy. As soon as the green light flashes on he steps on the accelerator and weaves his way frantically through the traffic.

Fortunately the streets of Strubensvallei are not busy and he is able to keep up the speed until he parks in front of the Visagies' gate, which has been left open since today's festivities and Aunt Magda's hurried flight. He hoots persistently until Shortie comes out of the house and walks to the gate. At this stage he does not recognize Don as the man who once confronted him here.

'Where's Stevo?' asks Don.

'What do you want with Stevo?'

'I want to warn him to stay away from Kristin.'

'Stevo just came out of jail, man,' says Shortie. 'He's not doing any chick called Kristin. Plus he is getting married to Aunt Magda.'

So, Magda was stringing him along after all. She is not only with the Visagies but of the Visagies. He has no time to cry over his lost money. He must find Stevo.

'I'm talking about the magistrate, you fool. Where is your brother?'

Only now does Shortie recognize the man as the magistrate's bodyguard. He begins to panic. He must tell this guy the truth. It may be the only chance of stopping Stevo before he does something foolish. He is even more fearful when it dawns on him that if the bodyguard is here, it may mean that the magistrate is unprotected, wherever she is. One never knows what Stevo might do to her. He does not want to lose his brother.

'You're too late, my china,' says Shortie. 'He's gone to talk to your Kristin.'

Don gets out of the car and opens the passenger door.

'You're coming with me,' he says.

'Oh, no, I'm not going nowhere,' says Shortie. 'You can't involve me in this.'

Don grabs Shortie by the collar, imploringly rather than aggressively. 'You are involved already, *my china*. You got to talk to your brother. You don't want him to do something foolish and end up in jail.'

'That's exactly what I said to him but he still left,' says Shortie.

'You'll be implicated too,' says Don. 'If he kills Kristin you'll be implicated. You just told me here that he told you what he was going to do and you didn't report it to the police.'

This convinces Shortie. There may still be time to save his brother. That is his main concern. Not so much the magistrate. He does not give a damn about saving her. Not after what she did to the Visagie family. And she plans to grind them into the ground too. Stevo said so.

Shortie gets into the car just as Ma Visagie comes out of the house.

'Hey, where are you taking my little boy?' she shouts.

Don speeds away with her little boy ensconced among the garbage bags.

He is speeding on Ontdekkers Road when his cellphone rings.

It's Jim Baxter. He needs him urgently. There is an armed robbery in progress. Guards from VIP Protection Services in an armoured vehicle have been waylaid by a gang armed with machine guns on the M1 Highway to Pretoria and there is a shootout.

Jim Baxter rattles on like an AK-47 and Don misses a lot of the details; his mind is not at the cash heist but in Weltevreden Park.

'You need to come over immediately, Don,' says Baxter. 'You need to be at the command post. You are the CEO now.'

'Not quite, Jim. You've not yet handed over officially. But I'll be there. Not immediately though. I am more than an hour away.'

Of course he is lying. He is less than fifteen minutes away. But he must get to Kristin first. He has to take her to a place of safety. Then he will attend to VIP Protection Services' problems.

Don is frantic as he works his way through the traffic. Shortie sits uncomfortably among the garbage bags. He is beginning to have second thoughts about his role in all this. He does not know what the call to Don was all about. He hopes it does not mean something has happened to his brother.

'Stevo's gonna kill me for this,' he sighs resignedly.

'Yeah. But after that he's going to thank you,' says Don.

He is dialling a number on the cellphone.

'I'm calling ten-triple-one,' he says.

'Hey, you can't call the cops on my brother,' screams Shortie, trying to snatch the phone from Don.

'Don't be stupid, Shortie. The magistrate's life may be in danger as we speak.'

Shortie gives up and Don dials again.

The magistrate has reached the lowest ebb ever. She is sitting at the dressing table mirror making herself up in the garish manner of prostitutes. She gets into her 'whore' costume with grace and deliberation as if it is something sacred.

She takes a bow and applauds herself, and The Clapper switches on the music and the lights. She begins her 'whore' dance, at first slowly as if it weighs heavily on her. As if the dance is resisting her. As if her body has forgotten the well-practised moves. But soon it picks up. Moments later she is completely immersed in it.

The music is throbbing and the strobe is flashing, creating a bizarre slo-mo effect. She is so immersed in the dance that she does not notice the dangerously armed man who walks into the room and stands at the door watching. After a while he speaks.

'Good evening, madam,' he says, in what he thinks is a genteel voice.

But the magistrate is oblivious of him. She continues with her dance. This annoys the man. He grabs her shoulders with both hands and yells in her face.

'I fucken said good evening, madam!'

She claps her hands to stop the music and the disco lights. House lights rise and she is face to face with Stevo Visagie. She freezes and lets out a blood-curdling shriek. Stevo slaps her face hard, which immediately silences her.

'Now, you gonna dance for me,' says Stevo.

He sits on the bed and places his carving knife and his gun next to him. He lights a cigarette and puffs with aplomb. He is really enjoying himself. The magistrate's lowest point is his highest. He claps to switch the disco lights on. But it is not the appropriate rhythm, so nothing happens. He tries again. Nothing happens.

'OK, bitch,' he says. 'You do it. Switch the damn thing on.'

But the magistrate just stands there looking at him.

'Never mind,' says Stevo. 'On second thoughts, I want you to dance with the normal lights on. I don't want any of your fucken disco lights. I want to see every sexy move.'

She just stands there stubbornly.

'Dance, bitch!'

He grabs the knife and approaches her. She reverses until she has backed into the wall. He slashes her arms—just a little bit—enough for some blood to flow and enough to drive it home to her stupid head that he means business.

She begins to dance slowly and reluctantly. He goes back to sit on the bed and gulps wine from a bottle he finds on the nightstand. Then he stands up again because he is not satisfied with the way she is dancing. He brandishes the knife in front of her face.

'Listen, bitch, I want you to dance the way I saw you dance when you didn't know I was here. I want you to dance like the whore you are.'

He grabs her and forces a slurping kiss on her lips. Then he pretends to throw up.

'*Sies! I* kissed a whore! Dance, whore! Dance!'

She begins to dance again. He turns his back to reach for the bottle of wine and she seizes the opportunity and tries to escape.

'You won't get away, bitch.'

He chases her into the living room, round the furniture, while she grabs items like flower pots, vases and even books and throws them at him. All the while he is ducking and charging at her. His head spins a bit when an ashtray hits it, giving the magistrate a chance to escape into another room—the guest room that used to be Don's bedroom.

'I'm going to kill you for this, bitch,' says Stevo, wiping blood from his forehead with the back of his hand.

The two cats are curled on up a mat next to the bed. They are woken from their nap by the commotion. Stevo creeps into the room and steps on Snowy's tail. Both cats snarl and screech and attack him, scratching and tearing the leg of his pants.

'*Eina*! Goddammit, man,' he screams, and then under his breath, 'I'm gonna kill Shortie for this.'

The cats escape out of the room.

The magistrate is hiding inside the built-in closet and is whimpering with fear. Stevo looks everywhere for her. He looks under the bed, behind the cupboard, behind a sofa. Then he stops and listens. There is silence for a while. He hears faint breathing and whimpering. He knows exactly where she is but he bides his time and whistles to himself. That should give her enough chance to wet her pants. Then he tiptoes to the closet and opens it swiftly. There she is, snivelling in the corner. He drags her out.

'What do you want from me, Stevo?'

'I want you to dance for me, sweet lady. That's all I ever wanted in my life.'

He drags her by the hair like a caveman, back to her bedroom. She stands defiantly in the middle of the room. Stevo sits on the bed, lights a cigarette, and drinks some more wine. He reads the label on the bottle and shakes his head in disgust.

'You drink this kind of shit?' he sneers. 'Only *bergies* drink this kind of shit. You're a magistrate, for God's sake.'

She does not move.

'OK, dance, bitch,' he says.

She is defiant. He walks menacingly towards her, wielding the knife.

'You're a stubborn little whore.'

He looks at her big stuffed breasts and pretends to drool.

'When did you become *ou* Pamela Anderson, your worship? The last time you sent me to jail your chest was very flat. Like a boy's.'

She instinctively reaches for her breasts, but her hands escape just in time as Stevo slashes her bosom. The pieces of cloth stuffed in the bra fly out.

'Oh, they are fake!' says Stevo in mock shock. 'Our little whore has fake titties.'

She cannot stop the tears from streaming down her cheeks. She is utterly mortified.

'Fuck you, Stevo Visagie,' she says, almost in a whisper. 'Fuck you!'

Stevo slaps her hard on the face. Again and again. Her face is smudged all over with lipstick and blusher and mascara and tears and mucus.

'Who is not a man now, eh?'

He slaps her again.

'Who is playing with little girls? OK, OK, it's me—not so? I'm in fucken chains in jail and you tell me to my face I'm not man enough, I play with little girls. Guess what? You were right, bitch. I play with little girls and you're the little girl I'm playing with tonight. Let's see your big boobs again.'

He slashes the second breast with the knife and the stuffing flies out. Then he puts the knife against her chest and snaps what remains of the bra. Her small breasts are left exposed.

'Oh, look who's a little girl now,' says Stevo laughing and staring at her breasts.

He slashes her arm and blood spurts out.

'Who is a scared little boy now, eh?'

She can't just stand there stubbornly any more. She tries to escape again. But he is at her heels.

'Who is a little wiggly worm?'

She falls down but he hauls her up.

'Please, Stevo,' she begs. 'Please.'

'That sounds nice,' says Stevo lasciviously. 'Like you're fucken coming. It's good, isn't it? It wants you to scream, "Please, Stevo, please."'

She is now crying shamelessly.

'Who's a crybaby now, bitch?' asks Stevo. 'Who's a fucken crybaby? OK, enough of your games. Dance, bitch, dance.'

He fiddles with the stereo manually and the music throbs again. She begins to dance.

'Faster, man! Faster! I hate lazy bitches!'

She dances faster and faster.

Neither of them hears a car stop next to the Visagie delivery van, or Don and Shortie opening the door. The security grille is wide open; Stevo found a way to pick its lock. That was why it took him so long to get here—he had to go to Soweto first to get Fingers Matatu, who in turn had to get a younger lock-picker who came to Weltevreden Park with Stevo, fiddled with the lock and then drove back to his interrupted tavern-drinking as soon as he had unlocked both the security grille and the door.

The magistrate dances for a few beats and then stops.

'Who said you should stop?'

'Please, Stevo, I'm tired.'

He slashes her skimpy dress, exposing her frilly panties.

'*Sies*, lady, you don't have any taste at all,' he says laughing heartily. 'My hookers are more high class than you. They don't wear stuff like that.'

She spits at him, right in his face. This stops his laughter short and infuriates him no end.

'You know what? I've had enough of your shit,' he says. 'I am going to kill the fuck out of you.'

He has the knife ready to slit her throat when the door flies open and Don barges in, his gun drawn. Stevo reaches for his gun and fires blindly. Don's gun drops as he takes cover. Stevo is going to kill them both. He raises his arm and aims, ready to pull the trigger. But Shortie rushes in yelling, 'No, Stevo! Don't do it!'

His brother's voice takes him by surprise. Don takes advantage of this distraction and lurches at Stevo. But Stevo is too fast for him. He fires a shot and Don falls to the floor.

'Ma will be really mad at you, Stevo,' says Shortie.

'Get out of here, Shortie, or I'll kill you too,' says Stevo.

The magistrate seizes the moment and kicks Stevo in the balls. While he is reeling Shortie gets hold of him. Stevo kicks his legs trying to break free but Shortie's grip is a firm one. The magistrate grabs a chair and knocks Stevo out cold. She rushes to Don and kneels beside him, sobbing. He opens his eyes and she is relieved that he is not dead.

Stevo has recovered and is trying to reach for the gun on the floor. Don kicks it away and trips the still groggy Stevo. Stevo falls down and Shortie holds him in his tight grip again. Both Don and the magistrate hit him with whatever is in sight until he loses consciousness.

While the magistrate is trying to stop the bleeding on Don's arm with the rags from her torn bra, Shortie is sobbing over the unconscious Stevo.

'Ma is gonna give me shit for betraying Stevo,' he cries.

Police sirens can be heard outside.

'Stop whining, man, you did the right thing,' says the magistrate.

Two police squad cars with blue lights flashing stop outside the yard. Police leap out of the cars and dash into the house.

Don has spent two days at the Johannesburg Hospital when he gets a visit from Jim Baxter. He fills him in on the cash heist. Two VIP Protection Services guards were killed. They were transporting cash in an armoured vehicle from one Johannesburg branch of a bank in which Dr Molotov Mbungane is the majority shareholder to a branch on the outskirts of the Tshwane Metropolis. The heist was carried out with military precision; the robbers fired their AK-47s mercilessly. It was clear that they intended to kill every VIP Protection Services guard. However, they had not reckoned with the guards in unmarked cars that always discreetly follow armoured vehicles. One robber was killed during the ensuing shootout. Another one was injured and is in police custody. The rest—estimated at about eight or so—escaped. But, praise the Lord, none of the cash in the armoured vehicle was missing. The reputation of VIP Protection Services was saved by the brave men who sacrificed their lives. If the crooks had managed to take the cash the company would certainly lose Dr Mbungane's contract.

But the main reason Baxter came is that there is a strange development in the case. The police have discovered that the armed robbers were former guerrilla fighters in the liberation movement.

'I thought you should know since you are a former guerrilla yourself,' says Baxter, who has never failed to mention that fact in company because it proved how open-minded he is; at the time Don was fighting in the bush Baxter was a colonel in the South African Defence Force.

'Have the police questioned the guy they caught? Was he able to say who the rest were?'

'They have questioned him,' says Baxter. 'But he won't talk. He is under police guard here at the hospital. I told the police about you. They think if you see the guy privately you may be able to talk some sense into him.'

Don does not think he is up to the task. But Baxter is a very persuasive man.

In the afternoon Don hobbles on crutches to the private ward where the prisoner is being held. Don's arm is in bandages and he is in agony, especially in the area of the ribs. The policeman at the door has instructions to let him in.

He cannot mistake the figure of Fontyo chained to the bed and guarded by three policemen armed with machine guns.

When Fontyo opens his eyes there is Don's pained face hovering over him. He just stares back at him and says nothing.

'So this is the trip for which you stayed sober, comrade?' says Don. Tears are streaming down his face.

'Bova is dead. Your people killed Bova, you bloody capitalist pig.'

And he turns his head to the wall. That is all he is prepared to say.

Don hobbles back to his ward.

Kristin is waiting beside his bed with a bunch of flowers.

'You've been crying,' she says looking at his blood-shot eyes.

'It's OK,' he says.

He does not know what to say next. She doesn't either. She could say 'thank you for saving my life' but that would not sound like her. That would sound too maudlin.

'When are you coming home?' she asks instead.

'I have no home,' he says matter-of-factly.

'Home is where your cat is,' she says.

He smiles for a while, and then says quite earnestly, 'For now . . . maybe. Me and Snowy . . . we can no longer be kept.'